Implications

An Arthur Blake Mystery Novel

by

Richard Davidson

Richard Davidson

Also by Richard Davidson:

Self-Help:
DECISION TIME! Better Decisions for a Better Life

Mysteries:
The Lord's Prayer Mystery Series:
Lead Us Not into Temptation
Give Us this Day Our Daily Bread
Forgive Us Our Trespasses
Thy Will Be Done
Deliver Us from Evil

Anthology: (Editor)
Overcoming: An Anthology by the Writers of OCWW

"Implications," by Richard Davidson.
ISBN 978-0-9829160-6-3
An Arthur Blake Mystery

Genesis 19:24 - Then the LORD rained upon Sodom and upon Gomorrah brimstone and fire from the LORD out of heaven;   (Bible, King James version)

CHAPTER 1 – ASSIGNMENT

"Arthur, wake up. Bishop Chandler's on the telephone for you; he says it's urgent."

"What time is it, Irma? I feel as though I just fell asleep."

"It's two thirty a.m.; you'd better snap to, and wrap your wits about you. He sounds upset."

Arthur stumbled toward the desk, where the telephone handset lay next to a pad of paper, a pen, and a glass of water. Irma had always been better at responding to nocturnal alerts than he had. Her arrangement of these items reflected years of experiencing nighttime callouts for crime scene pathology and forensics. Arthur sat down, swallowed some water, and picked up the handset.

"Hello, Bishop, how can I assist you?"

"I regret having to rouse you out of your sleep, Arthur, but it comes with your new position as consulting trouble-shooter for the Northern Illinois Conference. You no longer have pastor's hours for your assignments."

"You're saying that something has happened that needs my immediate attention. What is it?"

"One of our United Methodist churches is on fire. It's in the village of Amboy, Illinois. Do you know where Amboy is?"

"I do; it's southwest of Rochelle. I should be able to get there within an hour. Is there anything suspicious about this fire, Bishop?"

"That's your assignment. Figure out whether we should be worried about one or more arsonists on the loose. We had a huge fire in our United Methodist Church in Robinson, Illinois last Christmas night; the parsonage at the Epworth Church in Chicago has burned twice; and there have been fires in significant old churches in other denominations across the state. You're our best bet for discovering connections among these fires. Check it out, and let me know as soon as you have something."

Bishop Chandler disconnected, and Arthur turned to Irma. "Back when I worked as a NASA engineer, we used to call our trouble-shooting of mission problems *putting out fires*. It looks as though I'm back in that business, examining the possibility of deliberately set church fires. The Amboy United Methodist Church is on fire tonight, and I'm charged with finding anything suspicious in that blaze."

"Fill your Thermos with coffee, Arthur, while I get dressed and grab my evidence kit. I'm going with you on this one. When I was a kid, our local church burned, and I always wondered whether someone kindled that blaze. A church is an easy target for an arsonist."

CHAPTER 2 – AMBOY

When they arrived in Amboy, the fire was the center of intense activity. Fire teams from several surrounding towns assisted the Amboy volunteer firefighters. Irma and Arthur had just left their car when a huge fireball roared up through what remained of the roof of the church. The heat grew intense, even at a distance. Several firefighters who had been working close to the building beat a hasty retreat. They prepared to advance again, anticipating the receding of the burst of fire for lack of sustaining fuel.

Arthur approached the Amboy Fire Chief and identified himself as the Bishop's representative. Chief Webster shook his hand and indicated he'd meet with him after the fire was under control. He aimed Arthur across the street toward the bus stop where he had last seen the local pastor. Arthur knew that Irma would be pursuing her own independent investigation, so he accepted Chief Webster's advice to seek out Pastor Lorna Dyner. He expected that she was the tall woman at the center of a group of young people on the other side of the street, beyond the fire engines that filled both the parking lot and the blocked-off thoroughfare. As he neared their group, Arthur realized that the Amboy pastor looked barely older than the youths who surrounded her.

"Pastor Dyner, I'm Arthur Blake. I served as pastor of the Parkville United Methodist Church, and I'm currently working for Bishop Chandler. He asked me to come over here and learn all that I could about the circumstances and seriousness of this fire."

She excused herself from her young friends and motioned him toward a tree that stood isolated because its widespread branches prevented a clear view of the fire.

6

They shook hands and shouted in order to hear each other above the surrounding din.

"Hello, Arthur; I've heard of you and some of your investigative exploits. You're practically a legend among the younger pastors in the Conference."

"That's a bit out of proportion to what I've done. I may have entered the ministry later than most after my engineering career with NASA, but I had my own church for only five years, prior to getting this staff appointment. I have only slightly more seniority than you. Can you tell me anything about the way the fire started?"

"That's a mystery to me. We had a youth gathering that lasted until ten o'clock, and then we all left. The fire started about three hours later. We came back when we heard the sirens."

"From what I've seen so far, rebuilding may be an iffy proposition. How do you feel about that?"

"I'm afraid our church is a goner. Because it's ninety years old, we avoided many of the latest code requirements, thanks to grandfather clauses in the regulations. If we were to rebuild it, we'd have to comply with every chapter and verse of the rules. Our insurance wouldn't cover it, and it would require a lot more money than we could ever hope to solicit from contributors. Amboy has only about twenty-five hundred people, and only about two hundred of them attend the United Methodist Church. I'll probably be reassigned elsewhere, and our members will have to drive a little farther to attend church in one of the surrounding towns."

"Has your assignment to this church been a positive experience for you?"

"I'd give that a strong affirmation. The church had its untidy situations before I arrived, but we've had fun together and increased our membership too."

"What were the earlier situations, Lorna?"

They heard a loud crash as a section of the church roof, along with the steeple that had straddled it for ninety years, collapsed to the ground. After initially recoiling from the resounding impact, they both stepped forward, beyond the overhanging tree branches to see what had happened. Showers of sparks speckled the sky. Once they saw the flames decrease, they returned to their conversation spot under the tree.

Lorna remained silent for a minute. Then she returned to their earlier conversation. "I'll miss this old building. Even though we United Methodist pastors transfer to different churches every few years, this one has been like a home to me. Because of that, I have to hesitate before airing any of our dirty laundry to you or anyone else. Before I arrived, the church had a bunch of problems. I take no credit for solving them; it just took time."

"Can you give me some specifics?"

"To start with, we had a member who faced charges of having murdered his girlfriend during an extramarital affair. The gossipmongers convinced themselves and most church members that he had killed her. His wife made him move out of their house because of the accusation and the constant malicious chatter. It turned out that the authorities didn't have enough evidence to justify an arrest. He died in a single-car accident during the investigation; technically, the case is still open. We also had a seminarian training here, who had an affair with a different married member of the congregation. The Conference ruled her unfit for ordination. Her lover was so ashamed of himself that he left town. Finally, we had some discrepancies in the church bank accounts that led to our requesting that our former treasurer leave the church. We didn't file a formal complaint, so that problem simply evaporated over time. We added a couple of fund-raising events each year until we finished making up for the cash shortfall a couple of months ago."

"That's quite a litany of troubles. I'm impressed by your ability to right the ship after that storm, Lorna."

"Unfortunately, that ship won't survive tonight's disaster. If this fire puts me in search for a new position, I'd appreciate your recommendation, Arthur."

"You'll have it. I see my wife, Irma, heading toward us. She's been off talking with the firefighters. I'd like to have you meet her."

"I'll do that, but then I'll have to get back to those members of my flock who cared enough to come out here in the middle of the night."

Irma joined them; they exchanged introductions and those few pleasantries that were tasteful under the glare from the burning church. Then Pastor Dyner departed, leaving Irma and Arthur free to discuss their preliminary findings.

Irma said, "This is very tentative, but my talks with the firefighters and my own observations suggest that this was an arson fire. The perpetrator probably used an accelerant, because there were two very active hot spots, one fire concentrated in the sanctuary by the altar – that led to that huge fireball we saw as we arrived – and the other hot spot in the church basement below the entrance to the sanctuary. The lower-level fire burned a large hole in the floor above it."

"That fits with my tentative conclusion that quite a few people may have had a conflict with this church." He told Irma about the past problems in the church, and she agreed that there would be several people with enough of a motive to be considered possible arson suspects."

Arthur and Irma heard shouts from the firefighters and felt vibrations through their feet as another section of the church's roof structure collapsed and struck the ground. They moved out from under the shroud of the tree's branches to face the disturbing contrast of an emerging beautiful sunrise over the still-burning skeleton of the ninety-year-old church.

CHAPTER 3 – BISHOP CHANDLER

They sat in two wingback chairs in front of Bishop Chandler's office fireplace cradling their cups of coffee, just as they had on many happier occasions.

"Are you the bearer of good news or bad news, Arthur?"

"I'd say that it's mostly bad news with just a hint of something that will ease your stress, Howard."

"Well, give me that glimmer of daylight first; it may make it easier to swallow the bitter medicine that follows."

"That sliver of good news is that your fears of a serial arsonist going from church to church appear to be unfounded. Irma and the fire investigators consider it likely that the Amboy UMC Church blaze was a case of arson. However, my conversations with Pastor Lorna Dyner suggest that this was an isolated crime committed by someone who had a grudge against that local church."

Bishop Chandler leaned forward. "Then you suspect a particular person?"

"Unfortunately, that church had some serious problems prior to Lorna's arrival. She described them to me, and I have to conclude that there are several identifiable suspects connected with the church, plus other outsiders who might have reacted to the misdeeds of church people. The police will have a large number of leads to investigate."

Bishop Chandler stood and looked down at Arthur. "I appointed you to this position to handle internal investigations and to keep their results from generating bad publicity for the church. I want you to privately investigate this incident and determine who is responsible for it."

"Your desires are noted, but I would have to cooperate with the authorities. Withholding evidence and interfering with an official investigation are crimes, and the Conference should not want legal problems. I'll do what I can to minimize bad publicity, but I can't guarantee anything."

"I'll have to live with that, I suppose. What can I do to make a positive impact?"

"You might consider the recently improved dynamics and membership at the Amboy Church and look into the possibility of the Conference supporting a rebuilding effort. That would generate good publicity."

"I'll consider that, but our funds are quite limited. Some church leaders are actually suggesting that we should emulate the airlines' strategy and have fewer churches so that each would have a larger attendance."

"I'll offer a counter-analogy. Politicians say that all politics are local. I could argue that all religious enthusiasm is local also. We can't expect our people to travel far. They'd attend competing local churches instead, or drift away from regular church attendance anywhere."

CHAPTER 4 – AFTERMATH

By mid-day, Arthur and Irma had joined the arson investigators from the Illinois Fire Marshal's office. Wisps of smoke still rose from various points within the church ruins. A few firefighters remained on the scene to water down any hot areas that reignited.

Dennis Mikken, the lead investigator, pointed to the gaping hole in the floor of the church sanctuary. "That hole tells us that the fire in the basement was ignited directly beneath it, generating more heat there than anywhere else."

Arthur said, "Pardon my ignorance, but why couldn't that mean that the hot spot was on the floor that collapsed rather than underneath it?"

"That's a good question. I have three clues to back up my conclusion. First, because most of the heat from a fire tends to move upward, I looked at the remains of the choir loft that overhung the hole in the floor. The bottom of that loft is mildly charred, but it didn't ignite. This shows that the heat was higher at the floor level than at the underside of the loft. The basement shows greater charring, with more furnishings and carpeting consumed beneath the floor hole than at the other end of the room. Finally, when we went down into the basement, we saw that charring was greater on the underside of the boards surrounding the floor hole than it was on the top surface of those boards. Therefore, the fire started in the basement, spread across the ceiling, but burned through the floor above the initial hotspot. This also suggests that an accelerant was used in the basement, because the intensity was very high beneath that floor hole."

"That's all very logical. I assume you used the same logic to identify the second accelerated hotspot near the altar table."

"That was even easier, because the altar table was completely consumed as was the church's end wall adjacent to it. The fire burned the fabric banners on the wall and then climbed the wall to the roof of the building, where it burned through the beams and caused that end of the roof to collapse. Damage to the floor and ceiling beams between those two hotspots was significantly less."

Irma had listened as Dennis and Arthur exchanged these comments. She asked, "Have you identified the accelerant yet?"

"No, we'll cut out pieces of the wooden floor around the altar and take them back to the lab for analysis. We'll also take chunks of concrete from the basement, but the wood will be easier to test."

Arthur banged on the floor with the blade of a shovel he had found. "I know you're not a structural engineer, Dennis, but what's your opinion on the practicality of rebuilding this church. Because it's so old, some of the flooring and beams are quite a bit stronger than the new-growth wood that they use today."

"I'll grant you that, Arthur. My guess would be that while you could use some of the old materials and perhaps even preserve a portion of the floor, you would want to have a new design for a replacement building, making it smaller and more suitable for heating and cooling. These old churches were impressive, but extremely costly to maintain."

They walked out of the remains of the building into the parking lot where they removed their hard hats and gloves."

Dennis said, "We'll get lucky if it turns out that our arsonist used an unusual accelerant. Then we might be able to discover its source and the purchaser. If he or she used gasoline, we'll lose that identification opportunity.

Then, we'll take a look at other arson cases, especially those that have involved churches, to see whether a similar technique pattern emerges."

Irma tapped Arthur on the shoulder. "I don't know whether you caught that, but Dennis just told us that he thinks our arsonist was a professional."

They both looked at Dennis, and he nodded his head in confirmation. "This person knew how to be sure that the fire departments would not arrive in time to save the building. I suspect that he or she has worked on arsons in insurance fraud cases."

CHAPTER 5 – LIFESTYLES

Upon returning to their Parkville apartment after examining the church ruins in Amboy, Arthur headed for his usual mug of coffee, while Irma browsed through the newspaper. When he came back into the living room from the kitchen, Arthur knew from his wife's expression that she had some kind of project in mind for him.

"What's happening? You have that energetic 'Let's tackle something.' look."

"You're now officially on assignment as the Northern Illinois Conference trouble-shooter. We've already agreed that we don't have to concentrate on activities at the church in Parkville. You're no longer the pastor there, and you're not supposed to interfere with the way the new pastor handles things."

"That's a preamble to some declaration of independence from the church. What are you thinking?"

It's time for us to graduate from apartment living to our own house. I've found several possibilities in the paper. Let's take our first shot at house-hunting."

Arthur finished his mug of coffee and set it down on his desk. "Is this a come-as-you-are party, or do I have to dress to make an impression?"

"You're fine the way you are, and we'll leave now, before you change your mind."

Five hours later, they returned to the apartment carrying several brochures and a yellow legal pad full of notes on the houses they had visited. They laid down their paperwork, got drinks, and sprawled on soft seats in the living room.

Arthur leaned back on the couch and took two swallows of his beer. The hot day ruled against consuming

15

his usual coffee. "I never realized that there would be so many decisions required to select and buy a house. We agree on most things, but we've run into some major taste differences. Before we look any more, we should try to find common ground on the kind of house we want."

"That's a good idea, Arthur, but you don't have complete freedom of choice. We have to limit ourselves to the houses that are on the market. We could decide we want something that is simply not available."

"Let's start with location. I'd like a house that's no more than thirty miles away from Parkville, because we'll want to maintain our relationships here. Do you agree with that, Irma?"

"I'll go along with that thinking, but I'd rather not hang my hat on a specific number of miles from Parkville. We have to remain open to something that might turn out to be very attractive or a great value, even if it's a little farther away."

"What did you think of that ranch-style house we saw today?"

"It was cute, but it had only two bedrooms. We should have three, because we need a guest room plus a room for the child we've talked about adopting. We'd probably want a second floor because it would give us more space."

"What if we adopted a girl and a boy?"

"Four bedrooms would be fine with me if we could afford such a house."

"How about finding the house of our dreams and then worrying about its cost?"

"That's not very realistic, but I love the sentiment." Irma left her chair to curl up on the other end of the couch, facing him.

"Would you like to live in open country, or would you like to have nearby neighbors and shopping?"

"We haven't discussed that one before. I think I'd like to be away from town and in a wooded area if possible. Open farmland doesn't do anything for me."

Implications

"Would you ..."

Irma interrupted him. "No fair, Arthur; you're asking all the questions. It's my turn."

"Good – ask me something."

"Would you prefer an older house or new construction?"

"New construction has the advantage that we might be able to design something uniquely ours, but I think I'd really prefer a house that has a history. I am the son of an antiques dealer, after all."

"Now we're getting interesting. Your folks don't have a house that's very old, despite their love of antiques."

"You're right, but they live in an older town where everyone appreciates the value of things with some age on them."

Irma reached for the pad of paper that was on the table next to her end of the couch. "In summary, we would like to buy a two-story older home, nestled in the woods with three or four bedrooms, located reasonably close to Parkville. Would you like to have a stream running through the property?"

"That would be ideal. Why did you ask that?"

"... because I saw a newspaper listing for a house like that in Amboy. If you'd consider Amboy as a possible location, we could check it out when we next go to inspect what remains of the church."

CHAPTER 6 – HOUSE OF MING

Parkville, Illinois, located remotely northwest of Chicago, sheltered Parkville United Methodist Church where Arthur had been pastor for five years, the Blakes' apartment, plus the homes of their closest friends and associates. Parkville Police Chief Bobby Andrews and his wife Renee, a former police officer, had assisted Arthur and his then girlfriend Irma, a former County Medical Examiner, in investigating several local cases involving the Parkville Church. Penny and Joe Gonzalez, principals in a small federal investigative agency, had met Arthur while investigating a matter in Parkville, and had later joined Arthur and his local associates in solving cases that involved interstate and international crimes. A few years later, when Penny and Joe found themselves continuing to make frequent trips to Parkville because of Arthur's cases, they had decided that they could work just as efficiently and with a better home environment if they exchanged their DC apartment for a home in that northwest Illinois village.

These six friends and associates worked well together in solving unusual and complex cases with far-reaching implications. They also enjoyed each other's company on a social basis. Whether the purpose was investigative or social, they usually gathered at House of Ming, the Parkville Chinese restaurant operated by Arthur's friend Tony Fleming, who had truncated his surname for business purposes, in order to make his establishment sound more Chinese.

Friday evening found them all sitting at their favorite circular booth in the darkened rear corner of House of Ming, their conversation focusing on the subject of the Amboy UMC fire.

Implications

Arthur said, "It looked like a straightforward case of arson by someone local with a grudge against the church, until the state fire investigators concluded that the fire had been set by a professional. The whole concept of an arsonist being professional bothers me."

Bobby said, "It's always possible that a local person paid a pro to torch that church. What do you think, Joe?"

"That local person would have needed to have a lot of money or a very intense hatred against the church. It sounds more like an act of terrorism, except for the remote location that wouldn't get much notice and the lack of injuries to anyone. Usually terrorists want maximum attention, and they want to scare people by killing the innocent. Hence the *terror* part of their label."

Penny said, "Arthur, when you raised this subject, I assumed that you and Irma would be tackling this case on your own. Amboy is outside of Bobby's jurisdiction, and the burning of a rural Illinois church is not normally a federal affair. However, if the state fire investigators say that this was the work of a professional, we could justify consulting with you to the extent of checking church fires in other states for any that were set in the same manner. We've had a large number of church fires in various states, especially in the south, and some of them were definitely arsons."

Arthur said, "I question whether many of those were professionally set. When Bishop Chandler expressed his fear that the Amboy Church fire had been set by a serial arsonist, I did some research and found an article indicating that fires damaged or destroyed more than a dozen United Methodist Churches across the country within the past year or so, and that five of those had been instances of arson. My first reaction was to suspect local responsibility in most or all of the arson cases."

Joe said, "That's probably enough background to justify our checking into investigation results from past fires. Some of them could be hate crimes or terrorism."

"The UMC article suggests that insurance payoffs are much less than the costs of reconstructing these churches, so I doubt very much that there is an insurance fraud angle to any of these fires. Under our Conference rules, the local congregations wouldn't get to keep insurance money if the church wasn't rebuilt."

Irma said, "I think that's enough shop talk for this evening. The more important news is that we've begun to look for a house. Apartment living will soon be in our rear view mirror. We want to be homeowners like you"

Renee and Penny congratulated Irma. The men exchanged glances and shrugged.

CHAPTER 7 – OLD HOUSES

For their house-hunting trip to Amboy, Irma drove her black Mustang, which she considered her almost-living pet. Arthur enjoyed the opportunity to relax and absorb the scenery as passenger instead of driver. He noticed many signs and buildings that hadn't registered in his consciousness when he had previously driven the same route. The online material they had studied about Amboy indicated that the village dated back to 1852, so they looked forward to seeing a fair number of houses from the late nineteenth and early twentieth centuries.

Because they wanted to familiarize themselves with Amboy, Arthur and Irma had decided they would simply drive the streets and neighborhoods, stopping at houses bearing For Sale signs when they appeared interesting. They saw several interesting older houses, usually of frame construction and quite spacious due to their several additions over the years. However, it didn't take them long to realize that their dream of a home that was a hundred or more years old came with a flaw they hadn't anticipated. There were many such homes, and some of them were for sale, but none of them had the kind of location they wanted.

During the early days of Amboy, and most other Midwest villages, settlers had built their homes in a cluster, within relatively easy walking distance of each other to encourage mutual support. As the village expanded, the older area became its downtown district. Subsequent razing of those homes that were in poor condition or in key locations led to construction of stores, schools, and small industrial shops within one or a few blocks of the older homes that survived. The Blakes found some still-elegant Victorian homes from the late

21

nineteenth century, but those homes all lacked the charm of a relatively isolated neighborhood. The house described as having a stream on the property turned out to be in the business district and adjacent to railroad tracks used exclusively for freight trains.

Arthur had just suggested to Irma that they look farther out of town, perhaps at farmhouses, when his cell phone rang.

"Hello, this is Pastor Arthur Blake speaking."

"Hi, Arthur, it's Lorna Dyner. You may want to come back to our church site in Amboy. The state arson investigators found something very disturbing. It turns out that our church had a sub-basement that I never knew about. Perhaps the builders intended it to be a tornado shelter. Anyway, over the years everyone forgot about it. The investigators found a trap door leading to the sub-basement this morning and just came up after exploring it."

"We're actually in Amboy right now, so there's no problem about coming to your church. Is there something unusual about this sub-basement?"

"I'd call it unusual. They told me they found three bodies in there."

CHAPTER 8 - SURPRISES

Arthur Blake set down his phone after learning about the discoveries at the Amboy church and started to relay that information to Irma. The ringing of his telephone for a second time interrupted their conversation.

"Hello ... Arthur Blake speaking."

Arthur expected that this second call was again from Lorna Dyner, but he was surprised to hear the voice of Penny Gonzalez.

"I have interesting news for you. We have a lead as to the whereabouts of our old nemesis Karl Simitski, ancient artifact collector turned counterfeiter. Our agents have quizzed a number of his past archeology and art associates, and Steve DuBois came up with a couple of key connections. Steve will brief us at our house tomorrow at eleven o'clock. You and Irma are welcome to attend the session. Steve hinted that his news would require us to take some serious actions. Would you like to join us?"

"We'll be there, Penny, and we may have some news of our own by then. Just prior to your call, I received information that there are new developments in connection with that church arson investigation. We're heading over there now. It sounds as though things are heating up on two fronts."

He ended the phone conversation and turned back to Irma. "I think our house-hunting will have to be postponed for a little while. Let's head for the Amboy church. I'll fill you in on the fire news from Lorna while we drive. We also have a meeting at Penny's house tomorrow morning to learn about new developments in the search for Karl Simitski, who escaped arrest when we wrapped up our last case."

CHAPTER 9 – DEEP SECRETS

As Arthur and Irma walked from their car toward the burned-out skeleton of the church, State Fire Investigator Dennis Mikken emerged from the remains of the building to meet them in the parking lot.

"Hello, Arthur; hello, Irma; Pastor Dyner told me that she called you with my preliminary findings about our discovery. She tried to get more details out of me, but I didn't give her the whole story because I thought that you, as the Bishop's representative should hear it first. Certain aspects of our discovery require that we keep the details confidential. For both church and political considerations, it would be wise to suppress publicity until we solve this mystery."

Arthur said, "I'm glad you're sensitive to the dangers of releasing information prematurely. The Bishop specifically charged me with being careful to limit access to details or reports that might embarrass the United Methodist Church or the Northern Illinois Conference. What have you found that might fall into that category?"

"I may have already said too much when I told Pastor Dyner that we found three bodies. I hope she will be discrete about spreading that information."

"I'll talk with her about that as soon as we finish our discussions."

"Good. The sensitive part is that the subbasement appears to have been a warehouse for smuggled liquor during the Prohibition Era. There are still a large number of cases of old booze and a few oak barrels in there. I know that the Methodist Church was one of the major institutions that pushed for Prohibition, and here's a liquor warehouse right under one of their buildings."

Irma said, "Wow; that is a shocker! I grew up in a different church, but even I knew that the Methodist Board of Temperance was the driving force behind passage of the Eighteenth Amendment to the Constitution and the laws that governed Prohibition. The bootleggers were thumbing their noses at the Methodist Church by building that facility."

Arthur said, "They more likely expected that no one would look for such a warehouse here. They would have been right, too, because nobody ever found and emptied it. What are your political considerations, Dennis?"

The State of Illinois and the City of Chicago have been trying to eliminate their Prohibition Era criminal image for decades. It's bad for tourism, and it's bad for those who want to emphasize modern technological and social advances in our area."

Arthur nodded. "That's understandable. There's no separation of church and state here. We have a common interest in restricting access to this information. What can you tell us about those bodies, Dennis?"

"They're quite puzzling. If they could speak, they'd have intriguing stories to tell. Two of the bodies are virtually skeletal remains; they probably died during bootlegging days. The third body is much more recent, but dead too long to have been our arsonist."

Irma said, "That says that someone knew about that warehouse room during recent years. It almost sounds like the tales of treasure chambers in the Middle East where the ancients set death traps for anyone who might gain entry to them."

Dennis laughed. "Hopefully, we'll find a more logical explanation than that. When you were last here, Arthur told me you had a background in forensic pathology. I'll have to inform my superiors about this situation. In order to keep a lid on things, they may choose to ask you to assist our team in examining the bodies. Would you be available for that?"

"Certainly, Dennis, I'd be happy to help."

Arthur said, "I'd better find Lorna Dyner and make sure that she doesn't spread any premature information about that subbasement. I have two questions we're going to have to address in the near future, Dennis."

"What are they?"

"Was that chamber built specifically for warehousing liquor, and how did they get the booze in and out of there without arousing curiosity among the church members?"

CHAPTER 10 – BRIEFING, PART 1

The next morning, promptly at eleven o'clock, Irma led Arthur to the front door of the Gonzalez home in Parkville, carrying an offering of homemade chocolate swirl Bundt cake to accompany their meeting. Joe answered the door and invited them in with a sweeping arm gesture.

"Ooh, that cake smells good; you must have just baked it."

"We professional bakers preheat our ovens as the sun rises in order to give you early morning pastry delights."

Penny had been listening to this entryway banter. "Irma, I doubly welcome you. Joe and Steve depleted my snack supply while they watched television last night. I'll second Joe's comment about that freshly-baked aroma."

Arthur cleared his throat loudly. "All this welcoming of Irma and her cake – please note that I'm here too. Seriously, she is pretty special at baking; she'd be a welcome addition to Walter Hadley's staff at his bakery if she were interested in a side job."

Irma glared at him. "What do you mean by staff? If I wanted that work, I'd open my own shop and compete with him. Anyway, I have too much fun investigating strange criminal activities with all of you."

Steve DuBois, who worked with Penny and Joe at their clandestine federal agency, came downstairs and exchanged greetings with the newcomers. "I'll be sharing info about some bizarre developments today; how about you and Arthur?"

Irma said, "If this were a competition, you wouldn't stand a chance. I'm sure that we'll win the strangeness trophy for today."

Penny said, "That sounds like a cue for us to settle down. Grab your drinks and goodies, and we'll get started.

While we do that, Steve, please inform Irma and Arthur of your new status."

"I'm pleased to announce that married life suits me very well. Ellen, stepson Eric, and I have enjoyed life together for six months now in Paul, Idaho. Penny and Joe have promoted me to manager of the Washington office, justifying a larger apartment there to provide space for Ellen and Eric during school vacation periods. My final tidbit of news is that our high-schooler, Eric, will soon be babysitting for a new brother or sister; we're old-fashioned enough that we're foregoing a gender test."

Arthur said, "That is a cornucopia of good news. Congratulations on all counts."

Irma gave Steve a hug and a kiss on his cheek. "We'll have to come visit you soon in either Idaho or Washington. Our family isn't expanding yet, but we are looking to replace our apartment with a house."

Taking her cake and iced tea to the table, Penny sat down. She motioned for the others to do the same. "Sorry, Gang, but it's time for us to get to work. Steve is our houseguest and has come the farthest, so we'll let him speak first."

"Thanks, Penny; as you know, we've been trying to locate Karl Simitski ever since he altered his interests from collecting Middle Eastern antiquities to counterfeiting currency. He was originally an Iraqi citizen with a different name and had been a member of Saddam Hussein's government. He became wealthy when that government fell and he used fraud to help himself to a major portion of one of Saddam's bank accounts. He then came to the U.S. and assumed the guise of Karl Simitski, a collector of art and artifacts. As we were closing in on him for attempting to steal a major antiquity and possibly harboring loot from the Iraqi National Museum, he used his wealth to gear up for counterfeiting currency and then disappeared.

"After several months of investigating false leads, I made contact with one of Karl's former associates at the

University of Wisconsin at Madison. That contact, Dr. George Smetzger, a professor in the Department of Anthropology proved valuable to our cause when I visited him. In order to put him at ease and avoid the possibility that Smetzger would alert Karl to our interest, I posed as a fellow academic."

He approached the door of the Department of Anthropology, handling his bamboo cane as an orchestra conductor's baton rather than a tool for support. He greeted the receptionist with a wave of the cane and a smile.

"I'm Dr. Wilfred Stevens, and I'm hoping to have a brief meeting with Dr. George Smetzger. I called yesterday and left a message, but I don't have an appointment."

"I believe that Dr. Smetzger is in the building. Please take a seat while I try to locate him." She reached for her telephone.

He browsed through a scholarly journal about Middle Eastern archaeology while concentrating on the receptionist's telephone search comments. She obtained suggestions for Smetzger's location on her first two calls, and located him with the third.

"Dr. Smetzger, this is Paula at the reception desk. I have Dr. Wilfred Stevens here to see you. He mentioned that he called yesterday and left a message. Would you be available to meet with him?"

Wilfred noted that the person on the other end of the line spoke to the receptionist at length. At first, he took this to be an indication that Smetzger was rejecting his contact, but Paula smiled as she put down the phone.

"George will meet you in his office in five minutes. Turn left as you leave this room, and it will be the last door on the right at the end of the hall. Before he would agree to the meeting, he had to tell me a funny story about a priest, a minister, and a rabbi each trying to make a convert out of a bear. Sometimes I think George should have become a stand-up comedian instead of an archaeologist,"

"I've been on a number of digs, and I can assure you that a good sense of humor helps keep you sane while you're spending months searching for a few bones and artifacts."

He gave Paula another wave of his cane as he left the department office and walked down the hall as directed. The door of the last office on the right was open when he approached it. A bald man with thick glasses peered over three piles of papers on the desk.

"You must be Wilfred Stevens; come on in and have a seat. I'm George Smetzger."

"Thanks for meeting with me on short notice, George. The receptionist was laughing when I left her, after hearing your story."

"Paula is a good audience. I try to have a joke or humorous tale handy when I speak with her. What can I do for you, Wilfred?"

"We have a mutual friend, Karl Simitski. I haven't heard from him since last November, but I remembered him mentioning you. I wondered whether you knew where he is. When I last spoke with him, he mentioned the possibility of a dig in Iraq. Do you know where he is, and whether that field work took place?"

"Karl's an interesting guy. Whenever we were together, I'd tell people we worked comedy clubs together as Smetzger and Simitski. Try saying that ten times fast. Anyway, despite the name fun, I found him to be a moody one. He could be the life of the party, or he could be mad as Hell at someone who wouldn't cooperate with him. I had heard that he organized that field trip to Iraq that you mentioned, but I'm not sure whether he went himself. That would have been for the best, because I also heard that local terrorists ambushed the party, with some serious casualties."

"I had heard rumors of that, but I wasn't convinced they were true. The person who gave me that second-hand report said that Karl hadn't been over there. Would you know where he went after he left his house in Missouri?"

George turned to the pile of papers on the right-hand side of his desk. "I think I have something for you; it should be about three inches up from the bottom of this stack. Yes, here it is. Bob Philkins at M.I.T. mentioned in a letter that he had seen Simitski on a dock in a Maine fishing port, but that he had received a brush-off from Karl when he tried to talk with him. I told you that Karl's moody and hard to understand. Anyway, that meeting took place only two months ago, so Simitski could not have been a casualty of that Iraq expedition."

"That is good news, although I can't imagine why he was so rude to Bob Philkins. Karl must have some problems on his plate ... I've hit you with all this business about Karl, but what kind of projects are you pursuing, George?"

"We don't do major work in archaeology here, Wilfred, but we look for students with an affinity for the field. The main Wisconsin campus for those who want to specialize in archaeology is La Crosse. I have a liaison connection with them, of course, and I am planning to organize a dig in Israel in January of next year. Perhaps you'd like to come along with us?"

"Now that would be fun, but I'm not sure my schedule would permit it. I'll take one of your cards from the pile here, and I'll let you know in a couple of months. Thanks for the contact information on Bob Philkins. Right now, I have a project in Arizona to complete. I've enjoyed meeting you, George, and learning a little about your department. I may be back in touch with you in connection with a book I'm writing. I'll send you more details later."

Steve continued relating his story of tracking Karl Simitski. "The next lead came via a telephone conversation with Bob Philkins at M.I.T."

He prepared himself to be in character when Bob answered the telephone. As he heard the line go live, he thought, *show time*, and said, "Bob? This is Wilfred Stevens calling. I'm contacting you at the suggestion of George Smetzger from the University of Wisconsin. I'm trying to locate Karl Simitski. We're past associates, but I've lost track of him lately. George said that you saw Karl in Maine recently. Would you be able to tell me anything about his current activities or location?"

"Any friend of George's is a friend of mine, Wilfred. That George is a real character and a lot of fun at any party. I wish I could say the same for Karl. I did see him in Maine; it was an accidental encounter on a dock in Boothbay Harbor. He looked astonished to see me and at first pretended that we were strangers. I think he was doing something he didn't want witnessed, but I couldn't stick around long enough to find out. Simitski escorted me to the side and suggested that I leave because he was involved in a test for a classified government project. I complied because I didn't want to cause a fuss even though I have a high-level clearance, but the people there and the boat they were loading looked pretty unusual."

"In what ways were they unusual?"

"His assistants weren't speaking English. I couldn't quite pinpoint the language, but it might have been Arabic. I thought that strange for people supposedly working on a U.S. government project. Also, the boat they were loading didn't look like your typical Maine fishing boat; it was too streamlined and powerful."

"Was there a ship offshore that day?"

"That's a very interesting question, Wilfred. You're right on target. There was a freighter about a half mile out, and it didn't appear to be moving. My impression of it was that it was pretty nondescript and rusty. I didn't really focus on it."

"You were very observant, probably because Karl's behavior surprised you. When you're shocked, memories become indelibly recorded."

"Interesting observation; are you a psychologist, Wilfred?"

"Actually, I'm an archaeologist, but I'm also a student of the people around me. Let me ask you one more question, Bob."

"Go right ahead; I'm enjoying this conversation and the opportunity to rehash what happened that day."

"This one may be more difficult for you. Can you remember the date of that encounter?"

"That one's easy, Wilfred. The date was May twenty-sixth, the Monday on which we celebrated Memorial Day this year. I had left Cambridge for a Maine excursion over the Memorial Day weekend. It was a kickoff for changing to summer lifestyles and traveling. Will any of this help you locate Karl now?"

"You've at least given me some clues that are worth pursuing. I agree with you that it was a strange situation. It's always possible that he was working with Arabic speakers to set up a new archaeological expedition, but I'll have to check further on that. Thanks so much for this conversation, Bob. I'll let you know what I find out from additional inquiries."

"Please do that, Wilfred, and stop in for a visit when you're next in Cambridge."

Steve continued addressing those seated at the table. "Following my conversation with Bob Philkins, I wrote all of my notes from that contact in my logbook so that I wouldn't forget any of them. Karl's only government-related work would have been the export of counterfeit currency."

Joe said, "And it would have been a very large amount of currency to require a freighter to transport the cargo. What do you think, Penny?"

"I think Steve, as Wilfred, did a great job. I also think that Karl may have been shipping by freighter because ships don't receive the same security scrutiny as airliners."

Arthur said, "Joe, your agency should have connections for determining what freighter would have been offshore at Boothbay Harbor on May twenty-sixth."

"If the vessel was well-maintained, it would have Automatic Identification System or AIS electronics for collision avoidance and satellite tracking. Philkins described this freighter as run-down, so I wouldn't bet on the ship's announcing its identity, especially if it's involved in some kind of illegal business. Even so, its position and route might show up on marinetraffic.com or on some of our satellite records. We'll check on that."

Irma said, "The freighter may have been in poor condition, but that ocean-worthy speedboat should be easy to spot along the Maine coast. There can't be too many like that. What do you think, Penny?"

"I think you have a good point, and we'll check it out. I'm also concerned about the reference to Arabic-speaking assistants or freighter crewmembers."

Arthur took a piece of coffee cake from the serving dish. "We know that Simitski had invested in equipment and special paper for counterfeiting. It's logical to suspect that he was loading a shipment of counterfeit currency onto that freighter. If that was the case, he's probably decided that there's less risk in passing bad currency overseas. If he's printing money here and shipping it abroad, he would probably have his presses set up near the coast. My guess is that he'd still be somewhere in that area. He'd have no reason to suspect that bumping into a casual acquaintance would alert the authorities."

Implications

Penny said, "Let's not forget that Simitski is probably not his current alias. He was originally Iraqi, and we know that he changed his name since we last encountered him."

Joe said, "Steve, or should I call you Wilfred, you've done a great job in obtaining this information. I suggest that you start tracking that ship right away. Penny and I will discuss the strangeness of the Blakes' case with them while you work online in the other room."

Penny said, "That's pretty abrupt, Joe; why the rush? Simitski was sighted on May twenty-sixth, close to two months ago."

"As I recall, freighters often spend two to three months at sea. Whatever Karl loaded onto that ship may not yet have reached its destination. We have to try to find them before they get there."

CHAPTER 11 – BRIEFING, PART 2

Penny refreshed the supplies of drinks and snacks during the short break before the Blakes would start their presentation. Once the two couples had returned to the table, she said, "Now we're ready to hear about your unique case, Arthur. Do you still think it's stranger than shipping counterfeit money or other illicit cargo covertly from the Maine coast?"

"You can judge for yourselves after we relate our tale."

Arthur set the stage by reviewing his awakening by the Bishop's call and their witnessing the fire at the Amboy United Methodist Church. He repeated the litany of past problems in the church that he had received from Pastor Lorna Dyner, and he had Irma discuss her impressions while the fire was still raging through the building. Then Arthur dropped the bombshell of the surprise unearthed by Dennis Mikken and his state fire investigator partner.

"Up to this point, you may have felt that we have a traumatic, but not unprecedented, case of an arsonist torching a church. The strange part is that Dennis and company discovered a second basement level below the main basement. You get into it through a hidden trapdoor that became visible only after the basement furnishings burned away. When they opened this chamber, they found that it had been a warehouse for liquor from Prohibition days. It still contained a large inventory of smuggled spirits plus the remains of three people, two skeletons that probably date to the period when that warehouse was active, plus a more recent body that is no more than a few years old."

Penny said, "That is strange. You may have won the weirdness contest. Have you been in that subbasement yet?"

Irma said, "No, the fire investigators are going to pretend it doesn't exist until all of the news media people finish reporting about a generic church fire and go home. They aren't even revealing that they think an arsonist set the fire. Once interest in the burned-out church wanes, we'll be invited to view the chamber. I'm looking forward to joining the fire investigators in examining the body and skeletal remains. They're shying away from using an official pathologist in order to minimize the number of people who know about this find."

Arthur refilled his coffee mug. "This is almost going to be a case of time travel. We're going to have to unravel all the threads of a tapestry that someone wove during Prohibition days. Would your agency like to be involved in the process? There are federal angles because of liquor smuggling, interstate commerce of then-prohibited substances, tax evasion, and mob conspiracies. Irma and I will continue to investigate the case on our own because these crimes occurred on church property, but we won't have any official legal standing. We may have some mutual interests here."

Joe laughed. "Preacher, you're still giving sermons. You don't have to sell us on involvement. This will be a fun case and a great history lesson. What do you think, Penny?"

"I especially like the irony of putting a bootleg liquor warehouse in the basement of a Methodist church. The temperance faction in that church instigated the whole Prohibition movement. This would definitely qualify for investigation as a very cold case."

Irma cleared her throat to get attention. "Before we get too carried away with Prohibition ironies, let's remember that we also have a current case of arson to solve. We don't know whether the perpetrator might strike again at another church."

Arthur said, "Irma's right to address that issue. I calmed the Bishop's fears by suggesting that this was an isolated fire set by someone with a grudge against the Amboy church, but I haven't convinced myself of that. The state investigators think that a professional arsonist started this fire, and my research of Conference documents about past fires in churches revealed that last year, an arsonist hit Living Waters UMC in Centerton, Arkansas and destroyed the building in a similar way. Someone poured gasoline over the altar and ignited it. After the fire department extinguished that blaze, the arsonist came back the next night and used more gasoline to set a fire in the basement that traveled beneath the flooring and completed the destruction of the building. The attacker of the Amboy church used this same technique, lighting accelerants at the altar and in the basement beneath the other end of the sanctuary. The only difference was that he or she lit fires in both places at the same time, with more devastating results. We don't yet know whether the accelerant was gasoline, but the pattern is too similar for us to ignore it."

Joe said, "Your point is well taken. We'll work together on the arson as well as the Prohibition aspects of the case. If this person did follow the same arson pattern as in an Arkansas church fire, this definitely falls within federal jurisdiction. The constitutional right to freedom of religion also implies that a worshipper should be safe in his or her religious building.

"Consider us partners with you on this case, and keep us informed on all progress. We'll notify state authorities of our interest, but we'll also have to support Steve in his pursuit of Karl Simitski, so our efforts will phase in over the next few weeks."

CHAPTER 12 – KARL SIMITSKI

You never know what to expect. It was unbelievable that that Philkins guy from M.I.T. would stumble onto the dock in Boothbay Harbor while we were ferrying our load to that ship. He even yelled out to me as Karl Simitski, a name that I haven't used for months. Most of those crewmen who were doing the loading spoke only Arabic, but there were a few Africans who spoke both English and Arabic. By now, they've spread the story of my different name.

I doubt that Philkins continued to think about the incident after I got rid of him with that government project story. He's a person with tunnel vision, concentrating on his own project and treating interruptions and distractions as peripheral events. I'm less concerned about him than I am about messing up my cover story with that ship's crew. I'll have to convince them that Simitski was a name I used for one particular mission, and that my current name, Frederick Boynwik, is my real identity. I haven't revealed yet that I understand their Arabic conversations. That gives me a big advantage, even if they turn on me at some time. I'll be flying over to meet the ship when it reaches its final destination. When I get there, I'll have another chance to show my loyalty to the cause, but I'll have to be consistent about how I present myself to everyone.

This is very much like the period when I worked for Saddam Hussein. Everyone has to put the cause and organization first, and never appear to anyone to be a lone wolf. When I used the Karl Simitski name, I was my own cause and organization. I enjoyed that. I'll have to be very careful to evaporate from the scene when I next want to go out on my own. If those around me detect advance clues of my plans, they'll arrange for me to disappear permanently. I'm lucky that this outfit had nothing but contempt for

Richard Davidson

Hussein. The key leaders know about my walking off with half of one of his bank accounts, and they treat that as a plus for me rather than a sin. One of the best tactics I ever learned was to identify the dominant power group and join up with it. They'll have to depend on me as long as I keep the counterfeit money factory hidden and beyond their reach.

CHAPTER 13 – FIRST ENTRY

Penny Gonzalez had notified the State Fire Marshal that her federal agency wished to establish a task force combining their two groups' efforts to investigate the church arson and related matters, because of interstate aspects of serial church arsons and probable violations of federal laws. The Office of the State Fire Marshal concurred, and Penny designated Arthur and Irma Blake, consultants to her agency, for assignment to the case. They arranged all of this without revealing the existence of the Amboy United Methodist Church subbasement or their interest in it.

After the fire, Pastor Lorna Dyner had accepted an offer from the pastor of Franklin Grove UMC to conduct joint worship services until the Amboy congregation could rent or build new facilities. This resulted in very few people visiting the sight of the burned-out Amboy church beyond the first week following the fire. Dennis Mikken decided that interest in official activities around the church had subsided sufficiently for the new task force to make its first inspection on the following Monday, the weekday of least activity for all churches.

Penny, Irma, and Arthur met Dennis in the Amboy UMC parking lot and then walked toward the framework of the burned-out church. Arthur mused that the building looked like a skeleton, and they would soon be viewing similar human versions. Dennis and his assistant Celia, a tall muscular African-American woman, repositioned the protective fencing. Then Celia peeled back the tarp that covered the hole in the sanctuary floor to reveal a ladder set up for descent to the basement.

41

"The stairs to the basement are blocked by debris, so we'll use this ladder today. We didn't want to disturb the scene up to this point. Later, we'll clear the stairwell for easier access."

They lowered their equipment on ropes and then climbed down the ladder. Celia and Dennis switched on four well-spaced tripod-mounted battery lanterns to illuminate the whole room, albeit dimly. Penny, Irma, and Arthur meandered around the basement to get a feeling for the size of it.

Penny said, "This basement is larger than I expected. Given the age of the building, I thought this place would be divided into smaller rooms, but there are wooden columns supporting the floor structure above, in order to provide a large amount of open space. They must have designed this place for holding social gatherings and other large functions."

Arthur approached the wall that faced the parking lot. He pulled a piece of scorched paneling slightly away from the wall and looked behind it, using his flashlight for better illumination. "I think I see the answer to one of my questions. This paneling covers up a boarded-over gap in the concrete wall. At one time, they had a large doorway there. My guess is that they had a ramped driveway leading down here. They must have filled in the ramp recess outside to make it part of the lawn. This explains how the bootleggers moved cases of liquor in and out of here."

Irma said, "That leads us to the next discussion. Dennis, please show us how you discovered the entrance to the subbasement. I haven't noticed it yet, so it can't be obvious."

"To give credit where it is due, Celia was the first one to notice the anomaly. She should have the honor of revealing the entrance."

Celia gave a slight bow of thanks toward Dennis and walked toward one of the wooden columns near the back corner of the room. "Let me preface my comments by saying that for years, the church had carpeting covering the floor of this basement. I never would have located the entrance to the subbasement if that carpeting had not burned in the fire. The first thing I noticed was a pair of handles on the side of this column. At first, I didn't give them much thought because we had so many things to check and clean down here. Then, I observed when we had set up larger floodlights, that I could see light through a gap at the top of the column. This meant that it wasn't supporting the ceiling. This particular column is near the back corner of the basement, so the ceiling would have adequate support from the two concrete walls that join there."

Penny said, "Good awareness, Celia. You get extra points for that. Please continue."

"I looked at everything around that column, and I observed that its base sat on the corner of a square section of the wooden floor that was separated from the rest of the floor by cracks. It looked like a trapdoor to me, but there weren't any hinges. After staring at it for a while, I figured out how it works. The handles are mounted on opposite sides of the column. When I grabbed those handles and lifted; the square section of flooring moved upward along with the column, allowing me to rotate the whole assembly and reveal stairs leading down to a room on a lower level."

"Irma asked, "Did it look as though that room had been dug out as a modification to the building, or do you think it was part of the original construction?"

Celia motioned for everyone to follow her toward the back corner of the basement.

"It looked like original construction to me, but you can judge for yourself." She grabbed handles on the sides of a column; then she lifted and rotated it.

Arthur said, "That rotating slab of flooring is bigger than I expected. It's about four feet square. That would provide plenty of space for someone to climb the stairs carrying a case of bottles. I'll conclude that this chamber was built at the same time as the building and that it was designed for warehousing liquor."

Dennis nodded his head in agreement. "That conclusion implies that this church was designed and built by a construction company controlled by bootleggers. It is about the right age for that, Arthur."

"Do you have lights set up downstairs, or will we have to use flashlights?"

"There are battery-powered lanterns on stands down there also. I'll go down first and switch them on. Then the rest of you will have no problem following me."

Penny said, "You're saying that there's enough space for all of us down there."

Celia smiled. "You won't feel crowded downstairs."

Irma raised her hand like a student. "Before you lead us down, Dennis, have you taken precautions to secure the crime scene? If we have bodies in that chamber, we won't want a bunch of people corrupting the evidence before we do a thorough analysis of everything and everyone in that room."

"Good point; I do have yellow crime scene tape isolating the key areas, but to be extra-cautious, let's limit ourselves to two people in the subbasement at any one time. Take a brief break while I go back to the truck and get sets of plastic coveralls, gloves, and shoe covers for each of us."

CHAPTER 14 – FREIGHTER

Steve DuBois stood with Jefferson Lee of the Secret Service at the railing of a high-speed naval craft that they had temporarily borrowed from the joint task force operating against Somali pirates. In complete darkness, they scanned distant activity off the southern coast of mountainous Al Hallaniyah Island, located off the southern coast of Oman. Al Hallaniyah, the largest of the Khuriya Muriya Islands, was famous as a fishing paradise, but in the darkness of this night, it hosted a large freighter showing minimal lights as it prepared to offload cargo to several small powerboats.

Jeff lowered his binoculars and turned to Steve. "It's about time for me to give the signal. We want to grab them before the shipment gets split up among those boats."

"I agree. If these local boats spread the cargo to multiple staging areas and then fishing boats distribute it throughout the Middle East, we'll never recover all of it."

Jeff Lee raised his radio to his lips. "Close in now, and try to capture all of the small craft as well. Our principal may be on one of them."

Sounds of multiple engines broke the nighttime silence, and powerful lights pierced the darkness as twelve well-armed high-speed pursuit craft with crews at their battle stations converged on the freighter and its client vessels. An amplified voice from the lead naval craft commanded the freighter captain to allow a boarding party without resistance.

On board the freighter, crewmembers scurried to hoist the anchor and get under way. Others uncovered machine guns and aimed them over the railings toward the encircling boats. The captain had chosen to resist.

Suddenly, a roaring sound from the southeast heralded a low pass over the freighter by two jet fighters from the aircraft carrier assigned to the anti-piracy force. As they circled for their second pass, the freighter lowered its anchor again, and the crew removed the machine guns from their railing positions.

Steve and Jeff had just congratulated each other on the avoidance of violence, when one of the speedboats that had been awaiting its cargo share broke out of the ring of naval boats and headed for the southwest corner of Al Hallaniyah Island.

Jeff said, "They're heading for the harbor. We're faster than they are." He gave the order to pursue them.

Steve scanned the horizon as the first hints of morning softened the darkness. "There's nowhere for them to go. If they land in the harbor, their only hope is to hide in the island's mountains. Eventually, they'd either be found or starve."

"Unless they're local people - there aren't many who live on this island, but they could disappear among the others."

"I'm not worried about the locals, Jeff, but if Karl Simitski is in that boat, he'll have a harder time hiding."

The fleeing boat remained a mile ahead of them as it approached the harbor entrance. At that point, another larger boat emerged from the harbor and pulled alongside the smaller craft. Jeff and Steve watched through binoculars as three people transferred from the smaller to the larger craft. As a fourth person prepared to transfer, the first man onto the larger boat turned and shot him three times. The other two transferees threw the gunshot victim overboard. Then the smaller boat continued into the harbor, while the more powerful craft rounded the point at the southeast corner of the island and headed full-throttle for the Oman mainland north of the island.

Steve said, "We should try to rescue that man, if he's not dead already. Something made them turn on him.

We'll never catch that second boat anyway. They had a contingency plan in case something went wrong. Those three people who switched boats may have included Karl, or they may have been other leaders. I'm sure they were the most important people here."

Jeff directed the crew to head for the site of the splash and retrieve the victim. By the time they reached him, the man had partially submerged, but they were able to snag him with a pair of boat hooks. When the crewmen rolled the body over, Steve announced that it was Karl Simitski, and he was quite dead. Apparently, his associates had blamed him for the attack on the offloading operation.

Jeff said, "You have your man, and we prevented this shipment of phony money from getting into circulation, but our job isn't done. We still have to find that counterfeiting plant and learn whether Simitski had a partner who will keep it running. At least we'll have plenty of samples of Simitski's currency. Our analysts will be able to pinpoint its flaws and alert police agencies around the world to watch for it."

Steve said, "Simitski's death ends our involvement. He was the last loose end for our earlier investigation. CIA will want to check out the group that had been working with Karl. Jeff, when you find that counterfeiting plant, you may also find the collection of art and antiquities that Simitski accumulated with Saddam's bank account money. This will be a Secret Service case from now on, but our agency is available if new developments lead you beyond searching for the funny-money people."

CHAPTER 15 - DOWNSTAIRS

Shrouded in pale blue sterile vinyl, Arthur Blake followed Dennis Mikken down the stairs to the battery-lantern-illuminated subbasement. As he descended, he discovered that the lower level room was much larger than he had expected. It was at least half the size of the main basement above it. Decades-dried hardwood shelves supported many cases of whiskey. Oak barrels contained subtly varying liquids. He wondered whether all those quarantine years had improved the taste, potency, and value of this stash.

To the right of the bottom stair, separated from the nearest set of shelves, stood a round table surrounded by four chairs, centered within a larger area bounded by yellow crime scene tape. Upon the table sat an open bottle that must have once contained whiskey, along with two empty shot glasses. A pair of skeletal figures occupied two of the surrounding chairs. The third chair occupant, red plaid flannel shirt and blue jeans bulging slightly with not-yet-completely-decomposed flesh, leaned forward, face down on folded arms. The fourth chair sat angled away from the table as though inviting a future occupant.

Arthur shook his head as he surveyed the tableau. "The person who killed the most recent visitor to this place has a sick sense of humor. He or she arranged the body and extra chair for maximum impact upon later tourists like us."

"That's interesting word choice, Arthur. If these figures were wax clones, they would be appropriate for tourists in a museum. Unfortunately, they're real and gruesome."

"God rest their souls, regardless of their life stories."

"Amen to that. They've probably been dead too long for us to learn their histories. We'd better go upstairs and let the others come down. I don't think we should keep this place open for too long until the forensics people have examined everything. The only thing that kept that latest body from decomposing completely was cool dry stale air. Fresh circulating oxygen will accelerate decay."

"I agree with you about minimizing the open time for this place to retard decomposition, but I do expect that we'll learn these people's stories before we're through with this case."

Dennis and Arthur climbed back upstairs. The next two people to descend were Celia and Irma. Then Celia returned to the main basement level, allowing Penny to join Irma, who had stayed below to photograph all aspects of the three sets of remains and their surroundings.

"Irma, it's amazing to me that these unfortunates were down here for so long while normal church activities were going on upstairs."

"Actually, I met Arthur under similar circumstances, when I officially examined a body he had found in the attic of the older Parkville Church building. Corpses can't cry out for help or tell people where they are. There have been many occasions of murderers having sealed up their victims' bodies within buildings or buried them underneath houses."

"How romantic; you met Arthur while examining a corpse, and you still married him."

"In those days, corpses and cops were my only associates, so I think I did pretty well."

"Given those circumstances, I won't tease you anymore. It's too early to ask about the most recent victim; he'll require an autopsy. Can you say anything about our two bony friends?"

"I can; they were shot in the back, either while sitting at the table or as they tried to leave."

"And how did you deduce that so quickly?"

"You can't see it from where you're standing, Penny, but the shreds of shirt on the person on the left show two bullet holes, and the person on the right has a chip on a rib in the back, but not in the front. The chip geometry suggests impact from the rear."

"What else have you already figured out?"

"It is intriguing that the one on the left is male, while the one on the right is female. She would be an oddity if she had been one of the bootleggers. Even in crime circles back then, females had a hard time getting to play a featured role."

"That is interesting. I wonder if they were a couple and if there was a romance angle to their deaths."

"Penny, I like the fact that when you're away from Joe, you think about romantic aspects of life and death. We spend too much time on the objective details of investigations; we concentrate on the words, but sometimes miss the music."

"Ooh, I like your thinking. Maybe we should have you work with me and have Arthur work with Joe more often."

"I'd like that, but we should get back up to the main basement. I'll get back down here later to do a more thorough check of the bodies and other forensic evidence."

They climbed back up the stairs to the main basement, where Dennis, Arthur, and Celia awaited them.

Penny said, "We've all had a look at that chamber and its contents. Irma has deduced that our skeletal friends are a male and a female, and that they were both shot in the back. We'll have quite a puzzle to solve before we determine how and why those three got there."

Dennis took a step toward Penny. "I'm afraid that Celia and I won't be joining you on that quest for that scene's history. While you were downstairs, I received a call from the head of my department. She told me that our jurisdiction ends with studying the fire and trying to determine who set it. Illinois has critical budget problems, and there are too few of us fire investigators on the payroll to allow for investigations that exceed our chartered duties. They won't hire or borrow anyone else, so we're on a tight leash and budget. Penny, I'm sorry that we won't be able to pursue this mystery, but we'll unofficially consult if you come up with questions that we can justify as related to the fire investigation."

"I understand, Dennis. We'll keep the task force going by assisting you with your limited objective. Steve DuBois is coming off a special assignment to wrap up one of our older cases. I'll have him contact you shortly. We won't have this Amboy church matter resolved until we catch the arsonist and also learn the stories behind our subbasement residents.

CHAPTER 16 – APPRENTICESHIP

Bearing official task force credentials, Irma's forensics kit, and two cameras, Arthur followed his wife down the apartment stairs and into his Saturn Vue.

"How come I have to carry everything?"

"Because today you're my apprentice, and I'm in charge. I thought that I would be assisting some Illinois official in analyzing and documenting the contents of the hidden chamber, but given the state's inability to spend money, we're on our own. It may be a better approach, because we'll have fewer opportunities for some public servant to leak information to the press."

"Very good, Dr. Frankenstein; I will be your Igor."

"That's funny, but I don't expect to bring anyone back to life."

They drove to the Amboy UMC and found the parking lot empty and the church surrounded by connected portable sections of chain-link fence to protect people from accidents and the remaining church structure from looting. They retrieved the padlock key from beneath the stone specified by Dennis to be its hiding place, and unlocked the gate section. Arthur gathered their equipment and followed Irma into the open-roofed building carcass. He was happy to find a note near the covered hole in the sanctuary floor, indicating that Dennis and Celia had cleared the basement stairway of rubble.

"Now that I'm a pack mule, I appreciate niceties like being able to use stairs instead of a ladder to go to the basement." He wrote *Arthur thanks you* on the note and put it back where he had found it.

Irma led the way to the basement and lit the battery-operated lanterns. Arthur set his load of equipment down near the hidden entrance to the lower level, and they both donned vinyl protective coveralls and gloves so that they wouldn't further contaminate the crime scene below. Irma grasped the handles on the side of the special column; then she lifted up and rotated the square of flooring out of the way, following Celia's earlier example.

"That was a lot easier than I had expected. I had thought that Celia's strength would be a requirement for opening the portal, but that's not the case. When we get set up downstairs, please make a note that even someone with quite limited strength could gain entry to that chamber."

"I almost offered to open it for you when I saw you grab the two handles, but I realized that you were testing the degree of difficulty of the process. Now we know that young or small people can't be rule out as suspects."

"That's an interesting comment, Arthur. You're treating this as a current murder investigation. This happened so long ago that the perpetrator is probably just as dead as the victims."

"I expect that we'll work out the circumstances of that long-ago crime, but remember that there's also a more contemporary body down there. I'll wager that his murderer is still alive."

"And I'll wager that Bishop Chandler would prefer that you didn't use gambling terminology in your reports. Speaking of your boss, have you told him about this hidden chamber and the human remains inside it?"

"I have specific instructions from him to keep things quiet and to avoid any publicity that might be detrimental to the church. I've decided that his words give me leeway to keep our entire investigation confidential until we have results. The state did us a favor by keeping the arson investigation separate. We'll be able to discuss the fire inquiry without even indicating the existence of a second investigation on a federal level."

Richard Davidson

"That's fine with me, Arthur; now gather up the gear, and we'll introduce ourselves to the downstairs neighbors."

CHAPTER 17 – STEVE AND DENNIS

Steve DuBois arrived ten minutes early for his first meeting with Dennis Mikken. A few minutes later, Dennis and Celia entered the departmental lobby. After introductions, Celia excused herself to attend a meeting of her own while the two men headed for Mikken's office.

Dennis offered Steve a can of soda from his personal refrigerator, and Steve accepted, selecting a root beer.

"I had to lobby long and hard for this little refrigerator, but I prevailed based on my argument that I spend so much time at hot fire scenes that I'm always dehydrated and need to consume as much liquid as possible."

"That sounds like a valid argument to me, Dennis. Do you spend enough time in the office to get much use out of it?"

"They do keep me in the field most of the time, but at least I have drinks during the tedious process of writing up my reports. At any level, governments run on paperwork for fuel. Tell me, Steve, have you had much experience with fire investigations?"

"In other words, am I going to be useful to you as we work together? I'll say my experience has been limited, but that I'm glad it has been. We work on two different aspects of the fire problem. You investigate them after they happen. I watch for signs of pending terrorism and try to keep fires and explosions from happening at all. When I visit a fire or explosion scene, it usually means that we've already failed by allowing it to occur. We also have to treat some arson fires as accidental, both to tell the public that terrorism hasn't occurred, and to keep the terrorist from realizing that we know about him or her."

"That sounds as though you'll be very useful. One of your statements interests me. I've tracked down only one female arsonist. Have you seen many of them?"

"Terrorists want to be difficult to detect. Women have the advantages of arousing less suspicion and of being able to wear seemingly normal clothing that accommodates a hidden bomb or incendiary device."

"I think we'll make a good team for this case, Steve. There are far too many church fires for us to accept them all as independent events. There have to be serial arsons, whether the Amboy fire fits into such a chain of incidents or not."

"That's why I'm pleased that Penny nominated me to work with you. I've read about some of the recent church fires, and I haven't pinned down the indicators for a terrorist or a hired gun at work. You told Arthur and Irma that you felt a professional arsonist had set the Amboy fire. What led you to that conclusion?"

"You're going to make me defend my statements. Thanks, Steve; that's a valuable contribution. I'm not as sure now as I was when I reached that tentative conclusion. The earmarks of a professional arsonist are usually the nature of the accelerant, the precision with which it is applied, a pre-existing pattern of similar fires, and the existence of a motive that either directly rewards the fire-starter, or makes it worthwhile for someone to pay him. I initially suspected a pro because I had the feeling that the accelerant was something specialized. Since then, the lab people have processed the samples I sent them, and they've concluded that the accelerant was only gasoline. The two hot spots where fires started reminded me of previous church fires, so I thought it suggested an arsonist's standard operating procedure. As to a reward for destroying the church, I haven't discovered any. Consequently, I'm ready to back away from that *professional arsonist* theory until I find more supporting evidence."

Implications

"Good, Dennis; your willingness to reconsider fits with my gut feel about the prematurity of that *professional* statement. Can we review the photographs and notes you and others took during and immediately after the blaze?"

"Sure, Steve, but I didn't get there until the next day. The photos and videos taken during the fire were from amateur, fire department, and news media sources."

CHAPTER 18 – FORENSICS

Once in the subbasement, Irma's personality changed subtly as she prepared for evidence gathering and analysis. It was as though she had donned her *cloak of objectivity*. Arthur noticed the transition and prepared to assist as required while she took the lead.

"The first phase of our forensics procedure is observation. Before we disturb anything, tell me what you see, especially anything unusual."

"Fair enough, Irma; I wonder about the deterioration of clothing. My mother had a ragbag in the basement for decades, and those rags didn't change much at all over that period. She could remove a piece of an old dress or shirt and use it for a patch or a square on a quilt without any problem. Here, I see that almost all the cloth draped on the two skeletal figures has disintegrated into shreds, while the clothing on the more recent corpse is more intact, although it looks grubby and moldy."

"That's a good observation, Arthur. The bodies of the older victims completely decomposed, and their clothing pretty much suffered the same fate. The organisms that processed the body tissue attacked the clothing that was in contact with it also. The fact that the newer victim's clothes appear to be intact tells us that he hasn't been down here long enough for the decomposition process to spread from his flesh to the fabrics. I'll amend that statement by saying that the fibers in his clothing have probably lost their strength by now, even though they appear to be intact. What else do you see that's significant?"

"Getting away from the bodies, I notice that the shelves near the stairs have fewer cases and loose bottles of whisky than the shelves farther into the room. Those shelves also have less dust and fewer cobwebs on them. I'll speculate that someone entered this chamber within the last decade or so and started to remove the whiskey. Something must have happened to limit the amount of whiskey that he or she could take. That also means that this ancient bootleg whiskey still has value."

"Do you think that the more recent victim with his head on his arms at the table was involved in removing that whiskey?"

"He may have been, but I'll need more evidence to reach that conclusion if I want to be objective."

"Arthur, you are good at this exercise. I agree with you."

"Before you ask, I'll add that at least one of these people was shot down here rather than having been brought here after being shot elsewhere."

Irma looked around, but didn't see anything to confirm his statement. "Are you showing off or playing games? Why do you say that?"

"Look at the third case from the left on the second shelf up from the floor. That's not a dot over the *"i"* in *Whiskey*; that's a bullet hole. We'll have to search to see whether there are others."

"Your bullet hole at that low level says that someone was shot with a downward trajectory by a taller person, or that the victim was shot while sitting down."

"You're probably right, unless this was a stray shot that missed its target. The location suggests that someone shot the two skeletal victims in the back while they were sitting. They may have been playing cards or counting money at the table. I'll guess that the newer fatality was not sitting when shot. His body was arranged at the table afterward."

"I see your logic. Who would willingly sit at a table with two skeletons? That would be creepy."

"On our last visit, we noted that someone, probably the killer of the more recent casualty, arranged the fourth chair in a position to invite someone else to the table. That suggests that he or she stage-managed the final scene, and that the latest victim was placed in his chair after he died. Is it acceptable for us to touch things now? I'd like to look for bullets while you work on the bodies."

Irma moved her forensics kit closer to the table. "Those bullets should either be under the skeletons if they remained within their bodies, or in the walls or whiskey cases. There may be one or more within the fleshy corpse too."

Arthur photographed the bodies around the table, the overall layout of cases on the various shelves in the chamber, and the stairs to the main basement. Then he photographed the whiskey case with the bullet hole. He pried open the top of the case with his pocketknife and took a picture of the two broken bottles inside. The bullet had passed through the side of the case, then through the nearest bottle, and came to rest inside the second broken bottle beyond it. Arthur removed the whiskey case from the shelf, placed it on the floor, and used long tweezers from Irma's kit to extract the bullet and place it in an evidence bag. He marked the bag with the specifics of where he had found the bullet.

Irma wrote in her notebook that the newer male body showed signs of blunt force trauma to the back of the head from a heavy object. She suspected that the weapon that caused the wound had been some kind of metal tool rather than one of the many bottles in the room. Apparently, the killer had either been very angry or wanted to be very sure that the victim died, because he or she had also shot the man in the forehead.

She probed through the fracture on the back of the skull to try to get the bullet, but found she couldn't reach it. Then Irma retrieved her bone saw from the bottom of her forensics bag. She had only used it under sterile conditions before, but her long-sitting *patient* wouldn't mind. She carefully removed the top of the skull, and then used an angled clamp to push aside the small amount of remaining brain matter and grab the bullet. She placed it in an evidence bag and marked the critical reference data on the label.

Irma cleaned her saw as well as possible and returned it to its case. She heard Arthur working on something behind one of the sets of shelves and walked toward him. As she did, she heard scraping and thumping behind her. She turned around in time to see the trapdoor at the top of the stairs swivel to a complete closure. A final thump vibrated the wooden panel as a heavy object landed on it. Someone had sealed their exit and trapped them with three dead roommates for company.

CHAPTER 19 – PENNY AND JOE

Joe finished washing his and Penny's cars and returned his bucket and supplies to the garage. He joined Penny on the patio where she sat concentrating on her computer screen.

"The cars are ready for our next outing. You look pensive; did your research lead to something disturbing?"

"I did a search to try to get a feeling for the frequency of church fires in this country. I discovered that it's a major problem. I found a relatively old report from the U.S. Fire Administration in 2002 that indicated that there were at that time thirteen hundred church fires per year in the United States, and that twenty-five percent of them were instances of arson ... that's four hundred twenty-five church arsons per year, and the numbers will likely be higher now."

"Churches are easy targets, because they're usually open and rarely patrolled by security personnel."

Penny stood and stretched after sitting so long. "We're looking into that one church fire in Amboy, but how can any agency get a nationwide problem of this magnitude under control?"

"I appreciate your compassion and concern, Penny, but all we can do is to investigate each individual fire. There may be a few serial arsonists involved, but most of these fires are likely the work of someone who has a grudge against a particular church or who is against religion in any form. In my own searching, I even found a case where a church was destroyed by its own pastor, to cover the fact that he had stolen collection money."

"OK, Joe; we'll concentrate on the Amboy UMC fire. You haven't even seen the remains of the church. How about heading over there now, so that you'll have a better feeling for this church and the way somebody torched it?"

"Maybe later this afternoon or tomorrow, Penny; I have to check with Jefferson Lee at Secret Service now, to learn whether they've made progress on finding that counterfeiting plant."

CHAPTER 20 – TRAPPED

Arthur climbed the stairs as far as he could and pushed upward on the panel above him. "The person who locked us in here must have put something very heavy on top of this trapdoor. I should be able to push it upward and swivel it out of the way, but I can't budge it at all."

"I already checked that cell phones don't work in this subbasement, so we're on our own as far as figuring how to get out."

"I think we'll be able to handle it, but it may take a while. You can continue studying our three dead amigos if you like, while I work at opening up this panel. Do you have a drill in your kit, Irma?"

"I have a small one for drilling small holes in a skull or bone, but it's not going to open big holes in that panel."

"Let me have it. I want to make enough holes to keep us supplied with air while we work on our escape."

Arthur began drilling a pattern of holes in the panel, but the tool's battery grew weaker as he worked and failed completely by the fourteenth hole.

Irma switched off one of the battery lanterns. "We have three battery lights. I'll switch off two of them; the batteries will last much longer with only one operating at a time."

"We won't lack for light. I'll tear strips off the bottom of my shirt to serve as wicks, and I'll make alcohol lamps using bottles of whiskey that are still sealed." He opened a pocketknife and started to cut shirt strips.

"That's good thinking, Arthur, but the burning lamps will use up some of our oxygen."

"That's why I drilled the holes in the panel."

Arthur found a full bottle of whiskey, dipped a braid of shirt strips into it and lit the end with a match. The resulting flame cast new light on their surroundings.

Irma said, "That surprised me. You don't smoke, but you carry matches."

"You take a forensics kit on field trips; I carry a small survival kit. The knife and the matches came out of that."

"What else do you have in there?"

"I'll let you know the other items when they become useful. Right now, I'm going to take my new alcohol lamp and explore this chamber a bit more. I'm hoping to find some useful tools."

Arthur took his lamp and started searching up and down each aisle, being sure to check the contents of all the shelves plus the walls and corners of the warehouse chamber. He returned after about ten minutes carrying an open whiskey case with several objects in it.

"From the look on your face, I assume you found something useful."

He placed his burning alcohol lamp on the table and the wooden case on the bottom step. "I have several interesting items. Please accept into our evidence collection two probable murder weapons, a very old revolver and a small crowbar with hair sticking to it at the curved end. These might be useful in assisting our escape, but I suggest we avoid contaminating them unless we get desperate. I also have about twenty feet of strong rope and a claw hammer. I discovered an old two-wheel cart that they must have used for moving cases of liquor, but I couldn't see any immediate need for it, so I left it in the back corner against the wall."

"That's very good, Arthur; those weapons may even have fingerprints on them."

"We'll consider that possibility later. The top priority right now is to get out of this place before we have to go on a whiskey diet to survive. Hand me your bone saw. It's probably too delicate to completely open up the trapdoor panel, but it will at least give us a start."

Irma handed Arthur the saw. "You do realize that the saw won't do you any good unless you have a slot in the panel for inserting the blade to start its cut."

"Fear not; I planned ahead. When I drilled those air holes, I arranged them in two straight lines at right angles to each other. Now I'll hit the back end of my knife with the hammer I found, in order to connect the drilled holes and make two places, at right angles, to insert the saw blade. I'll try to open a hole for us with the saw. If it breaks before we're done, I'll burn the rest of the panel, setting it on fire with the alcohol lamp."

"That sounds like a good plan, but I think it will take a long time. Let me take turns working at it with you, so that we'll always have someone resting while the other one is working. It will take extra effort because we'll be working over our heads. We should also remove our coveralls before we get too sweaty."

Irma gave Arthur a pair of goggles from her forensics kit to protect his eyes as he worked beneath the panel. The hammered knife technique worked well to connect the drilled holes, except for the two times when the knife stuck in the groove. On those occasions, they had to wiggle it and hit it sideways with the hammer to work it loose. After thirty-five minutes of effort, Arthur had opened the two slots enough to insert the bone saw blade.

Irma changed places with Arthur for the initial sawing work, both because she had experience using the saw and because she had more energy than he did after the knife blade work. She found that the saw blade was sharp enough to cut the panel but that the hardness of the wood made progress slow and tedious. She had finished the first cut from the panel center to one edge when Arthur said that it was time to change off again. She welcomed this respite because her arms ached from having worked so long above her head.

Implications

Arthur took over with the bone saw, cutting from the center of the panel toward the other side of the corner in order to complete the square cutout that would free them from their cave-like chamber. It didn't take long, sawing over his head, to appreciate Irma's strength and stamina. His progress was slower than hers had been. His cut was halfway to the edge of the panel when the saw blade twisted and snapped. Only a short piece of the blade remained attached to the handle, allowing only a minimal cut with each push-pull stroke. Arthur tried hammering the panel square loose, but it seemed as firm as ever.

Irma asked, "Will you have to burn the rest of the square away?"

"Burning is a possibility, but I'd rather not if I can avoid it. Fire is too uncontrollable."

"It's too bad the drill battery failed. That short piece of saw blade is probably long enough for cutting out the webs between adjacent drilled holes."

Arthur set down his tools and hugged Irma. "You're a genius. Thank you."

"What are you talking about? We can't drill any more holes."

He laughed. "The last time I looked, holes were holes. We can't drill any more holes, but I can remove a nail from one of the whiskey cases and hammer a row of nail holes through the panel. Then we'll connect those holes with saw cuts, just as we did before."

The process turned out to be harder than Arthur had expected. After just two holes, the nail bent. Arthur removed a dozen nails from the whiskey cases, used each until it bent, and then continued his job with the next nail. After forty minutes, he finally had a row of nail holes all the way to the side edge of the panel.

Irma said, "I'll take over now. I've always been good at connecting the dots."

Because of the broken blade, the saw cuts were very short, but the remaining saw teeth were sharp, and before

67

long, Arthur joined Irma to hold the cutout square in place while she extended her sawed path all the way to the edge of the panel. Finally, Arthur lowered the sawed-out panel square to the floor and they could look up into the room above them.

One problem remained. In order to have room to work with their tools, they had cut their square opening over the bottom of the set of stairs rather than at the top where the short distance between the steps and the panel would have made drilling, hammering, and sawing impossible. Now they would have to find a way to hoist themselves out of their chamber.

At first, they discussed the possibility of Arthur interlacing his fingers to form a step for Irma, but they agreed that that tactic would still not get her high enough to climb all the way out. Then, after a few more minutes of brainstorming, Arthur announced that he had an idea he thought would work. He left Irma by the table, and disappeared among the whiskey shelves, returning two minutes later with the wooden two-wheel cart.

"Here's my plan. This thing is made of hardwood, and its back has crossbars like a ladder. I'll raise it into the air upside down and hook the edge of that square opening with the L-shaped cargo platform. Then, I'll keep the cart pressed against the edge of the opening while you climb up its back like a ladder. Can you do that?"

Irma stared at him. "I think you'll find it too heavy to lift up that way. I also think the plan is too dangerous. However, if you can actually raise it up there and hold it steady, I'll climb it." She gave him a long kiss that felt like a just-in-case goodbye.

Arthur moved four whiskey cases alongside the stairs so that he would have a platform to stand on. Then he swung the cart upward so that it hooked the edge of the cutout opening. He braced himself to keep the cart pressed against that edge while keeping its back framework vertical, and nodded for Irma to climb up. She blew him a kiss and started climbing, first onto a concrete step and then onto a board on the back of the cart. She tested her weight on the first crossbar and then, having satisfied herself that it would hold her, climbed the remaining length of the cart back as fast as she could. She had to squeeze through the opening because of the cart's wheels and axle, but she made it.

Once out of the subbasement, Irma assessed the problem of getting Arthur up too. "There's a big rock on top of the platform. It may be too heavy for me to move. There's also a pipe wedged between the top of the swiveling column and the ceiling so that the platform couldn't be lifted far enough to rotate, even without the rock on it."

Arthur said, "Let's worry about the rock first. Lift this cart out of the opening, and use it to move the rock. It should give you more leverage."

Irma pulled the cart up, with Arthur lifting the bottom of it to assist her. She realized as she did so how heavy it had been for Arthur to raise it above the panel without any support. She tried to insert the cart platform blade under the rock, but the rock was too heavy for her to tilt it.

"I can't move the rock at all. What's plan B for getting you up here?

"Come back to the opening. Plan B calls for me to throw you the rope. Tie it around that swiveling column, and I'll do my best to climb up."

"That's a good plan, but I'll improve it. Throw me the rope, and before you try to climb out, I'll tie spaced knots in the rope for you to use as steps. In the meantime, extinguish that alcohol lamp, and take a swallow of whiskey to fortify yourself. You're damn tired already."

"Will do, Captain, but cussing at a pastor and making him drink ninety-year-old booze is highly irregular."

"And the other events of this afternoon aren't?

CHAPTER 21 - INTERPRETATION

An enhanced group sat around Joe and Penny's dining room table that doubled as a conference table. Three hours had passed since Irma and Arthur had escaped. Evening had darkened the skies, but not the thoughts of those who were present. Steve DuBois had invited Dennis Mikken to join the group as Irma and Arthur reported on their potentially fatal experience.

Arthur had deferred to Irma, who had just reached the end of her story.

"... Then Arthur tied my forensics kit to the end of the rope with the spaced knots and climbed up. We pulled the kit up behind him, and used it to dust for fingerprints and photograph the rock on top of the panel and the cutout we had made in order to escape our prison. That's our survival story; we're open to questions and comments."

Several people started talking at the same time. Irma said, "I'm going to play the schoolteacher here. Those who want to speak, raise your hands. Very good; I'm going to let Dennis, as the latest addition to this group and the state's representative, speak first."

"Thanks, Irma. Please don't take this the wrong way, but your traumatic entrapment in that lower chamber excites me. I have to conclude that the person who locked you down there was the arsonist. I believe that he or she torched the church so that the ruins would be left deserted, allowing free access to that chamber. I've already remedied that security lapse by arranging for a twenty-four hour per day State Police detail at the church until we make alternate security arrangements. Your imprisonment suggests that our arsonist knew about that subbasement before starting the fire. You said that you dusted for fingerprints once you escaped. Did you find any, Irma?

"We found a partial fingerprint and a partial palm print on the handles that are used to lift and turn the swiveling column, but they're too smudged for identification use. It's possible that they could help corroborate the correctness of an arrest by showing that they aren't incompatible with the prints of the accused perpetrator. That's the greatest value I can give them." She pointed to Joe for the next comment.

"I have to apologize and say that I promise to accept Penny's suggestions in the future. She wanted to drive to the Amboy church in the early afternoon so that she could show me the details of the fire and subbasement. I declined that visit because I wanted to do something else first. If I had accepted Penny's suggestion, we would have scared off the assailant ... sorry, Arthur."

"Joe, you're overlooking the possibility that if you two had come earlier, there might have been four of us locked in that warehouse chamber. Hindsight is irrelevant. You have to play the ball whichever way it bounces. Beside, our imprisonment may have expedited the solution of this case. We found weapons that may have been used to kill the people who had been sealed into that chamber, and we have that fingerprint and palm print that Irma mentioned."

"Penny asked, "Irma, do you think there might be usable prints on those suspected murder weapons?"

"We handled and bagged them carefully. We don't think we destroyed any print evidence, but who knows how clear prints would be after all this time? We'll give you the revolver and crowbar to check through the State Police Laboratory."

Steve said, "I've done some checking of my own that might be useful. Dennis told me that they found the entrance to the subbasement only because the main basement carpeting had burned during the fire and had to be removed. I contacted Pastor Dyner, and I asked her when the church had installed that carpeting. She checked with some of the long-time members, and they said that the basement has had carpeting for many years, but that they had installed the current carpeting as a replacement three years ago, about six months before she received her appointment here.

Arthur looked at Irma, and she nodded back, indicating both that she agreed and that he should speak for the two of them. "That period three years ago, when the old carpeting had been removed, probably coincides with the addition of the more recent corpse into the chamber. While Irma and I were down there, we noticed and recorded that someone had removed some of the whiskey cases close to the stairs within the past few years, but that the number of cases taken was relatively small. We estimated that timing because of the differences between the amounts of dust and cobwebs on the clear shelves as compared with the full shelves. We wondered why the unknown persons hadn't taken more whiskey. If the main basement floor had been free of carpeting for only a brief period, then that interval would have set a limit on the amount of whiskey that someone could have removed. One might assume that body number three had been someone helping with the removal of cases of liquor and that he died when his partner or partners turned on him. The removal of whiskey cases would have ended when new carpeting resealed the warehouse entrance."

Joe said, "That fits, Arthur, but if I wanted that whiskey, wouldn't I just come back a little later and cut out the carpeting over the subbasement entrance?"

Irma said, "Perhaps that's the argument that got our third victim killed. His partner may have had a strong reason for keeping the existence of that liquor warehouse chamber quiet. Dennis, you raised your hand again. You may speak, but I think from now on we can contribute our thoughts informally, without raising hands."

Implications

"Do you think that this partner of the dead man would be our arsonist, returning three years later?"

Arthur said, "That's a definite possibility."

CHAPTER 22 – APPROACHES

The next morning at breakfast, Irma figuratively donned her doctor hat. "As the wellness expert for our family, I think we should take it easy today. We had quite enough stress and exercise getting ourselves out of that subbasement."

Arthur nodded but raised his index finger to introduce a point of counter-argument. "I agree, but I propose a restful technique for continuing with the case. I'd like to arrange for a few peaceful interviews today."

"I suppose that would qualify as taking it easy, who are we going to interview, or is this a solo venture for you?"

"I'll start off by checking with Lorna Dyner to find out the names of older people in her congregation. Then we'll go talk with them to see whether they remember anything about the construction and early days of that church."

"Even if they have someone more than ninety years old, they're not likely to have been at that church since childhood."

"I agree; it's possible, but not likely. However, an older person in the United Methodist Church might know some other elderly person, who has lived in Amboy all his or her life. It may require talking with several older people, but I think we'll learn something useful about the history of that church."

"Wouldn't it be easier to start by going to the Village Hall and asking for old photographs and blueprints they might have on file?"

"Steve already did that in preparation for working with Dennis Mikken. He found that nothing that old was available. By the way, Amboy is a city rather than a village. It's smaller now than it was when it was a maintenance and freight hub for the Illinois Central Railroad."

"Then we'll follow the interview route you suggested. It's more fun learning about the past from people's memories than studying files full of old documents, anyway."

CHAPTER 23 – MEMORIES

Pastor Lorna Dyner had suggested that Arthur and Irma speak with Billy Woffort, a member of Amboy UMC who was ninety-one years old and a World War II veteran. He lived in a small house, not far from the church. When they called ahead for an appointment, he invited them to come right over, but asked that they bring some doughnuts and coffee because he had nothing to serve them.

Forty minutes later, Billy Woffort opened his front door and invited Arthur and Irma to enter.

"I don't get much company anymore, so this will be a treat for me, as will the doughnuts and coffee. Thanks for bringing them; I hope you didn't mind my request."

Irma said, "That's the least we can do for you, in exchange for good conversation and your memories. I'll set our goodies on the coffee table in front of the couch."

"You two take the couch. It's a little soft for my back, so I don't sit there too long at one time. I'll sit in my old wooden rocking chair. I made it myself a long time ago, and it's more comfortable for me than just about any chair I've tried. What can I tell you that you don't already know?"

Arthur passed the box to Billy, who pulled a glazed chocolate doughnut from underneath several others. "We appreciate your talking with us, Billy. You know about the fire at the church, don't you?"

"I sure do, Pastor. I was out back watching it. That thing was so hot that I was tempted to put a marshmallow on a stick and hold it up in the air for toasting. I won't be able to go to church anymore unless they arrange for a bus or something."

"That's a great idea, Billy. I'll suggest to the Bishop that the Conference should help pay for bus service to another church."

"So you get to talk to the Bishop, do you? I saw him once at some big meeting. Is he a regular guy or different from the rest of us?"

Arthur noted Irma's smile but maintained eye contact with Billy. "He's definitely a good thinker and easy to approach. He sent me here to find out more about the fire and the church history. My wife, Irma, and I were wondering whether you remember anything about the time when that church was first built, either from having been there or from talking with others."

"I'm afraid I can't help you there, Pastor. I've been in this church ever since I got back from the War in 1946, but the church is or was a lot older than that. I lived in Milwaukee when I was growing up. I can't think of anyone in the church who would remember its beginnings."

Irma leaned forward. "What about someone who isn't a member of your church? Do you know someone your age who grew up in Amboy? Building the church would have been a special thing for kids to watch, and they might have known some people who attended Amboy UMC after they finished the building."

Billy tilted his rocker forward. "You folks should talk with Midge Drinkwater. She's a girl I occasionally date who has lived in Amboy her whole life. She's in the Catholic Church. At one time, I hoped to marry her, but she said she'd had enough of marrying. She outlived three husbands and then decided they were more trouble than they were worth. I came along too late for her, but we're still good friends. Midge is the best cook I ever met, including my mother, who was pretty darn good."

Irma asked, "Where does Midge live? Can you give us her phone number?"

"She lives in a big white house in the countryside north of Amboy. It's outside of the town, but she grew up in a small house not far from here. Her first two husbands left her some money, and her last husband wanted status, so he bought that big house for her; it's older than she is."

Billy stood up and handed Arthur a small address book from a shelf of the bookcase. "You can copy her address and phone number from here. This book is the most valuable item in this place. It has all my girlfriends' contact info in it. Men die off sooner than women; so if you're one of the lucky few who survive, you have lots of female friends."

Arthur and Irma thanked Billy for the conversation and information. They shook hands and left. As Irma walked by the front window, she noticed that Billy had pulled his third doughnut from the box and was smiling as he ate it while leafing through his little black book.

Irma drove her black Mustang to Burger King, where they stopped for lunch. Before they went inside, Arthur called Midge Drinkwater to introduce himself and schedule a visit. She sounded enthusiastic about receiving company.

One hour later, ninety-two-year-old Midge Drinkwater opened her front door for her guests and revealed that she enjoyed dressing for company. She wore an antique white dress with lace on her collar and sleeves plus a big welcoming smile.

"Please come in. I have a pitcher of lemonade and some homemade apple strudel for us to enjoy while we talk."

Irma made a mental note that multiple interviews in a single day could be very fattening. Aloud she said, "Your dress and your house are lovely. A three-story house like this is unusual."

"It's an old Queen Anne style. The house is more than one hundred years old. Even so, it's in very good condition."

Arthur said, "I don't mean to pry, but are you able to handle all the stairs to the other floors?"

"That's not a problem, Pastor; my late husband Albert had an elevator installed alongside the stairs. Getting up and down is simple. I do appreciate your concern though. Come into the living room and sit down."

Midge led them through an archway on their left into a large room that surprised them because of its modern furniture.

Irma took a seat on a leather-covered chaise lounge. "I see you aren't a purist about matching your furniture to the age and style of your home, Midge."

"I figure that if I'm this old and like modern cars – there's a Chevy Corvette in the garage – the house will have to accept modern furniture. Anyway, I'll probably have to give up all of these pleasures soon. My kids have all been after me to move into a senior residence facility. I have to admit they do love and appreciate me. At least I won't have to worry about them fighting over my money when I'm gone. I gave it all to them already and set up a living trust to handle my expenses while I'm still here."

Irma asked, "How many children do you have?"

"I have three with my first husband, three with my second husband, and my third husband came with four of his own, so the answer is ten."

Arthur said, "That's quite a family. I won't even ask you to count the multiple generations of their offspring for us. As I indicated on the telephone, we'd like to ask you some questions about things that happened in Amboy a long time ago. Billy Woffort said that you've lived in this town all your life."

"That Billy is a sweetheart; did he tell you that he wanted to marry me? I still date him from time to time. Yes, I have been here forever; so ask away, and I'll try to remember the days before my hair turned white."

"We're checking on the history of the Amboy United Methodist Church. It burned down recently, and it would help us if you remembered anything about its construction and its early years of operation."

"Gee, Pastor, I thought you were going to ask me something hard. We used to call that place the creepy church. Kids kept away from it in the early years because they were superstitious about it."

"What made you think of it as creepy?"

"That was the only church I ever heard of that was built by an undertaker. My dad told me that old Milton Jergens, the undertaker, paid for the entire construction of the church in exchange for being able to use the basement for wakes and as a funeral chapel. They had a ramped driveway to let the hearse back down to the basement level for delivering and picking up coffins. Jergens built a small building on the other side of the parking lot that he used for his office, salesroom, and embalming workshop."

"Did you ever go to a wake there?"

"I did, Pastor, and that's what made it feel extra creepy. My friend Betsy's dad died in a railroad yard accident, and my folks took me along to the wake. I was only six or seven, and that was my first experience with death. I stayed out of the way in the back section of the basement, and I heard scary noises while I was staring across the room at the open coffin. I had nightmares for weeks afterward."

"Can you remember what the noises sounded like?"

"That's a bad question, Irma; now I'll have nightmares again. I heard thumps, scraping sounds, and evil laughter. At the time I thought that there were ghosts surrounding me, and they dragged chains and heavy objects behind them as they tried to get back up to the daylight."

Arthur asked, "Then these sounds seemed to come from underneath you?"

"I don't know. At the time, I thought they were all around me. That was too long ago for me to remember much more. All I know is that I tried to stay away from that church whenever possible after that. I thought it was haunted, and so did some of my friends. Once Mister

Jergens went out of the funeral business and into something else, I didn't mind it as much. They stopped having dead bodies in the basement, so that made it better. Anyway, it's time to change the subject and have some strudel and lemonade."

They relaxed and enjoyed the refreshments. The strudel was so good that Irma asked Midge for the recipe. The two women went out to the kitchen to copy it, while Midge invited Arthur to look around the house.

Arthur returned after twenty minutes to find Midge and Irma enjoying each other's company. He was surprised to find Irma doing most of the talking.

Their talking stopped as he entered the room.

"Ladies, don't let me interrupt you. Midge, you have a very interesting home here. I've never been in this style of house before."

"Well, perhaps you'll see it again. Irma says that you two are looking for an older house to purchase, and I know that my children are going to talk me out of this place before long. If you're interested, and we can agree on terms, we might have some mutual benefits here."

Arthur laughed. "Billy Woffort was wrong. He said that you had this house because of your first two husbands' estates and your third husband's desire for status. I'll guess that your business savvy had a lot to do with increasing the value of all your husbands' estates. Am I right, or am I wrong?"

"I have brokered a deal or two in my day, but I prefer that friends like Billy see me as humble and folksy."

"You are both of those, but I don't think I'd want to play poker with you. Regardless of characterizations, it's a lovely house, and I'd like to discuss it further with you if Irma would."

"Indeed I would, Arthur."

"Don't sound enthusiastic; she's a poker player."

"Not actually, but I always thought I would do well at that card game. This isn't poker, though. I know that I'll have to sell, and you know that this house might be more than you could afford if it were in a prime location. Out here, there's not a huge demand for large old houses, so we'll just figure out what you can afford and strike a deal. How does that sound?"

Irma said, "It sounds too good to be true. Don't take a loss for our sakes."

"Profits and losses don't mean so much when you're my age. Besides, I may get extra brownie points when I make that final trip if I did something nice for a pastor. Let's do it! The only catch will be that I'll expect Irma and Arthur Blake to visit me and be my friends until that final moving day comes."

Irma hugged Midge. "We'll be your friends forever."

CHAPTER 24 – *MILTON JERGENS (Titles in italics are flashbacks.)*

Milt gazed at his unique creation from across the parking lot. "Finished at last; I'll bet there's no other church building like it in the world."

Sammy, his right-hand man, nodded his head in agreement. "I wouldn't take that bet, Boss. We should get our parts of the building set up before we invite Pastor Baxter to bring his flock."

"Take Mario with you to John Sbarboro's funeral home in Chicago. Johnny T. says we have a shipment waiting there for us. Take the hearse, with two empty coffins. Put the cases you pick up into the coffins, so that no one will be suspicious if they see you unloading when you get back here."

"Will do; but with that ramp leading down to the church basement, they won't see what we're doing anyway, when I back the hearse down there."

"Patience, Sammy; we're professional undertakers, and we can't have the public see us doing anything out of character. Johnny T. always advises businesslike behavior, and I agree with him. The beauty of building this church is that it won't attract any attention from the law or the feds. That's why we put it so far out in the country. We have a big rail freight terminal in this town if we want to service someone at a distance, but we're so far out from Chicago that we won't get involved in any of the competition there."

"It is getting wild. Deany O'Banion tried to pull a fast one on Johnny Torrio with a raid by crooked cops, and now O'Banion's suffered the consequences. Do I have to worry about anything at Sbarboro's place?"

"Just remember what I taught you. You're a professional taking care of a transaction between funeral homes. John Sbarbaro has a foot in every camp. Everyone needs him. He's an assistant state's attorney, a bootlegger, and undertaker to all of the different factions. You'll be on neutral ground in dealing with him."

"I'll try to get on good terms with him and his people. We'll be making quite a few visits to his place before we fill our warehouse."

"Be careful in talking with them, Sammy. We're the only ones who know where the shipments go. Don't mention our warehouse or the church. For all they know, we're burying the stuff in graves."

Sammy shifted his weight from one foot to another. "What if they come out here to check on us?"

"They won't. We're small potatoes compare to what they move in the city. Besides, we have Johnny Torrio's blessing. Nobody's going to rock the boat. Now stop chattering, and get going."

Milt watched as his men drove off in the hearse. It had cost him a lot of his own money plus high interest loans to build the church. Stocking the inventory and generating an income stream would have to come fast to satisfy his *bankers*.

CHAPTER 25 – MISFITS AND MEMBERS

Once again gathered around Penny's dining room table in the Gonzalez's Parkville home, the four others listened as Irma summarized the conclusions reached by the State Police Laboratory from her collected evidence.

"We did get a partial fingerprint and palm print for the person who sealed us within the subbasement chamber. However, they're smudgy enough that the State Police couldn't search for a match in any of their databases. The lab staff corroborated my theory that the crowbar we found in the warehouse chamber is the weapon that fractured the skull of the more recent victim down there. The killer finished off that victim with a shot to the head. The bullet I retrieved from inside his skull matches the bullets used to kill the two older skeletal victims, and all these bullets were fired by the pistol we retrieved, a 1917 Colt 45 ACP Revolver, made for Army use in World War I."

Joe said, "Now that's interesting. All three victims died from shots that came from the same pistol, even though something like eighty years separated the killings of the first two victims from the third. That must mean that the killer of the first two left the pistol in the warehouse chamber, and the more recent murderer used it on the third victim."

Penny took a closer look at the pistol sitting on the side table. "This military weapon would do a lot of damage to someone at close range as in that subbasement. I'll suggest that the third victim's death wasn't premeditated. The killer didn't bring a personal weapon, but used one that was available down there. The murderer may have reacted to an unexpected disagreement. Even now, there's one unfired cartridge in the pistol."

Arthur said, "I'll add that one of the Prohibition Era workers in that warehouse probably served in the Army during World War I. The timing would have been right for that. The younger gangsters of that time would have been veterans, while the senior people in the gang would have been too old for wartime service. In other words, the killer of the two skeletal victims was a lower-level mob member, who may have acted on his own or may have had orders from a higher-up."

Steve said, "I like the way this discussion is moving. We're working out events that happened a long time ago. We now think we know something about the earlier killings. What can we say about the person who killed the third, more recent, victim? Was that murderer also our arsonist, or was that killing too long ago to have involved the arsonist? Any ideas, Irma?"

"That's good thinking, Steve. Let's bring our speculations closer to the present. I'll start by saying that the person who imprisoned Arthur and me in that chamber already knew about its existence and significance when he or she acted. That person could have been connected to the most recent murder, or could have been the arsonist."

Arthur nodded and said, "It's time for Irma and me to talk with members of this church congregation. We'll find out whether Pastor Dyner's version of past problems is correct and get some additional points of view. Then we'll ask for your assistance in tracking the involved parties since their departures from Amboy UMC. Several individuals there offended others and suffered the consequences; some people may have felt violated by the actions of the church or its leadership. Bitterness can be a strong motive for seeking retribution."

CHAPTER 26 – JEFFERSON LEE

Steve DuBois' cell phone rang. He glanced at the caller identification window and became more alert when he read *Jefferson Lee* there.

"Hi, Jeff; it's good to hear from you. How can I help you today?"

"I wanted to give you an update on the case we worked on together. Your Karl Simitski may have been good at art swindling and international intrigue, but he was a lousy counterfeiter. At first, we thought we were in trouble because a couple of boats did get away with cases of Simitski's currency from that freighter; but it turned out to be a positive development. The quality of his money is marginal at best and easy to detect. It never would have passed muster in the U.S. Anyway, we alerted the FBI and several friendly Middle Eastern governments. They've already rounded up a bunch of Arab terrorists from a previously unknown group by watching for people using his currency. We had to act fast before too many people had that money, but the tactic worked."

"Did you locate and close the factory, so that they won't produce any more of that stuff?"

"Simitski set it up in an abandoned supermarket two towns over from Boothbay Harbor, where Bob Philkins saw him loading cargo. He made the mistake of using a local trade student rather than a master printer as his production manager, causing the printing quality to suffer. We shut down that operation yesterday afternoon, so Secret Service is marking this case closed. It has been fun working with you ..."

Steve interrupted Jeff. "Hold it! You sound as though you're about to terminate this conversation and proclaim our relationship at an end. I'm glad that the counterfeiting case is complete, but I'd like to argue for us to continue working together. We have a current project with connections to events that occurred during Prohibition. Primary federal jurisdiction over Prohibition crimes was the responsibility of the Treasury Department, not the Department of Justice. The few investigative agents at Justice had not yet received the glory of the FBI label. We'll be looking for records of Secret Service actions during Prohibition. Do you think you might be able to access those records for us?"

"That was a long time ago, Steve, but if reports exist in the files, I'll be able to get them. You'll have to be as specific as possible with your requests, and then I'll take it from there."

"Thanks, Jeff; I appreciate both your assistance and the chance to keep working together. Who knows; we might find some incidents and gangster networks that have never seen the light of day before."

CHAPTER 27 – CHURCH SCANDALS

Amboy UMC had never been wealthy enough to own a parsonage for housing the pastor, so Lorna Dyner lived in an apartment near the center of the city. Amboy was a municipality the size of a village that had become a city early in its history, when it had a larger population and aspirations to grow still bigger.

Arthur climbed the three front steps and rang the bell for Lorna's apartment. She buzzed him through the security door, and he went up to the second floor, where she awaited him, standing in her open doorway.

"Welcome, Arthur; come on in. I'll enjoy a sit-down session to relieve my tension from everything that has happened."

He went in and accepted the reclining chair she offered.

"Thanks for meeting with me, Lorna; I need some information about the church and its members that only you would have."

"That makes me feel important, but I expect that others would have the same info, even though you might have difficulty identifying them. By the way, I have both lemonade and beer if you want something to drink."

"I'm normally a coffee guy, but it's a warm day, and the beer will be fine."

She went out to the kitchen and returned with two bottles of beer and a bowl of pretzels. "Is this the way you like your beer, or would you prefer a glass?"

"The bottle is perfect. How well have you coped with the commute to your temporarily shared church?"

"It hasn't been bad, but some of our folks are staying home in the face of that long journey."

"Given that situation, I'll give you some good news. I talked Bishop Chandler into paying for bus service on Sunday mornings. For the rest of the week, you're on your own, but on Sunday, you may charter a bus and send the Conference the bill for it. The bus won't accommodate everyone, but it should be adequate for those who don't or won't drive."

"That is good news, Arthur; thank you for speaking up on our behalf. What information can I give you in exchange?"

"It's not a matter of payback, but I'd appreciate it if you would identify some of the people involved in the earlier church problems we discussed, so that I might contact them."

"The only reason I can attribute to your wanting to meet them is that someone has decided that our fire was not an accident. Is my logic accurate?"

"Let's say that we're trying to be as thorough as possible in our investigation. Until we have evidence of something unusual about the fire, I'd like you to treat it as an unfortunate accident. The Bishop wants to avoid potentially harmful or sensational publicity, and we don't want to spook a potential suspect by advertising our suspicions."

She shifted her position to sitting cross-legged on her straight-back chair, "I can keep a secret, and I love the idea of being part of a conspiracy. What details do you need from me?"

"I basically want all the underlying information from your earlier account. It may require some research on your part, so write down my questions now, and put your answers on paper when you have them. Call me when you're ready, and then we'll meet again so that you'll be able to give me your findings in person. I want to avoid emails for confidentiality."

"That will work for me." She walked over to her desk and picked up a notebook and pen. "Go ahead with your questions; I'm ready."

"First group of questions: Who was the man suspected of murdering his girlfriend, and what was her name? What was the name of his wife who kicked him out, and what was the approximate date of the car accident in which the man died?" He waited until Lorna stopped writing.

"Second group of questions: What was the name of the seminarian whose affair got her into trouble? Where did she grow up, and where did she go after leaving Amboy? Who was her lover who left town, and what was his wife's name?"

"Third and final group of questions: Who was the treasurer who mishandled the church funds, and where did he go after leaving Amboy? What were his education and work backgrounds?" Once again, he paused while she wrote.

Lorna looked up. "I have it all, Arthur, and I know that this will require a lot of digging and subtle questioning so that I don't arouse suspicions among our members. Since I'll have to put so much time in on this, you'll have to pay for my effort."

Arthur raised his right eyebrow. "How much do you want?"

"This will cost you exactly two sermons preached at our temporarily shared church. I'll be too busy to handle them and this also. Do we have a deal?"

"A deal it is, and you may even select my sermon topics."

CHAPTER 28 – *SAMMY*

Sammy yanked on the hearse's hand brake, opened the door, and ran over to where Milt Jergens stood waiting for unloading to begin. "Boss, there's trouble!"

Milt stiffened and escorted Sammy to the back of his sales office building for privacy. "What's happened?"

"That feud between Johnny Torrio and O'Banion's gang erupted. Torrio thought that with O'Banion out of the way, the remaining northsiders would toe the line and not be difficult. It didn't work out that way."

"Don't tell me Torrio's dead."

"Not quite, but pretty damn close to it – Hymie Weiss and the rest of O'Banion's gang ambushed Johnny as he got back to his apartment after taking his wife shopping. Torrio's in the hospital in bad shape, but he's still alive. That Capone guy who started as a bouncer at Johnny's Four Deuces place has taken over. He has men guarding Johnny in the hospital and others going after Weiss, Drucci, and Moran. I got out of the city as fast as I could. People could get caught in the crossfire among all those trigger-happy mugs."

"So, Alphonse has taken over. I've met Capone. He doesn't have the polish or the businesslike outlook of Johnny Torrio, but he has the toughness to keep the organization together. Johnny called him his protégé. Hopefully, that means that he taught Capone a few things along the way."

Sammy relaxed a bit. "So, you're saying we don't have to worry about Capone deciding he wants to take over our operation here?"

Milt patted Sammy on the shoulder. "He has more than enough to handle in Chicago. Besides, we're all Torrio's people. We'll see later whether Johnny comes back after he gets out of the hospital, or if Capone is the man in charge for the long haul. We'll keep our undertaking and warehouse businesses going here and cause no problems for anyone. We pay our cut to the organization; that's all that matters."

Sammy shook his head. "That's not all that matters. You've had Mario and me handling preparation and embalming of the stiffs. We're no good at it, and it ain't our cup of tea. We'll feel a lot better if you get someone on board who knows what he's doing. Those bodies deserve better than what we can give them."

Milt laughed. "Sammy, you have a good head for business after all. I saw the terrible job you two did on our last client. I was going to yell at you for it, but you have a better idea. We'll check out some of the funeral homes around here and find an expert who wants to jump ship. I'm sure we'll be able to persuade someone."

CHAPTER 29 – POSSIBILITIES

Arthur shut the apartment door behind him and called out for his wife's attention. "Irma, I'm back from my follow-up meeting with Lorna, and I have lots of information."

He heard no response, so he assumed she had gone out somewhere. Leaving his notebook on the dining room table, he headed for the kitchen to make a pot of coffee. Arthur had put a new filter into the coffeemaker and had opened the container of coffee before he noticed Irma sitting at the kitchen table with a large pad of paper. "Didn't you hear me calling out to you when I came in? You look so pensive sitting there; is everything all right?

"I heard you, but I didn't want you to interrupt my thoughts. You were calling out about the fire investigation project, and I'm working on something more important."

He added coffee and poured the water into the top of the machine; then he started the brewing process. "What's more important?"

"In case you haven't noticed, we have a life together beyond investigations. I'm making notes and sketches concerning what we might do with Midge's house after we buy it."

"Speaking of that house, we'll have to decide on our offer. We'll want to be as fair as possible to Midge, while realizing that she's promised us a bargain price."

"I think both she and I can count on you to come up with a fair price."

"In other words, you're expecting me to make the decision as to the amount of the offer."

"Yup; you're the pastor with the brownie points that will help her get into heaven."

"When she said that, I thought it was a cute comment. I have one other house question for you. Have you told anyone about it?"

"Not a soul; and you'd better not either. Too many things could go wrong before we finalize the deal. I'm taking no chances on jinxing my dream home."

Arthur poured the freshly-brewed coffee into the largest mug he had. "Let's discuss my new investigation information. After that, I'll draw up a formal offer for the house, and then we'll discuss your sketches and notes without any interruptions."

"I always get third billing, but I'll accept your sequence in order to get action on buying that house. It really would be perfect for us, even though it is larger than I ever considered possible. Now, what is the crucial information you brought home?"

He retrieved his notebook from the dining room and sat down at the table; she changed to a blank pad of paper and concentrated on his words.

"I don't know how critical the input I got from Lorna will be, but at least it gives us a bunch of leads to explore. I asked her for answers to three groups of questions, so let's discuss them in the same way."

"Fair enough..."

"First group of answers: The name of the man suspected of murdering his girlfriend was Rob Danten. Lorna couldn't find the name of the dead mistress. His wife, Trina, kicked him out of their home following the murder and subsequent vicious gossip. The single-car accident in which Rob Danten died occurred during the last week of March a few months more than two years ago."

"I've listed Lorna's responses."

"Second group of answers: The seminarian who had an affair that got her kicked out of pastoral training was Mandy Miller. She grew up in Minnesota and moved to

West Virginia after the scandal. Her lover's name was Jerry Tackman, and his wife's name was Ginger."

"... So noted."

"Third group of answers: The treasurer who helped himself to church funds was Kenneth Cantini. He had a history degree from the University of Iowa, and he operated a carpet cleaning business from his home."

Irma completed her notes. "You're indicating that all of these people are potential arsonists, except for the one who died in the car crash and the lover he supposedly killed. Don't forget that peripheral people such as relatives of these people might also carry a grudge against the church in Amboy."

"You're right, but we have to start somewhere. Each one we check out and eliminate narrows the field."

CHAPTER 30 – MIDGE DRINKWATER

This time, when they turned off the road and up the inclined driveway, Irma and Arthur saw Midge walking toward a red Corvette parked in the driveway. They pulled up alongside the sports car, got out, and greeted Midge.

Arthur said, "You didn't tell us it was red."

"You didn't ask."

Irma hugged Midge. "Did we come at a bad time? Are you leaving on a special errand?"

"Not at all; come on in, you two. I was only going to give Betty her exercise. I hate to admit it, but I haven't driven her anywhere all week. I'm getting to be such an old stay-at-home."

Arthur had been looking at details of the car's instrument cluster. He stood and joined the women. "My cars have always been named Betsy, so we use similar nicknames. That is a beautiful machine."

"She's my pet. My oldest son is salivating over the prospect of owning her once I have to stop driving; he's a very young seventy-six. My first husband was my high school steady boyfriend, so I got into the habit of producing offspring at a tender age. Anyway, when I go, I'll leave a whole bunch of people and trophies behind me."

Arthur took another admiring look at the Corvette. "One personal question if you don't mind, Midge; is Drinkwater your maiden name, or the family name of your most recent husband?"

"It's my maiden name. After I finished with all of my marriages, I went back to ground zero. It got complicated, keeping track of all those married names. Let's go into the kitchen and sit. I made a blueberry pie just in case someone stopped by. I'm still a bit psychic about anticipating events."

Midge had Arthur raise the top on the Corvette to shade the interior from the hot sun. Then they all went into the house and headed for the large kitchen with its handcrafted maple table.

Irma said, "I enjoy the contrasts of this house. It's very old, but it has amenities like air conditioning and an elevator. You enjoy modern furniture in several of the rooms, but you keep the kitchen traditional. This place is practically a time machine. You can feel as old or as current as you wish, Midge."

"Thank you, Irma. You understand the secret of my longevity. Past, present, and future all coexist within me."

Arthur had let his thoughts drift aimlessly, but he latched onto their conversation about the past. "Midge, one of the matters we're supposed to research in connection with that church that burned is a car accident at the end of March two years ago. It killed a man named Rob Danten. Do you by any chance remember that?"

"I do, because it was in the newspapers, and people were calling me about the sensationalism of the whole affair. He was supposed to have murdered his girlfriend, but the police had to drop their plans for a trial when he died. My old-timer friends were convinced that the accident was a suicide. They said that he drove deliberately into a tree on his way over to Northern Illinois University. He was a Professor of History over there. The woman he was supposed to have killed taught in the Journalism Department at Northern Illinois, but she was only at the instructor level."

"Wow; you do know what's going on around town. Did your friends also tell you anything about Danten's wife, who kicked him out of their house during that period?"

"They said a few things, Arthur, but the main memory I retained is that nobody liked her. One of my pals even suggested that the wife would have been a more likely to commit a murder than her husband. I attributed that comment to a touch of meanness, and I forgot about it until now. Love triangles are always dangerous, though. Did you folks come to ask me about local history, or may we address ourselves to more weighty matters, like blueberry pie?"

Irma said, "Don't call the pie too weighty, or I'll only allow myself a sliver. Let's pretend it doesn't have calories so that I'll be able to enjoy a generous portion. It does look good."

They enjoyed their pie, along with vanilla ice cream and root beer. When they finished, Arthur patted his stomach.

"This kind of old-fashioned food is probably not good for me, but it keeps my mind off of scheduled tasks and projects."

Midge said, "If you buy this place, I'll throw in a year's supply of ice cream. I subscribe to a service that delivers a three-gallon drum of ice cream each month. Irma, are you as comfortable in this house as Arthur appears to be?"

"Of course I am, but a good part of that comfort lies in the companionship. You'll have to promise to stick around here for as long as you like, even if we do buy the house. There's no urgency for us to displace you."

Arthur said, "That sounded like my cue. Midge, we did our calculations, and this is what we came up with as our offer for the house. I hope it will be acceptable to you." He handed her a file folder with several pages inside, stapled to the folder. "I gave you some backup details, so that you'd know our thinking as we did our calculations."

Midge examined the papers as Irma and Arthur sat silently, awaiting her reaction with slightly increasing tension as the seconds became minutes.

"I admire your transparency in giving me more information than is normal in real estate transactions. Your offer is more than I expected, but less than I would have asked on the open market. At this point, I should show my negotiating skill by asking you to increase your offer. As an alternative, I could place limitations on what your offer would cover in order to be acceptable. Arthur, I believe that you said that your father is an antiques dealer."

"Yes, he is. His shop is located in Richmond, Illinois."

"You also said that your apartment is furnished with antiques."

Irma wondered where Midge was going with this discussion. "We do have antique furniture."

"Therefore, I will negotiate by saying that for the price you have offered, I will sell you the house, but not the modern furniture. I'll include the traditional stuff like the kitchen table and chairs, but the modern furniture will go to my children and their families."

Arthur laughed and rose to shake Midge's hand. "We accept. You are an excellent negotiator, and you knew we would want to replace the modern furniture anyway. Thank you, Midge; this is a special moment for us."

Irma said, "And I meant it when I said that you're free to stay here even after we close on the transfer. This will be your home until you're ready to abide by your children's arguments against your living independently."

"I knew that I had chosen the right people for my house. Let me put my negotiating hat on once more. I have a suite, two bedrooms, a bathroom, and a small sitting room, at the west end of the second floor hallway. If you'll let me hire a caregiver and live in that suite after you take possession, I'll swap Betty for your black Mustang. That will counter all the family arguments that I should live in some old people's home. I'd be free until my time comes."

Irma said, "Midge, I'm sure we could work something out without your sacrificing your Corvette."

"It wouldn't be a sacrifice. I'd still get to drive it from time to time. The car is too powerful for my son anyway. He's better suited to a Mustang."

Arthur asked, "Would your family resent us for interfering with their plans?"

Implications

"Are you kidding? You'd be saving them a ton of money out of their inheritances for an old people's residence, and I'd be having someone with medical capabilities living under the same roof with me in my own home. It's the best of all possible worlds!"

CHAPTER 31 – SUSPICIONS

After receiving a telephone summons from Irma, Penny and Joe Gonzalez drove over to the Blakes' apartment in Parkville. Penny knew the excitement in Irma's voice signified that she had something momentous to report, but Irma had insisted on delivering her news in person, and at her place rather than Penny's. It had sounded mysterious but intriguing.

When they knocked on the door, Arthur opened it and escorted them into the living room where Irma awaited them, standing next to an end table upon which two hardcover books sat, covered by a pad of paper, so that the visitors could see only the edges of the pages. Irma noticed Penny eying the two volumes.

"Welcome, you two. It's time for us to discuss the case at our place rather than yours. You've had all of the hosting fun."

Penny said, "From the tone of your voice on the telephone, I suspect you arranged this gathering for more than the sake of hospitality. You look as though you're about to burst with your news. What's she up to, Arthur?"

"I'm a bystander today. This is Irma's show. You won't get any hints from me. You're family to us, so just head into the kitchen for drinks and snacks; bring them back here to consume while Irma enlightens you."

Joe said, "Aha; enlightenment - this will be a special session."

When they returned with their treats, Penny and Joe sat and looked at Irma expectantly.

"Don't get too excited. We're far from finding our arsonist, but we have discovered some interesting background information. You already know that the subbasement in that church served as a warehouse for booze during Prohibition days. What we hadn't discovered earlier is that an undertaker built the Amboy Methodist Church - *United* wasn't part of its name then. The builder was Milton Jergens, and he agreed to do the construction in exchange for using the basement as his funeral chapel for wakes. He made a ramped driveway into the basement for loading and unloading of coffins. He also constructed the hidden lower basement, and he delivered shipments of whiskey to it in his hearse, probably hidden inside spare coffins. He built a smaller second building on the other side of the parking lot for sales and embalming operations. This was a functioning funeral home business, but he made most of his money from bootlegging."

Joe said, "I'm impressed. How on earth did you learn all of that?"

"It's a combination of information from Arthur's examination of the remains of the church building and the recollections of our new best friend, who was actually at one of those wakes as a little girl. She even remembers hearing strange sounds there, which must have come from people working in the warehouse chamber."

Penny said, "Your friend must be in her nineties."

"She's very young for her age. I'll tell you more about her later." Irma paused for a drink of lemonade. "We've also learned that Rob Danten, the church member who was accused of murdering his mistress a few years ago, was a history professor at Northern Illinois University. The deceased mistress was a journalism instructor at the same school. He died in a single-car accident before they could charge him with her murder."

Penny said, "Since they're both dead, neither one could be our arsonist. What makes them interesting to you, Irma?"

"We researched the faculty at Northern Illinois, and when I saw that the Chair of the History Department is a woman, I volunteered to interview her. It turned out that we had a few friends in common, and we spent two hours exchanging stories and information. I came out of our meeting with some interesting and thought-provoking information. First, I learned that Rob Danten's special area of interest was the history of the Prohibition Era. His mistress, the journalism instructor, turned out to have been studying and writing about comparisons of newspaper accounts during the same period. Her goal was to determine which were factual, and which were sensationalized to sell more papers."

Penny said, "Their common interest in Prohibition brought them together, and may have led to those two books you've hidden under the pad of paper on the table."

"You're correct in both of your assumptions, Penny. I'll discuss those books shortly; but that common interest in the Prohibition Era may also have led to their deaths."

"That got my attention. What did you learn to justify that statement?"

"Our new friend, Midge, said that a few of her meaner friends had suggested that Rob Danten's wife would have been more likely to be a murderer than he would. Apparently, no one liked her. That thought was in the back of my mind when I learned from the Chair of the History Department that the maiden name of Rob's wife was Jergens. Trina Danten was born Katerina Jergens, and she is the granddaughter of the gangster and undertaker who built the Amboy Methodist Church. She may have been unhappy about information that Rob and his girlfriend had published."

Arthur stood up and placed his hand on Irma's left shoulder. "Your research has been fruitful, but we should avoid moving too rapidly toward conclusions. Assuming it is true that Trina Danten is Milton Jergens' granddaughter, we have no evidence that she has done anything illegal. We certainly can't say that she killed Rob and his girlfriend."

Penny said, "I agree with Arthur, but we should investigate her further. It's quite reasonable that she would belong to a church that her grandfather had built. She and Rob were probably married there. What do you think, Joe?"

"I'll follow Penny's thinking and add one step to it. Trina may have told her husband about her grandfather's criminal past, and that may have led him to specialize in the history of Prohibition."

Irma said, "I appreciate your thoughts, but they make me ask some more questions. If Trina knew about Milton's bootlegging activities, did she also know about the warehouse chamber underneath the church? If she told Rob about her grandfather's secret business, did she reveal the subbasement information to her husband? We have to consider anyone who knew about the whiskey warehouse beneath the church a murder suspect. Given such knowledge, Rob or his girlfriend could have killed the most recent victim down there, before they met death themselves."

Irma's questions led to a period of silent thinking by everyone. Finally, Arthur broke the silence with his own question.

"Do the two books on that table contain any hints as to whether the deceased couple knew the church's secret?"

Irma said, "I have to study them some more, but the sections I've read so far suggest that they didn't know about it. Both Rob Danten and Marie Chance, that was the girlfriend's name, write as outsiders, trying to learn from published materials and old interviews. Neither one of them cites anything about the Amboy church."

Penny said, "It would be helpful if you told us more about those books."

Irma removed the top book from beneath the pad of paper without revealing the cover of the lower book. "Rob Danten concentrated his research on the whiskey itself. His title is *Distillers Take a Back Seat*. It deals with the illegal homegrown and amateur distilling and brewing businesses that developed during Prohibition and the tricks that bootleggers used to import established foreign brands."

"What do you mean by tricks?"

"Well, Joe, the Coast Guard and other agencies patrolled the U.S. coastlines for three miles out from the shore. The bootleggers would regularly schedule a rendezvous with ships of foreign registry just beyond the three-mile limit. A favorite location for this was off the coast of Atlantic City, New Jersey. Ships would transfer liquor coming from the Bahamas, Cuba, and some of the French-colonized islands to high-speed boats that could outrun the Coast Guard cutters. As long as the transfers took place in international waters, the legitimate distillers and distributors from other countries could say that they had done nothing illegal."

"They were actually pretty smart to do that. The bootleggers didn't have to smuggle booze all the way from other countries in their own chartered vessels, and they probably got the legitimate foreign distillers to pay the freight if they wanted access to the forbidden U.S. market."

Arthur had gone into the kitchen for more coffee. When he returned, he walked to the center of the room to draw everyone's attention. "I agree that Rob Danten's book on the logistics of whiskey procurement is interesting, but it's academic and doubtfully important enough to be a motive for murder. His girlfriend died first. Whether Rob, his wife, or some third person murdered her, they would have needed a motive. Rob's wife might have killed her out of passion, but if so, why would she frame her husband for the crime? Let's look at Irma's second book to see if it might have motivated someone to kill its author."

Irma accepted Arthur's prompt and picked up the second book. "The title of the book written by Marie Chance is *Sifting for Facts: An Analysis of Prohibition Era News Reporting.* It's not a catchy title, but it suggests that it might draw attention to some events or people who reporters overlooked at the time. That kind of revelation could be a motive for murder by someone who wanted to protect a family's reputation."

Arthur added, "... or perhaps to avoid shining light on the illegal sources of a family's wealth."

Penny said, "That line of thinking would suggest that we should look for someone who is not at all obvious and who is a seemingly outstanding citizen. Unless we can pinpoint the threatening information in that book, it would be nearly impossible to find Marie's murderer, especially after three years have passed."

Joe said, "We might not even have jurisdiction in such a local murder. Would we have any reason to believe that her murderer was also our arsonist?"

Irma returned the book to the end table. "We don't have enough data to answer that question, but I'm convinced that the answers to all aspects of our mystery stem from events that occurred during the Prohibition years.

CHAPTER 32 – *ROB AND MARIE*

The university parking lot sat abandoned except for two side-by-side cars, gradually becoming less obvious as the twilight deepened beneath a moonless sky. Inside one of those cars, Rob Danten and Marie Chance shared kisses, caresses, and concerns.

Marie patted Rob's crotch signaling the end of their sexual frolicking and buttoned her blouse. "We're grabbing pleasant interludes like a couple of undergraduates. When are you going to tell Trina that it's time for you to divorce her, so that we can get married?"

Rob tucked, zipped, and buckled. "You know that I want the same thing, Marie, but frankly, I'm afraid of her family. When I first started studying gangland history, I thought that only her grandfather had been involved in the mob. Now I believe that the offspring of several of Milton Jergens' friends and some of their kids may have continued to work in the family business. I'll have to manipulate Trina into wanting a divorce, or she might request a heavy-handed favor from one or more of her friends."

"And how do you expect to get her to want a divorce?"

"I found proof that old Milton double-crossed Capone by dealing with Canadians for some of his booze. In the process, he reduced his kickback to Capone and the Chicago mob. I figure that she'll want to avoid getting the present-day Chicago folks mad at her family, and she'll let me go. I also found detailed personal information about current mob descendants."

"That kind of thinking could also get you killed. We don't know for sure that contemporary outfit people would care about sins from way back then, but it might work if your proof also shows that they're not the legitimate business people they now claim to be. Give me your proof, and I'll reference it in my book analyzing newspaper reports during Prohibition. You'll be able to protect yourself by saying you have an insurance policy. My book comes out in two weeks, so any time after that you can discuss divorce with her. I'll have a reliable person holding the key to finding the proof location in my book. I've become friends with a lot of newspaper editors while researching my material, and they'd be very happy to get and publish this story."

"I don't think Trina knows who you are. She suspects I've been seeing someone else, but it doesn't bother her too much. If she does identify you, we might have to leave town and become two other people."

"That would be fine with me, Rob. But I'm old-fashioned, and I'd rather marry you if we can get you divorced first."

"Good enough, Marie; in two weeks I'll start campaigning for a divorce from Trina."

CHAPTER 33 – JEFFERSON LEE

Steve DuBois answered his cell phone on the second ring while slipping a bookmark into the book that had been this morning's project. "DuBois speaking ..."

"Steve, this is Jeff Lee; I may have something interesting for you. You told me about that book by Marie Chance that might have evidence about crimes from the 1920's."

"Hi, Jeff; it's good to hear from you. I'm studying that book right now, but I haven't found anything unusual."

"About two and a half years ago, one of our Secret Service agents, Saul Sanders, was found bludgeoned to death next to a highway in northern Indiana. I've been studying Saul's files because he was our historian for crimes during Prohibition. I found a cryptic note on a file card in a locked desk drawer. The card was marked with three stars, and on it were the words *Marie Chance* and *Western Winnipeg Independent*. I checked, and no such newspaper or other publication appears in our records. I suspect that it may be a code phrase used between Marie and Saul."

"Hold on for a minute; Marie's book has an index of publications cited. That's a typical academic technique. Yes, there's one item under *Western Winnipeg Independent*. It's on page 247."

"Steve, when you get to that page, tell me if you see anything unusual about the layout. I have a feeling that she'll have marked that page to indicate its importance."

"I have it now. Uh-oh; I think someone read this article and understood its significance."

"What do you mean?

"Jeff, you said that the card in Saul Sanders' file had three stars on it plus Marie's name and the Winnipeg newspaper tag."

"Right ..."

"The article I found, attributed to that imaginary newspaper, is called *Stars of Tomorrow*, and the indicated writer is Sally Saunders. The article lists the children and grandchildren of Prohibition Era mobsters, along with their assumed surnames used to avoid the stigma of being members of gangster families. In some cases, the article lists their current locations. This could have easily angered someone. It may have led to the murder of Marie Chance and her boyfriend, Rob Danten. I know that Rob died in a one-car accident that some thought was suicide, but someone might have staged that. How did Marie die?"

"I checked that out, and the official ruling was death from strangulation, supposedly by her lover, Rob. Unofficial notes suggest that Marie's killer may have tortured her prior to the final strangulation."

"Given that information, I'll suggest that the torture led to Marie's revealing that Sally Saunders was really Saul Sanders, and that both Rob Danten and Saul died to eliminate people who may have been connected to this article."

"Thanks, Steve; we hadn't had any leads for why Saul was killed. If your theory is correct, someone probably pressured the publisher of that book to take it off the market. I'll check on that possibility. We may be about to solve the murders of three people if we can identify a person who pressured the publisher like that."

"There probably weren't many of these books sold because of their academic nature, but even the one book we have will be enough to upset a bunch of mob families."

CHAPTER 34 – INVITATION

Parkville Police Chief Bobby Andrews returned home for the evening to find his wife, Renee, waiting for him in the living room with two glasses of wine on the coffee table separated by a formal-looking envelope. He heard their daughter, Thelma Lou, singing downstairs in Momma's apartment.

"Hi, Renee; I sense something unusual about to happen. Momma's taking care of Thelma Lou, and you're here with wine glasses. Did I forget our anniversary? Is this a special occasion?"

"No, Bobby, but we're about to be part of one, and we should drink a toast to it. Put your police stuff away, and open that envelope next to the glasses."

Bobby complied, taking his attaché case, hat, jacket and holster to his office and returning with a red flowered Hawaiian shirt draping his massive chest and shoulders.

"Now I'm off-duty and informal. Let's see the mysterious envelope." As he opened it and read the printed card it contained, a smile removed any traces of tension from his face. "They've finally done it, and they kept the whole process a secret. Good for them!"

"As soon as I received the invitation, I called Irma for details. She wouldn't tell me much about their new home, but said that we would see it on Friday along with the others who are coming. I think they're having about twenty people. She gave me directions. Will you be able to come home on time Friday?"

"I wouldn't miss this grand unveiling for anything. Knowing Arthur and Irma, this secretiveness means that they expect this house to impress us. It also means that I'll get to find out about the latest case they're investigating. It's way outside of my jurisdiction, being in

Amboy, but I'll at least be able to tune in on what's involved."

"Just don't ruin the evening with a lot of shop talk. In the meantime, pick up your glass and join me in a toast ... to Irma and Arthur, may their new house quickly become a home filled with laughter and delight, and may it be the place where their dreams come true."

"This is good wine, and that was a great toast, Renee. You should repeat it at the party."

"That's why I'm rehearsing it here with you."

CHAPTER 35 – HOUSEWARMING

When Renee and Bobby Andrews arrived at the big white house, they took one of the last spaces on the long hillside driveway leading to the wide parking area above it. They walked up the slope, looking at the other cars as they did.

Bobby said, "I recognize some of these vehicles, but some I've never seen. They must be having a large and mixed crowd."

"Bobby, when you're on duty, they're *vehicles*; when you're at a social event, they're just *cars*. Anyway, look beyond the cars to the house. It's big, impressive, and very old. I don't know how they kept us from realizing that they had purchased this place."

"My guess is that they made a quick deal for it. They probably also bought it directly from the owner, so that they didn't have to have a lot of meetings with realtors representing both parties."

"Speaking of parties, please be on your best social behavior tonight. Keep the shop talk to a minimum, or at least discuss such things privately, away from folks who are here to enjoy themselves."

Bobby grunted affirmation and smiled at the way his tall, slender wife bossed him around despite his rugged bulk that intimidated many other people. They crossed the upper parking area, climbed the porch stairs, opened the screen door, and entered a room full of people who all seemed to be talking at the same time. Irma waved and wound her way through the crowd to greet them.

"Hi, Guys; did we manage to surprise you, or did this gumshoe know all about our buying this house?"

They each hugged Irma. Renee said, "We didn't have a hint that anything special was happening with you two.

Since that church burned, you've been out this way most of the time, so we had no clue."

"I don't think that Penny and Joe knew either, and they've been in Amboy with us much of the time. Did it feel like a long drive to you, or are we still within reasonable range for doing things together?"

Bobby nodded. "It wasn't bad at all, and once we start doing things with you here, or in-between, we'll work out some shortcuts to make the traveling feel casual. I recognize our usual investigative gang and some of the folks from the Parkville United Methodist Church, but there are quite a few who are new to me."

"Isn't it great that we have a place with room enough for a large gathering? Some of the people here are friends of Midge Drinkwater. She's the woman from whom we bought this place, and she's a treasure. Midge is in her nineties, and she'll be staying with us in a small apartment upstairs for as long as she wishes. This transaction worked out well for both sides."

Renee said, "It all looks and sounds perfect, but where and when do we get a tour?"

"Step one is to help yourself to drinks and nibbles at the tables over there near the entrance to the kitchen. Arthur's giving tours every thirty minutes or so, but if you want more information than he gives to his groups, come see me for a personal walk-around. Right now, I see someone I have to grab for something special. Go find people you know, and they'll introduce you to others."

Irma aimed Renee and Bobby at Wally Sanborn, Arthur's best friend and coffee buddy from the Parkville Church and then she headed over to where Steve DuBois had just opened a beer.

"Well, Steve, what do you think of our new-but-not-new house?"

"It's spectacular." He raised his bottle toward her. "I toast you and your domicile. Enjoy it, and turn it into a special place for family and friends."

Irma hugged him. "Thank you, Steve. Have you noticed that even though the house is old, it has some modern innovations? Have you seen our elevator?"

They walked over to the elevator shaft next to the staircase. Steve admired the open grillwork enclosing the shaft.

"This enclosure is like a big sculpture, and the fact that you can see between the brass wall design figures makes it less intrusive on the house. In other words, I like it. Does it work well?"

Irma raised her voice in order for it to carry over the party background noise and conversations. "Try it, Steve. Push the button to bring the elevator down from upstairs."

Steve's button push initiated a noticeable whirring and clanking as the elevator cage began to descend from the third floor. "That isn't as loud as I expected. I'll have to try it again another time when there isn't crowd noise ..."

The elevator appeared from above as he spoke, and his words trailed off as he saw that the cage held two occupants. Steve looked shocked as his wife, Ellen, and his adopted son, Eric, greeted him.

Together, they shouted, "Surprise!" Ellen followed with, "You thought you could go to a special party without us, huh?"

"But you two are supposed to be home in Idaho, getting ready to join me in DC next week."

"At Irma's suggestion, we altered our vacation plans slightly. Are you disappointed?"

Irma said, "I'll leave you three in order to perform my hostess duties. Enjoy yourselves. Ellen and Eric have been here since last night, Steve, so they'll be able to give you a private tour of the house." She patted Steve on his shoulder and walked away.

Eric said, "This is a neat place, Dad. I'm getting some ideas for how I could help you add a few more rooms to our house."

Implications

Ellen smiled as Steve absorbed the impact of Eric having called him *Dad* for the first time. It had been awkward for Eric, deciding how to address his mother's new husband while remaining loyal to his veteran father who had died in Iraq. Apparently, Eric had made his decision after a lot of soul searching and conversations with his mom. The final phase of new family formation was behind them.

Steve said, "That sounds great to me, Eric. The Blakes did us a big favor by arranging this get-together. How about you leading all of us on that tour that Irma mentioned, right after we all greet Joe and Penny? I saw them in the kitchen as I walked by the doorway."

The DuBois family entered the kitchen, where Joe and Penny were cutting three fruit pies into individual slices.

Eric led the way. "Hello Mr. Gonzalez; hello Mrs. Gonzalez; it's good to see you again. Dad told me you're working on a case in this area."

Joe and Penny both smiled in reaction to Eric's referring to Steve as *Dad*. Then Penny said, "It's good to see you too, Eric. How would you like to have the very first slice of pie? You can choose from apple, blueberry, or cherry. This is such an old-fashioned house that we wanted to have traditional desserts."

"Thanks; I'll have the apple. It looks perfect."

Eric took his pie out to the front parlor, and the four adults exchanged greetings all around.

Penny said, "Ellen, was Steve surprised when you and Eric came down from above?"

"He looked flabbergasted. Irma is terrific at keeping secrets."

Steve said, "Apparently the Gonzalez clan knew about it."

Penny said, "I did, but Joe didn't. Irma had to clue me in. I ferried Ellen and Eric from the airport yesterday. However, neither Joe nor I knew that the Blakes had purchased this house until the invitation came. It's a fine old building and very homey. I suspect that we'll be holding some of our meetings here."

Joe said, "Speaking of meetings, I have to touch base with Arthur on something related to the case. I promise I won't keep him from his duties as host."

He found Arthur outside by the open garage door, showing the red corvette to Shirley Hadley, his secretary during his time as pastor of Parkville UMC. Joe waited at a distance until they finished their conversation and Shirley departed. Then he walked over and put his arm around Arthur's shoulder.

"Congratulations, Buddy; this is an amazing place. Is that Corvette yours too?"

"We worked out an interesting but convoluted deal. I'll give you the details some other time, but part of the arrangement was a trade of Irma's Mustang for this slightly older beauty. I noticed you standing in the background while I finished up my chat with Shirley, so I suspect you have something on your mind worth waiting to share."

"I plead guilty to that. I wanted to let you know that I spoke with Dennis Mikken, our State Fire Investigator. He told me that Celia had earlier found that rock that someone used to trap you and Irma, and that she had left it in a wheelbarrow on the church's basement level. Apparently, the Sunday school teachers used the rock as a symbol of strength and steadfastness in their Bible classes. The point of all this is that because the rock was in a wheelbarrow, the person who put it on the swiveling panel to trap you did not have to be unusually strong."

"Then that person must have removed the wheelbarrow, because it wasn't there when we climbed out of that subbasement chamber. The disappointing aspect of your information is that we'll now have to expand our list of possible arson suspects. I had thought we were looking for a very strong person because of the heavy stone, but now we'll have to consider people with only average strength as well."

Arthur picked up a soft cloth and buffed the Corvette's fender where Shirley had touched it. Something about a special sports car made you want to care for it. He had selected all of his prior cars for their usefulness or value. As an outright purchase, the Corvette would have exceeded his budget. It was not particularly useful; but it sure was a beauty.

Joe could read Arthur's thoughts as he caressed his Corvette. "It looks as though you have a new mistress. Don't worry; I won't tell Irma. I've had my share of love affairs with cars too."

"It's as though I've moved out of my normal class and comfort zone. I don't like people who show off their fancy cars, and now I'm one of them."

"Keep pondering your new situation, Arthur. I have to get back to helping Penny serve the snacks and desserts."

Joe walked back across the parking area, and Arthur forced himself to do the same, following a few more strokes of polishing Betty. As he walked up the front steps, he spotted Midge sitting on a rattan chair at the far end of the long porch, and he joined her.

"Hi, Midge; thanks once again for making all of this possible. I hope the crowd isn't too loud or unruly for you."

"Don't kid yourself. Some of the parties I used to throw were ten times this size. I'm just enjoying my opportunity to do some people watching. Most folks don't realize how revealing they are when they mingle, or refuse to mingle, in a crowd."

"Has anyone stood out as particularly interesting to you?"

"I hope you won't take offense, given your profession, but that Amboy pastor, Lorna Dyner, doesn't fit with any of the other people at this party. She's tense and acts as though she wants to eavesdrop on other people. She keeps moving around from the fringes of one group to another, as though she wants to listen in on someone who's here but having problems identifying who that person of interest is."

"And you got all of that by just sitting here and watching her."

"I did cheat, Arthur. After she piqued my interest, I followed her enough to see how many groups of people she sampled. She was like a honeybee visiting many flowers in a garden."

"That's a very intriguing observation, Midge; thanks."

"I have a surveillance advantage; no one pays much attention to someone as old as I am."

"Well, I certainly do. I'm sure Billy Woffort does too. He'd like to be your boyfriend, and he's heading this way. I'll go check out Lorna's behavior while you spend some time with Billy."

"You have that only partially correct, Arthur. Billy is already my boyfriend, and don't get too shocked when I occasionally invite him to stay overnight in my second floor apartment."

CHAPTER 36 – MANDY MILLER

Arthur observed from a distance the eavesdropping behavior of Lorna Dyner as she moved among the housewarming party guests. He decided that it was time to have a talk with her. He would try to make her focus on a topic unrelated to the party and observe whether she tried to break off the conversation and return to her listening in on other guests. Arthur stopped by the kitchen for two pieces of cherry pie and worked his way through the groups of guests to reach Lorna.

"Hi, Lorna; we haven't had a chance to talk today. I need some more of your input on the history of the Amboy Church. Come sit with me and enjoy some pie."

She looked unhappy at the prospect of having to sit in one place. "Your house is such a classic, Arthur; why don't we talk as we walk through it. You can give me an abbreviated tour."

Arthur sat on a couch and patted the seat beside him. "I've been mingling on the run for too long. Sit and enjoy some pie."

Lorna reluctantly joined him. "What do you want to discuss?"

"I need to know about Mandy Miller, the seminarian that they asked to leave the program. Was she still at the Amboy Church when you first arrived?"

"She was, but I didn't feel that I could lean on her as a resource while I worked to get the congregation's acceptance as the new pastor. Mandy tried to make me feel unwelcome, but she ended up distancing herself from both the membership and me. Mandy's affair with Jerry Tackman had begun to lose its privacy. A few weeks after I arrived, Jerry's wife Ginger confronted him, and he admitted his sinning but asked for a divorce. Ginger retaliated by spreading the word of Jerry's taking up with what she called the *seminarian slut*. Many of the older and more traditional members began to write letters to the District Superintendent and the Bishop, requesting that Mandy be reassigned to another church or be kicked out of the program. I could hardly defend her actions if I hoped to gain acceptance as their new pastor, so I refused to get involved. I simply said that all decisions would be made at the District and Conference levels."

"I'm not quite clear on whether Jerry went with Mandy when she was told to leave or whether he returned to his wife?"

"Actually, Jerry left before Mandy's fate was decided. The publicity had embarrassed him. He knew his future would not be rosy with either woman, so he ran away from the controversy ... Arthur, would it be all right with you if we finished this discussion at a different time. A friend of mine is at this party, and I'd like to get to talk with him."

"Sure, Lorna, I'll contact you during the week to set up a meeting. Who is this friend of yours; we must know him if we invited him."

"Now I'm the one who's embarrassed. I've only talked with him on the telephone, about a possible date. During those conversations, he called himself Ralph, but I don't think that's his real name. I have a good ear for recognizing voices, and shortly after I arrived, I heard his voice in fragments of conversation within the crowd around the entrance. Since that time, I've been listening in on chatter within many smaller groups in the hope of identifying him. I'd like to get some assessment of the man before I agree to a date. I don't know whether you invited him; he may be here accompanying someone with an invitation. Either way, I'll probably refuse the date unless I can find him and learn more about him."

"It sounds as though you have a mission. Go forth and conquer."

CHAPTER 37 – TRINA JERGENS

With the housewarming party one week into their rear view mirror, Irma and Arthur sat on their front porch accompanied by cool drinks and clipboards, assessing the status of the church arson case. As usual, Irma did most of the writing and served as moderator of their two-person conference.

"I have to believe that the *Western Winnipeg Independent* article in Marie Chance's book will be the key to sorting out the players in our mystery."

Arthur drained his lemonade. "That's the one that listed the current family names of descendants of Chicago mobsters?"

"... that, plus current locations for some of them."

"Marie thought that the threat of revealing that information would force Rob Danten's wife to give him the divorce he wanted. Instead, it probably led to both of their deaths. Trina had lived her entire unmarried life as Trina Jergens, Milton's granddaughter. She had nothing to fear from Marie's threat. Milton had established himself as a reputable undertaker and a philanthropist who built a church. His daughter wouldn't feel she needed to hide her background."

"We don't know what happened to Milton after he built the church. The two old skeletons we found in the warehouse chamber suggest that he became involved with violence. We should try to find out how and when Milt died."

Arthur poured a fresh drink and made a note on his pad. "I think you have a good analysis there. Marie Chance wasn't stupid. She had to have a reason for feeling that she could control Trina with the threat of publicizing this article. What could it have been?"

Irma set down her clipboard and stared at him. "Sometimes you amaze me. That's exactly the right question. There's only one possible answer – even though I can't prove it. Marie thought this list would intimidate Rob's wife because Trina had compiled it. Rob must have found the list of names and locations at home and showed it to Marie, who copied it. Based on the information Steve got from Jeff Lee at Secret Service, Marie must have taken the list to Agent Saul Sanders. It had to be Trina behind that document. Who else but someone within a mob family could have generated that list? The gang kids and grandkids probably kept track of each other, even though they wanted to hide from the outside world."

"I'll applaud your conclusion. There's one way to test its plausibility."

"What's that?"

"Find out whether Trina is still alive and living in the open. If she compiled that list, and it cost Rob and Marie their lives, my guess is that Trina is either dead or hiding somewhere."

CHAPTER 38 – KENNETH CANTINI

As Irma and Arthur cleared the table after lunch, the telephone rang.

"Hello, Arthur, it's Steve DuBois; I have some feedback from Jefferson Lee that may interest you."

"What's new at Secret Service?"

"Jeff checked with the university press that published Marie Chance's book and found that someone did, indeed, pressure them to take that book off the market."

"What do you mean by *pressure*? Was there any violence involved?"

"None at all; an attorney simply informed the publisher that Marie's article, quoted as being from the newspaper he represented, was pure fiction and not anything that they had published. He told the press that the article invaded the privacy of the people mentioned in it, and he said that his firm would sue the publisher for libel if the book wasn't removed from their active list and all copies recalled from bookstores."

"I have a feeling that this attorney represented the *Western Winnipeg Independent*; am I right?"

"That you are, Arthur; It was actually a good strategy, because the gangland heirs did have a strong case for invasion of privacy, even though the article was supposed to have come from a fictitious newspaper. The publisher complied and stopped selling the book; he hadn't expected to sell many of them anyway."

"Who was the attorney, and can we connect him with any of the murders?"

Steve chuckled. "Here comes the interesting part. His name was Kenneth Cantini. If my memory and notes are correct, he was the treasurer who embezzled funds from that church that burned in Amboy. He wasn't an attorney at all, and we have another connection back to that church."

"His showing up in this context is amusing, but not if he was involved in murdering Rob Danten, Marie Chance, and Saul Sanders."

"Point well taken, Arthur; I apologize for my laughing at his pretending to be an attorney."

"It is interesting that, this long after Prohibition, there were so many people with gangster connections attending that church. It appears as though Ken Cantini took an active role in events that led to several murders. He may be an accessory to one or more of them. Have you or Jefferson Lee learned what he's been doing since that church treasurer scandal?"

"He sold his Amboy house and moved to Las Vegas. He may have been looking for anonymity there, or he may have been trying to use the money he stole from the church as seed money for a gambling habit. We're sure that he made contact there with the people who put him up to this lawyer masquerade. We don't know whether his connections lived there or were just passing through town."

"There are certainly Chicago mob family members living there. Do you know where Ken Cantini is now?"

"No one knows for sure. After he played his attorney role, he returned to his Las Vegas home. Recently, he flew from Vegas to Rome as part of a tour group. The tour guide said that Cantini disappeared while they were touring the Roman ruins. They took a break to eat, and after lunch, their head count was one short. She can't tell us whether Ken wandered away or if someone forced him to leave. The Italian police and Interpol are looking for him."

126

CHAPTER 39 – BACK TO BASICS

After disconnecting, Arthur joined Irma on the couch and relayed Steve's information. She looked perplexed as she unconsciously twisted her long brown hair around her fingers.

"Bishop Chandler assigned you to determine whether the burning of the Amboy Church was arson, to advise him as to whether they should worry about fires at other churches, and to minimize adverse publicity for the United Methodist Church. We're now involved in a bunch of additional mysteries: what scandals and deaths happened to people in that church several years ago; the identities of those bodies in the subbasement of the church and who entombed them; plus the murder of Secret Service Agent Saul Sanders."

"All those mysteries are related, and we don't know which one led to the arson attack on the church."

"I'll grant you that they're intertwined, Arthur, but it's also possible that the arson had nothing to do with any of those other things. Shouldn't we focus on finding the arsonist?"

"I'd be in complete agreement with you if we had a plan for zeroing in on him or her. In the absence of such a plan, the only thing we can do is attack these peripheral but related mysteries and hope they'll lead us to the person who set the fire."

Irma stood and looked down on Arthur triumphantly. "I have a plan."

His right eyebrow arched quizzically. "Your humble student awaits your wisdom. What should we do?"

"Let's concentrate on the *why* of the fire. What was the arsonist's motive?"

"That's a great idea, but do you think you can answer that question?"

"I can state some reasonable assumptions and make an educated guess at the motive."

"I think I see where you're going with this, Irma. We can conclude from everything else that we've discovered about the Amboy UMC, that this fire was not an action against a randomly selected church."

"Next step: we can assume that we were trapped in that subbasement chamber by the arsonist returning to the church to accomplish something."

Arthur nodded in agreement. "He or she didn't succeed that evening because we were in the way."

"And the arsonist still hasn't succeeded because Dennis arranged for a State Police guard on what's left of the church."

"Therefore, the objective of the arsonist is to retrieve something from the subbasement liquor warehouse."

Irma smiled triumphantly. "And that something is more valuable than the old cases of whiskey."

"That *is* a plan. Let's get Dennis and Steve to join us in doing a thorough search of that chamber; and this time, we'll have the State Police guarding the entrance.

CHAPTER 40 – *MILTON JERGENS*

Milton opened the door of his sales office building and called across the parking lot to the man standing next to the hearse. "Hey, Sammy, come over here."

Sammy jogged across the lot. That shout from the boss had sounded important.

"Yeah, Milt; what do you need?"

"I have a special assignment for you. Go to John Sbarbaro's funeral home in Chicago, and pick up a shipment. This won't be booze; it's a deceased client. Drive carefully so that you won't get any attention from the cops or Secret Service. This body has to retire to our country cemetery very quietly. People in the mob are used to you making trips to Sbarbaro's for booze, so they'll never suspect that this time our hearse will be doing its advertised job of carrying a corpse. Don't say anything to anybody. If someone asks you questions, play dumb. Just pick up the coffin that John has waiting for you, and bring it back here. Set it up in the basement for a wake, but keep it sealed. We'll put a photograph on top of it to satisfy any mourners or church members who might visit our chapel area."

"Will that photograph match the client in the box?"

"Like I said, Sammy, play dumb on this one."

CHAPTER 41 – PROSPECTORS

Dennis Mikken and Steve DuBois had joined Arthur and Irma in the basement of the burned-out Amboy UMC. They had gathered in response to Arthur's call for assistance in finding new evidence concerning the arsonist. When Arthur told him that they would be working in the subbasement, Dennis arranged for a second State Police car to be on church property to avoid a possible repeat of the warehouse entrapment episode. Arthur briefed the newcomers on the planned effort.

"Irma suggested that we should look for the arsonist's motive, rather than concentrating on identifying the individual from the evidence we've found. Once you take that approach, it becomes logical that the portion of the fire set in the church's basement had the goal of destroying the carpeting that hindered access to the subbasement entrance. Add to that the fact that the arsonist or an accomplice locked Irma and me inside the warehouse chamber, and we have to conclude that there is something valuable down there that he or she is after."

Steve said, "That makes sense, Arthur, but are you sure that the target isn't the old whiskey stored there? It might have quite a value to collectors."

"I'll grant you that the whiskey does have value, but now that we know about this warehouse, the theft and sale of its liquid contents would be an admission of guilt."

Dennis asked, "If not the booze, what do you think they're after?"

"I don't know, but with the three of us plus Irma exploring that warehouse, we should be able to do a much more thorough search than we did earlier. When the bodies were still down there, we had to be careful that we didn't disturb any evidence. This time, we'll be free to take things apart if necessary."

"Will we need to bring any special tools?"

"No, Dennis, Irma has a tool assortment already laid out for us down there."

The three men descended the steps to the subbasement to join Irma, who sat at the table completing sketches of the overall layout as a reference in case they had to disassemble the shelves or other items in the room. She looked up as the feet and legs on the steps became complete people.

"Hi, Guys; thanks for agreeing to search and dismantle this place as required until we find the treasure."

Dennis looked quizzical. "Are you convinced that there is a treasure for us to find?"

"I'd give it a high probability, unless someone unknown got to it first, like those grave robbers in Egypt. My arguments for its existence were strong enough to convince Arthur."

Steve asked, "What were those arguments?"

"Without going into all the details, the arsonist must have set the fire in order to drive the church people away and to burn off the carpeting that masked the subbasement access panel. Our firebug assumed everyone would abandon the church ruins after the preliminary fire investigation. Then he or she could have unobserved access to the subbasement chamber. The arsonist returned when Arthur and I were down there, and locked us in, hoping that we would starve and join the other corpses as permanent residents."

Arthur said, "That would have taken a long time, with all that old whiskey and beer to sustain us."

Irma gave him a scathing look. "Anyway, we'll give this place a thorough search and see whether we find anything valuable enough to be the motive for arson. As Arthur may have told you, we don't think it would be the whiskey itself, because anyone taking and selling it would be confessing the arson by that act."

Arthur noted that Irma had included him in that *we* comment. He did the wise thing and said nothing.

Irma assigned each of them to a row of shelving plus the walls, ceiling, and floor adjacent to it. Her plan was for them to each search one section and then work together to follow up on whatever they individually found. She distributed battery-powered lanterns as they scattered to their appointed areas.

Arthur had volunteered to search the shelving closest to the back corner of the large chamber, feeling that set would give him more adjacent walls and surfaces that might contain hiding places. He tried to attack his portion of the room in a very methodical manner, to avoid missing any part of it. Before long, he realized that he needed a better definition of his objective.

"Irma, would you be willing to say that we're looking for a single object that is relatively small, rather than a whole bunch of items? We need to focus our thinking, or we'll miss something important."

"I'll go along with your single object theory. I'd guess that it would have to be small or unremarkable to have avoided notice during other visits over the years. I think it dates from Prohibition days, so it would probably have no obvious value."

Dennis said, "We don't know what we're looking for, and we don't know whether someone already found and took it sometime during the last eighty years or more. This search is impossible, but I'll keep trying for a while."

They checked all of the shelves and all of the cases of whisky. Steve disassembled his set of shelves and emptied every case of whisky that had been stored there. He completed this effort and sat down at the table, looking frustrated.

Arthur chose to disregard the shelving and spend his time studying the floor, walls, and ceiling. He thought he would be looking for some kind of cavity or hidden compartment. He had no success within his assigned area, so he started to study the periphery of the entire chamber. He tapped surfaces, listening for a hollow sound; focused his light on each detail; and felt every surface with his hands. After about an hour of scanning everything, he discovered something unexpected.

"Hey, Folks; I just noticed that there's a gap between the top step leading out of here and the floor above it. It's about an inch and a half high, and I think I see some kind of lump in there. I'll need a long stick or wire coat hanger to fish it out.

CHAPTER 42 – *MILT AND SAMMY*

Sammy had responded promptly when Milt called him from the other side of the church parking lot. The tone of Milt's voice told Sammy that he was in trouble.

"What is it, boss?"

"Come into my office. I need to talk with you."

As Sammy stepped through the doorway, his tension ratcheted upward. Next to a wooden desk chair stood Mario, his huge hands sheathed in the thin black leather gloves he wore in his role as the muscle of Milt's outfit. Mario and Sammy had worked together frequently, but they had never been friends. Mario was all business and all muscle.

Sammy tried to be casual. "Hi, Mario; I guess this is a group meeting."

Milt closed and locked the door. "Sammy, you've given us a big problem. I told you not to open that coffin you picked up from John Sbarbaro. You broke the seal on it, and you removed something from inside."

"Honest, Boss, if it got opened, someone else must have done it. I never took a look at her."

"Who told you the person inside that coffin was a woman? I certainly didn't. You just confessed to opening that box. What did you do with the ring you took?"

Sammy was sweating, but he tried to sound reasonable. "Sorry, Milt, I guess I didn't think things through. I felt it was too nice a rock to bury, so I gave it to my girlfriend. She was very impressed when I put it on her finger."

Milt remained calm. "Tell us who your girlfriend is and where we can find her. We'll have to get that ring back."

"Sure, Boss; she's Wilma Schenkle, and she works at Johnson's Steakhouse as a hostess."

"Thanks for cooperating, Sammy. Now, you and Mario are going to go over to that steakhouse and bring her back here, along with the ring."

"Can we wait until she finishes her shift? It will only be a couple of extra hours, and the delay will keep her boss from asking questions or getting mad at her."

"I think we'll be able to do it that way. Just be sure to get her and the ring back here by six o'clock. Will you do that?"

"Sure, Boss; and you don't have to send Mario with me. I'll make sure she gets here on time."

"Mario's my insurance policy, Sammy. He goes with you; understood?"

Sammy didn't look happy. "C'mon, Mario; do you want to drive?"

Mario said, "You drive. I want my hands free."

At seven o'clock, the car returned, driven by Mario, with two passengers sitting stiffly in the back seat.

Milt came out to meet Mario as he walked toward the sales office building. "You're late. Does that mean they caused trouble?"

"Nothing I couldn't handle, Boss. They're tied up neatly in the back seat; and here's the trinket you were after."

Milt noticed a cut on the right side of Mario's forehead. "Did Sammy do that to you?"

"Naw; it was that little bitch of his. She scratched me with that rock on her finger. It's not on her finger any more, and I'll bet that finger hurts a lot from my pulling that ring off."

"Good work, Mario. Take them down to the warehouse. I'll join you in a few minutes, as soon as I make a phone call."

Ten minutes later, Milt descended the subbasement steps to find Sammy and Wilma sitting at the table with gags in their mouths and their hands tied behind their backs. Mario stood behind them with his right hand in his coat pocket.

Milt shook his head as he addressed the seated couple. "Sammy, you've deeply disappointed me, and you've involved poor Wilma in this mess. You should have followed my instructions exactly. The person in that coffin has to disappear quietly, and her prized possession has to disappear along with her. I suggest that you say your prayers."

Milt nodded to Mario and climbed the steps. As he reached the main basement, four shots reverberated through the warehouse chamber. He turned and called down to Mario, "Is it done?"

"Job complete; I put two in each of them to be sure. I'll clean up the mess."

"Good. Untie their hands, remove their gags, and leave them sitting there as a warning to any others who might get greedy and disobey orders. Stow the gun on a shelf in the back corner near the two-wheel cart. Then come see me in my office."

Fifteen minutes later, Mario eased his bulk into the armchair next to Milt's desk. "It's all cleaned up, Boss. I couldn't find one slug, but it's in the room someplace. I'll find it later."

"How did you feel about having to take care of Sammy? Did it bother you? Were you two good friends?"

"Sammy was always a little too different for me, so we never got to be buddies. I think he had ambitions, and in this line of work, that's dangerous. I learned in the Army to follow orders, so I don't worry about feelings; I just do what I'm told."

Milt stood and patted Mario on his shoulder. "Thanks for your loyalty. We need your kind of thinking around here. With Sammy gone, you'll take our new embalmer, Louie, with you on your pickup and delivery trips. Keep a close eye on him for a while. We got him from an unaffiliated funeral home, and it's going to take a while before we'll be sure he's dependable. I called him a little while ago and told him he'd be working with you. He sounded agreeable, but don't trust him until he proves he's loyal. Let's make sure he fits into our plans before you tell him too much or take him down to the warehouse."

"That sounds good to me, Boss. I don't talk too much on assignments anyway. You may want to line up a replacement embalmer just in case Louie becomes a problem like Sammy."

CHAPTER 43 – *JOHN SBARBARO*

Milt won his bet with himself as to who would be the next person to call him. He had already rehearsed his response. "Hello, John; thanks for checking with me. Yes, everything's ready for the funeral. We had one little problem, but it's been handled. You can pass the word that the client is ready for interment and the gravesite reservation has been made."

John Sbarbaro's voice carried a hint of the suspicious nature that had made him a successful prosecutor while still conducting his illegal hobbies. "I need the whole story, Milt. Al's not going to be happy if there's a slip-up."

Milt felt the sweat start to drip down his back. We're burying Capone's mistress. Either his wife, Mae, doesn't know about this floozy, or she was the one who pulled the trigger. I'd better play this straight, or I could end up on a slab too. "Here's the whole story, John. One of my guys couldn't resist breaking the seal on the coffin and taking a peak, despite my warnings. He told his girlfriend too, so we had to keep both of them quiet. They won't cause any more problems."

John's pause seemed to take forever. "...You say a civilian was involved. Describe her."

"...Brunette, about five foot four, a hundred and thirty pounds, twenty-six years old ..."

"And you say she's a local girl out there?"

"... She was a hostess at Johnson's Steak House."

"Thanks, Milt. I have it all. There won't be a wake. Complete the burial tomorrow. Don't put a stone on the grave."

"We'll take care of it quietly, John."

Milton Jergens breathed a sigh of relief and poured himself a glass of whiskey from the bottle in his right-hand drawer. John would give him a *good and faithful servant* rating when he spoke with Capone, and he hadn't even mentioned the ring! Milt noticed how warm that piece of jewelry felt in his pocket. He'd better return it to that woman's finger and do one or two last-minute things before certifying her as ready for burial.

The next day, Milt picked up his *Chicago Daily News* and read that a car had crashed and burned three miles outside of Amboy. The article indicated that the young woman driver inside had been burned beyond recognition and that police were looking through missing person reports in an attempt to identify her.

CHAPTER 44 – DISCOVERY

Steve, Dennis, and Irma joined Arthur at the exit steps of the subbasement warehouse, where his flashlight had revealed the silhouette of an object at the back end of a gap between the top concrete step and the floor above it. Irma took a coil of stiff copper wire from her forensics kit and straightened it out; then she bent the end of the wire to form a hook.

"Try using this to grab it, Arthur. If necessary, you can reform the hook to match the size of your object."

Arthur tried the hooked-end wire, but found that he could touch the object but not hook it. Then he duct-taped his pen crosswise onto the end of a yardstick and used that like a hockey stick to bring the lump closer to him. At first touch, the object felt like a stone, but as Arthur pulled on it, he felt it flexing, indicating some softness in the object or its wrappings. He noticed that they were all holding their breaths during the final moments of his dragging the article within range of his outstretched fingers.

"Got it! It's something wrapped in an old piece of cloth." Arthur carried the item to a clear spot on the table and uncovered it slowly. "I want to be sure that I don't lose any small fragments of this thing." Then he stepped back, and they all stared at it.

Dennis said, "So much for treasure hunting; I'm sure our arsonist wasn't after a piece of wood broken off of a whiskey case, wrapped up in an old cloth."

Irma held out her arm like a barrier in front of the others. "Not so fast! Even if this object doesn't turn out to be valuable, it's key evidence. Someone tore that cloth off the male skeleton's shirt. Here's a photograph I took earlier. The pattern matches, and it hasn't deteriorated because somebody tore it off that shirt prior to the body decomposing. The cloth and the piece of wood inside it date to the time when the first two victims died."

The others all stared at the photo and the cloth. Irma's conclusion was correct.

Arthur said, "All those years in forensic pathology pay off again. If the cloth is valuable evidence, then the piece of wood must be important also." He picked up Irma's bend-end tweezers and used them to invert the thin piece of wood.

"I was right. Someone printed a message on the reverse side of this board. It's pale after all these years, but I see *Binghampton 13NW 4SW*."

Steve looked at the board through a magnifying glass he retrieved from his pocket. "That notation was written with an old fountain pen. I can see where the line edges spread as the wood absorbed the ink. The writing comes from the right period to be important. Does anyone know what Binghampton might mean? The numbers appear to be some kind of coordinates keyed to compass directions."

Richard Davidson

CHAPTER 45 – GINGER TACKMAN

Ginger Tackman still wondered if she might have improved her handling of Jerry and his affair. By taking an aggressive stand against that *seminarian slut*, she had achieved the satisfaction of assuring that Mandy Miller would never be ordained in the United Methodist Church, but in the process, she had scared Jerry into leaving for parts unknown. She had made sure he would have no future with the seminarian, but he had decided that he couldn't redeem himself as a husband and had preferred to re-start his life's journey somewhere else. Ginger knew that Jerry would never return; yet her romantic outlook on life had compelled her to leave all of Jerry's belongings just as they had been when he left so suddenly. She was in limbo between a past life she craved, that would never return, and a bewildering future she refused to accept. Even recent attention from Lester Haynes, the paint store manager, could not convince her to hope for something new and better.

Ginger had grown up in a family where everyone had married for life. She couldn't recall any aunt or uncle who had been divorced or deserted. With Jerry gone, she felt like a cancer on her family's tradition of lifelong marriages. He had committed the sin, and had left her with the shame. She would like to have a long discussion with Pastor Lorna Dyner about her outlook, but Ginger wasn't sure that the never-married young preacher would have any beneficial advice to contribute.

Each afternoon, she looked through her photograph albums and tried to relive in her mind the good times she had shared with Jerry ... and each afternoon she ended her mental flights with the same question; what had transformed him into such a bastard?

CHAPTER 46 – BINGHAMPTON

It didn't take long for Dennis Mikken to discover that Binghampton was the name of the oldest cemetery in the Amboy area. He learned that this burial ground was located at the northwest corner of East Main Street, otherwise known as State Route 10, and Sterling Road. Some of the *residents* of Binghampton had been there since two decades before the Civil War, while others were quite current, the cemetery still being in operation. Because the burial ground faced Sterling Road, and that two-laner ran from southeast to northwest, the grave rows at Binghampton paralleled the road. Binghampton 13NW 4SW had to indicate a grave location. Dennis telephoned Steve DuBois to share this conclusion.

"Hi, Steve; it's Dennis, and I've figured out the meaning of that cryptic writing on the board we found in the lower basement. That note describes a grave location in Amboy's Binghampton Cemetery. If you're not busy, I'll drive by, and we can go check it out."

"That sounds good to me, Dennis. I'll bring my camera so that we can document what we find for the others."

When they arrived at the cemetery, they parked on the shoulder of Sterling Road, near the older gravesites. They walked among the headstones to get a feeling for the age of the different rows and sections.

Steve didn't consider himself superstitious, but he found himself patting the headstones as he walked behind the row of markers. "It's a combination of feelings for me. I walk behind the stones so that I can get close to them without walking on anyone's grave; I also feel an urge to touch them because that moves me to the timeframe when they died. That may sound crazy, but it helps me to realize how much different the adventure of life was when these folks lived."

"There's nothing wrong with that, Steve. I grew up on a farm, and that helps me understand people who lived when this part of the country was almost all farms. You learned to be independent, because there were no government facilities and services to solve your problems for you."

"Some of the graves have no headstones. Do you think someone stole them?"

Dennis bent down to examine one unmarked grave. "This one shows no sign that there was ever a marker. Some of these folks may have been too poor for a stone, or they may not have had any relatives who would want to check up on them."

"Let's see if we can figure out which grave is 13NW 4SW. I figure that it should be four rows in from Sterling Road and thirteen graves up from the beginning of that row."

"That sounds right to me. Someone printed the location designation on that board during the 1920's, so we'll have to look carefully to be sure we count from the first grave in the row. Some graves may have become hard to identify due to the passage of time."

They found the fourth row from the street without any trouble. Then, Dennis walked to the end of the row closest to East Main Street and compared the location of the end grave with those of the end graves on the other rows.

"It looks as though the end graves line up across all of the rows. I'll count to thirteen starting with this one."

Dennis counted from the foot end of the graves, while Steve counted from the head end. When they came to a stop, they were both facing the same unmarked grave."

Dennis said, "That makes sense. The only reason to record the grid location on a board and protect it for future retrieval would be because the gravediggers hadn't marked the grave after burying the coffin."

Implications

"Logically, I think you can go one step further, Dennis. They were deliberate about not marking that grave. That grave contains something that someone wanted to remain hidden forever. The person who recorded the grid location was disobeying instructions. He or she planned to go back later and dig up the coffin."

CHAPTER 47 – JEFFERSON LEE

Jeff had grown increasingly convinced that Irma Blake had found the key to the importance of the published list of information about mobster descendants – Trina Jergens Danten had to be the one who had compiled it. He was so convinced of this that in his mind he referred to that document as *Trina's List*. The problem he faced now was determining whether Trina had played a role in the deaths of her husband, Rob Danten and his mistress, Marie Chance. Trina wouldn't have had the physical skills to murder his fellow Secret Service agent, Saul Sanders, in such a brutal fashion. Would she have enlisted a professional hit man? Lee's ancestors on his oriental side might suggest that he meditate upon this puzzle, seeking enlightenment; but his instincts adhered to the logical principles of the western side of his family and his namesake forebear, Thomas Jefferson. Jeff had always considered his bearing of that great man's name to be both an honor and an obligation. He would reason his way to a solution.

He started to write notes on a pad of paper. From the information he had received from the Blakes and others, Jeff saw Trina Jergens Danten as a petulant woman who fantasized about the prestige bestowed on her by marrying a college professor and about the lost panache of Chicago mob figures. Trina would have compiled that list of mob descendants and their locations without seeking or getting permissions. By making that list, she would have felt part of a larger and more important group. Trina definitely would have felt fear from the publication of her supposedly private list; she also would have hesitated before letting that anxiety drive her to killing her husband. She wouldn't want to risk arrest and the loss of the prestige she valued. Trina would have been apprehensive, but smart enough to deny having made the list. She could have preserved her college faculty connections while granting her husband the divorce he wanted. There certainly would have been other professors to marry.

Jeff ended his notes with a circled conclusion that Trina was the kind of pain-in-the-ass person that people avoided, but that she would not have murdered anyone. She would have avoided murder because she would have had nothing to gain from it and everything to lose. He saw Trina as self-centered and one who would do what she saw as beneficial and self-aggrandizing. She hated others, but she loved herself more.

The killer of Rob Danten, Marie Chance and Saul Sanders was someone else, perhaps two someones. He could see Saul's assailant as being a person on the mob descendants list. If Trina hadn't killed Rob and Marie, who had? Perhaps their murders hadn't been personal but had been the result of something they had uncovered in their research on the Prohibition Era. Jeff thought about Steve's tales of the corpses in the bootlegging warehouse beneath that burned-out church and his visit to the old cemetery. Rob and Marie could have become targets for that most classic of reasons: they may have known where the bodies were buried.

CHAPTER 48 – EXHUMATION

Dennis Mikken and Penny Gonzalez made a joint appearance before Federal Judge Myron Ekklesworth to petition for authorization to exhume the contents of the grave in Binghampton Cemetery. They based their petition on the likelihood that those contents would lead to the identification of a church arsonist and possibly the murderer of a Secret Service agent. Judge Ekklesworth expressed his reservation that this sounded like a fishing expedition rather than an action likely to yield a specific result. Nevertheless, he granted their request because it demonstrated combined state and federal cooperation and shared goals.

The following day Penny and Joe presented the judge's order to Gilbert Wilson, the Manager of Binghampton Cemetery, accompanied by Arthur and Irma Blake, Dennis Mikken, and Steve DuBois. In keeping with their earlier agreement to minimize publicity concerning the church arson, they indicated that the exhumation was a federal matter, and Dennis did not reveal that he was a State Fire Investigator.

Gilbert Wilson expressed pleasure that something was happening to break up an otherwise monotonous day. "In case you folks didn't notice, our job here is a lot more upkeep than it is burying new clients. Our gravediggers, Lenny and Hank, will enjoy the change of pace and your interest in their efforts. I'll get them started on it right away."

Gilbert left to arrange the procedure, and the visitors adjourned to the gravesite to await the results. Twenty minutes later, Lenny and Hank arrived with their equipment and began to dig. Steve set up his camera to record the entire process.

Lenny and Hank enjoyed the attention of this group of officials, and they responded by showing off their efficiency. After a short but intense effort the gravediggers had uncovered and raised an old but sturdy coffin. Irma expressed surprise that it was essentially intact after approximately eighty-five years. They set it upon a wheeled platform and left the scene to allow the visitors privacy for examination of the coffin's contents.

Joe attempted to release the latches, but found them difficult to operate. Attributing their stubbornness to their age and the ground moisture, Joe reached for the toolbox he had brought. He oiled the latches and then forced them open with vise-grip pliers and a screwdriver. Then he raised the lid and deferred to Irma for inspection of the enclosed remains.

Irma stared downward at several locations without touching anything, making mental notes of what she saw.

With a touch of impatience, Penny said, "Well, come on; give us your expert opinion. Is there anything unusual in that box?"

"I've seen only two unusual things so far. There's a second male corpse on top of the primary female inhabitant, and the person on the bottom is wearing an ornate ring with the largest diamond I have ever seen."

She yielded her position to the others, one-by-one, but admonished them to avoid touching anything yet.

Arthur took his turn to view the coffin contents. "I think we can conclude that there's nothing romantic about the presence of the male body. Some third party bashed in the back and left side of his skull with a shovel or other blunt object."

Irma said, "I'll add that he was a last-minute addition, because his body wasn't embalmed. She's fully desiccated and in much better shape than he is. He's virtually skeletal. I'd have to say that whoever embalmed her did an extremely good job to have her remains currently dried out and discolored but in better condition than many other old corpses I've examined. The burial may have occurred at the beginning of a very cold winter that delayed early decomposition."

Dennis viewed the remains and nodded his head. "The winters are extremely cold in this county. I'll rate that diamond ring as a probable motive for the arsonist. He or she wanted to get into the subbasement to find this grave location information and go after the ring. I don't know what that ring cost in the 1920's, but it has to be worth a fortune now."

Steve said, "If that ring motivated the arsonist, that person would have had to know about the existence of the grave location notation on the scrap of board in the warehouse chamber. That says that the arsonist is probably a descendant of the individual who hid that board scrap."

Penny shook her head. "That's a good possibility, but it's not necessarily true. The arsonist could be descended from someone who was told about the hidden grave location information, or could even have been someone who was unrelated but read about it in an old diary or other document."

"You may be right, but I think this discovery supports my discussions with Jeff Lee about the importance of that list of mob descendants and their locations."

Arthur said, "There's one small problem in relating the contents of this coffin to that list. We don't know the names of either occupant of the coffin or if they were mob figures. We also don't know the name of the third party who killed the male occupant. How can you trace descendants of an unknown person?"

Irma said, "We could work backwards. We could take DNA samples from these corpses. Then, when we arrest someone based on other evidence, we could compare their DNA to these samples to look for a relationship."

Joe had taken his turn to view the bodies and the ring. "That's a good idea, Irma. Take your samples for possible future comparison use. We should take the ring and see whether we can find a jewelry expert who is able to identify the workmanship. Do you think you want to perform an autopsy on these two or have someone else autopsy them? We have to decide whether to tell Lenny and Hank to rebury the coffin."

Irma said, "I'll take samples for DNA screening. I don't think autopsies would add that much more information after all these years. His cause of death is obvious. If two of you would put on gloves and slightly raise the man's remains, I'll be able to take a closer look at her body right now."

Joe and Dennis donned crime scene gloves and raised the man, while Steve moved to take more pictures from a different angle, following the separation of the two bodies. Irma raised the woman's head and inspected it from several angles.

Can you determine how she died, Irma?"

"Steve, take a couple of pictures while I hold her head at this angle. I see two small-caliber bullet holes in the back of her skull. There are no exit wounds that I can see."

Arthur said, "That sounds like an execution-style killing."

Irma said, "That's about all we're going to learn. I hesitate to try an autopsy without a specific reason. It would have limited value. These remains are very fragile. Steve's set of photographs should reveal almost as much after all of the years since their original burial. If we do the DNA sampling to go with the photography, I'll vote for re-latching and burying the coffin so that we minimize the exposure of the corpses to air."

Arthur said, "That's fine with me. These two have already told us a lot."

Penny said, "I must have not been listening; what did they tell you?"

"Her clothing is stylish for the time. She was prepared properly after death per the instructions of someone who cared about her. The male's clothes are those of a professional funeral home worker. He may have helped to bury her before he got greedy and went for that ring. That also says that the third party who killed this man protected the ring and her body, and did not hesitate to take a life."

CHAPTER 49 – *LOUIE*

Milton says that I have to start escorting the bodies from the city and to the cemetery. I didn't sign on for that. I've always worked as an embalmer; that's a technical profession, and it gives me satisfaction when I do a good job and satisfy the family of the deceased. Why did Sammy have to quit? I wouldn't mind so much if I had to ride in the hearse with him, but that Mario is an animal.

This afternoon, Mario and I have to escort a coffin to Binghampton Cemetery. It's a nice enough place, and I do like to view some of the older headstones from before the Civil War, but to have to work at close quarters with Mario – ugh! What makes it worse is that I didn't even get to do the embalming on this one. Sbarbaro's guy, Frederick, did that in Chicago. The coffin arrived sealed. I'll bet he didn't do as good a job as I do. Anyway, I'll pick out some appropriate clothes for escorting patrons to their final resting place. I'm not even sure whether this one is a man or a woman. They don't tell me anything. I'm just a specialist, and now they're taking that title away from me.

Time to go; my new suit shows that I'm a professional. Mario's wearing that old dark thing that's his trademark. It may be his only suit. At least he won't bore me to death with his chatter. He never says much of anything, and if you ask him a question, he just grunts or mumbles. What a bore! I'm driving, so that will give me something to keep my mind occupied along the way. I'll have to remember to avoid speeding; this is a hearse, and I'll have to drive it with proper formality. If I save my money, and Milton decides to retire, I may be able to buy this business from him. I could be a classy undertaker, and I enjoy dealing with the public.

Richard Davidson

Here's Binghampton; if I had a long line of cars behind me, I'd have Mario flag them into appropriate parking spots. That would be nice – ordering him around. Anyway, it's just the hearse today, and the gravediggers have an open hole where we're supposed to stop. Good parking job. Mario's getting out. Time for the hard lifting; I hope this one's not too heavy. Mario's strong; I'll do my best to keep the coffin level. I don't want him to think I'm weak. There ... it's safely on the stand next to the hole. Mario will go off to tell the manager we're ready to lower the coffin and cover it. While he's gone, I'll see how Frederick's embalming compares with mine.

That's different; the coffin has an extra wax seal across the latch. Somebody wanted their loved one protected from evil spirits or some such thing. I'll ease it off the latch and peek inside while Mario's gone. He's too dense to notice the change. There ... it's open. I have to admit that Frederick did a good job; she almost looks as though she's only sleeping. Pretty girl; and look at that ring she's wearing. What a waste to bury that forever. I'll just take a closer look at it ... Oh, my God! Mario's back early, and my reaching for the ring doesn't look innocent.

"Mario, I'm just admiring ..."

CHAPTER 50 – *MARIO AND MILT*

Milt inserted his special ledger into its compartment beneath the floorboards where a second similar volume already resided. Then he focused on his desk calendar and wrote two reminder notes for the next day.

Mario opened the outer door, walked in, and plopped himself down on Milt's side chair. Milt noticed the smile on his face.

"Is something funny? Did you complete the burial?"

"Yes to both of those questions, Boss. I'm smiling because I was right in my thinking."

Milt leaned back in his wooden desk chair. "What were you right about?"

"Remember when I suggested that you might want to look for a new embalmer?"

"Yeah; I remember. Did something happen to Louie?"

"I caught him right after he opened the sealed coffin, as he was reaching to take the ring."

"That ring is nothing but trouble. What did you do with him?"

"I arranged for him to be close to that ring forever. He's buried in that coffin along with the dame."

Milt's face had an expression of uncertainty. "Was he alive or dead when you buried him?"

"As dead as two blows with a gravedigger's shovel to the side and back of his head could make him; I'm beginning to think we can't trust anyone."

Milt stood up. "Did the gravediggers witness your hitting him and stowing his body in the coffin?"

"Nope; they were taking their time coming from the office to the gravesite. By the time they arrived, I had the box buttoned up, and I'd cleaned off the shovel by using it to move a pile of dirt from one spot to another."

"That's good work, Mario, but I think it's time for us to be careful for a while. Did they give you a receipt with the grave location on it?"

"Here it is: Binghampton 13NW 4SW. What do you mean by being careful?"

"We'll close the underground warehouse, except for special visits by you and me privately, so that future employees including the next embalmer don't get nosy and find the bodies in there. We'll be legitimate businessmen who don't make a lot of suspicious trips to Chicago. I made a connection with some suppliers in Canada, and they can ship our booze to Amboy by train in padded coffins, set up so that the bottles don't clink during shipment. All we'll have to do is claim the boxes at the freight depot and bring them here in the hearse. I'll hire a couple of guys to help you, and we'll store the coffins sealed until we need what's inside. Does that sound reasonable to you?"

"Anything that reduces our risk sounds reasonable to me. How will we deal with Capone and the Chicago people? Will they get suspicious?

"We just did them a big favor by making that dame's body disappear. They'll be fine with us for a while. If we have to adjust things later, we'll do it. We've always been small potatoes to them. I think they'll just forget about us. Anyway, Prohibition won't last forever. I hear rumors that some people in Congress are working toward ending it. We need to push the undertaking as a business that will last longer than Prohibition. We may even want to buy into something else."

"I like the sound of that 'we' you keep using. Am I a partner now?"

"That you are, Mario. Start calling me Milt instead of Boss."

CHAPTER 51 – TRINA'S LIST

Secret Service Agent Jeff Lee had joined Steve DuBois and Joe Gonzalez for a visit to Arthur Blake's new home near Amboy. The purpose of their meeting was to analyze the list of current names and locations of Prohibition mobster descendants and to determine how to turn it into a useful resource. They had the house to themselves. Irma and Penny had driven to Chicago to meet with jewelry specialists regarding the ring worn by the woman in the coffin. Midge Drinkwater had gone to visit one of her grandchildren, accompanied by her hired caregiver.

The three guests arrived in Joe's personal red Jeep from his house in Parkville. Arthur greeted them at the door.

"Welcome all; come on in. Good to meet you, Jeff; Steve has relayed many of your shrewd insights for us to digest. Today, we'll get to exchange views in real time. I've set us up at the kitchen table, so that the drinks and snacks will be handy. The women are gone, so snacking and drinking will be a do-it-yourself affair."

Jeff shook Arthur's hand. "I've been looking forward to meeting you too. I've never worked with a pastor on a case before. I hear you're pretty good at these things."

"Let's just say I'm a facilitator. We all contribute key steps toward solutions, based on our experiences and backgrounds. Anyway, come on into the kitchen and grab a drink plus something to nibble. Don't report me to the women for not having a fancy spread of goodies."

They headed for the kitchen, Steve ushering Jeff aside for a quick tour, while Arthur and Joe brought out a few bottles and snacks. Once Steve and Jeff returned from their tour, the four of them settled into chairs around the big old table. Jeff distributed copies of the list that Marie Chance had published in her book.

Jeff opened the discussion. "We have one of the few remaining copies of Marie's book. It would never have been a best-seller, even in academic circles, and Steve has told you about the successful effort by mob-affiliated people to have the book removed from sales outlets. Even if it had been widely circulated, readers would have had difficulty discovering the list and its significance. Marie encoded it, so to speak, as an article that appeared in a non-existent Canadian newspaper."

Arthur nodded in affirmation. "That's a very good point, Jeff. She wanted the list to be out there, but not obvious. Why would she have done that?"

"Steve and I have discussed that point, and we've agreed that Marie's main motive was to threaten Trina Jergens Danten with publicizing the list if she didn't grant Rob a divorce. It would only have been a threat to Trina if she had been the person who compiled it, drawing upon her associations with other mob descendants."

Joe said, "If Trina had been cooperative, Marie would have let the list remain obscure and hidden. Why would she do that, Jeff?"

"She had no quarrel with the people on the list and expected that many of them would be completely innocent of their parents' and grandparents' sins. Frankly, I agree with that viewpoint. Some of the descendants may not even know about their ancestors' crimes and criminal connections."

Arthur doodled a family tree diagram as he spoke. "That list is a danger to mob offspring and successive generations of descendants. Some of the gangsters' sons changed their names and moved away. Johnny Torrio's only son George, born in Washington, Iowa, became George Miller. Even Alphonse Capone's son Albert changed his name. The female descendants change their names with each marriage, so their unsavory family connections would gradually become less obvious. I can understand how that list's existence would bother many people because it would be the key that unlocks the name-change puzzle."

Steve had listened to Arthur while going to the refrigerator for a can of soda. He put the can on the table but remained standing. "I don't want to hurt people who had mob ancestors any more than you do, but somebody isn't innocent. Somebody killed Marie Chance and tried to frame Rob Danten for her murder and his own suicide. That same person or some other mob offspring probably killed Saul Sanders from the Secret Service. How do we find those killers? I say we should go after them, and not worry about revealing identities of innocent people." Steve sat down and opened his drink.

Arthur responded, "Our killers may or may not be on that list, but they have a connection to it. We know that Ken Cantini, our sticky-fingered treasurer from the Amboy Church passed himself off as a lawyer to squelch distribution of Marie's book, and then he disappeared on a trip to Italy. We also think that people in Las Vegas hired Ken for the book-suppression job. Are we getting close to finding Ken or his Las Vegas contacts?"

Joe gestured to Steve and Jeff that he wanted to handle Arthur's question. "About two hours ago, I spoke with several people in cooperating agencies. Italian authorities have found Ken Cantini's body in a poor section of Rome. Somebody shot him in an alley, but he managed to crawl into a building and scrawl a name in a pocket notebook before he died from loss of blood. That name was Miller."

Steve and Jeff exchanged glances. Then Jeff said, "There were two Miller families on Trina's list. One was descended from Torrio's son, George Miller, and the other originated with George "Bugs" Moran, who was one of the three guys who tried to kill Torrio. Moran's relatives included the grandfather of Amboy UMC's ex-seminarian, Mandy Miller. The two Miller families are not related."

Arthur looked disturbed. "I'm surprised that the list included Mandy Miller's name. That suggests that she had wanted her seminarian assignment to be at Amboy UMC. I'm sure that the United Methodist Church doesn't allow seminarians to select the church where they will serve."

Jeff asked, "What if she got someone in authority to recommend a particular assignment?"

"I suppose that's possible, but who would have spoken up for Mandy?"

"Her mother's name is also on the list, Professor Martha Miller. She teaches New Testament Theology at Garrett-Evangelical Theological Seminary in Evanston, Illinois."

Arthur slapped the side of his head. "Ouch! I should have connected those two names. I took two of her courses at Garrett. Martha knows her stuff, and she's good at teaching it. Being part of a mobster's family doesn't exclude you from success in legitimate fields."

Steve asked, "Joe, did you learn anything new about Cantini's contacts in Las Vegas?"

"I didn't get anything definite about the people who hired Cantini, but several witnesses said they saw him with Jake Smathers, who is a mob attorney from Chicago. It's not much to go on, but it's something."

Steve said, "Maybe Jake coached Ken on how an attorney would act in dealing with a publisher. Even if that was the case, there's no crime involved. My adopted son, Eric, asks me all the time about how a G-man would act in different situations."

Joe smiled. "He really wants to go into the family business after he gets out of college."

"Fortunately, he has about eight more years before he has to decide whether he has a fantasy or a career choice there."

Implications

Arthur walked over to get another mug of coffee from the pot. "Joe's news suggests that we should check on the whereabouts of Mandy Miller. She's the only Miller who has a connection to both the burned-out church and Ken Cantini. They were together in that church at the same time. If she is or was recently in Italy, we need to talk with her."

Jeff said, "We'll check on her travels. She's the first concrete result from studying Trina's list. There may be more."

Richard Davidson

CHAPTER 52 – THE RING

After shopping in Chicago's North Michigan Avenue *Magnificent Mile* district as what they had jokingly called a warm-up exercise, Penny and Irma entered the understated jewelry store. This was the first time either one of them had visited Tiffany's; they found themselves suitably impressed by the store's décor and reputation. A well-dressed middle-aged man approached them.

"May I assist you, Ladies? My name is Selwyn Carpenter, and I'm the Assistant Manager here at Tiffany's. Is there something specific you're seeking today?"

They had already agreed that Penny would act as their spokesperson in this encounter. "We're pleased to meet you Mr. Carpenter. I'm Penny Gonzalez, and my associate is Irma Blake. We would like to discuss a piece of jewelry we already have in our possession, but we'd prefer to do so in a private area if you have one available."

"We do have a conference room for discussing custom and special items, but I would need to clarify the nature of your business before proceeding there. Tiffany does not purchase jewelry or loan money against it."

"That's not our objective. We have a special older item that is historically significant, and we would like to determine whether Tiffany or C. D. Peacock, the two foremost jewelers in Chicago at the time, created it. May we proceed to your private room?"

"Certainly, Ladies; you've not only assured me of the serious nature of your visit, but you've also piqued my interest. Please wait just one moment while I ask the staff to hold any calls for me."

He approached a desk bearing the sign *Appraisals*, and whispered something to the woman seated behind it.

She nodded and flashed a quick piercing look at Penny and Irma. Her posture straightened, suggesting that she thought something important was about to happen.

Mr. Carpenter returned and guided them behind a red velvet drape and down a narrow hallway to a door marked *Private*. Once through the door, they found themselves in a small but ornate conference room furnished with an antique mahogany conference table and matching cabinets displaying jewelry and chinaware.

"May I get you some coffee or tea before we begin?"

Penny said, "Thank you, Mr. Carpenter, but we stopped and enjoyed refreshments during a bit of shopping before we arrived. Irma, don't let me decline for both of us if you do want something."

"No, Penny, I'm in complete agreement. I'm refreshed and anxious to learn more about period jewelry."

Selwyn Carpenter opened a base cabinet beneath a glassed-in display, and withdrew a sturdy but old ledger book.

"By way of setting the stage, let me tell you that Tiffany gives a lifetime warranty with each piece of jewelry it creates and sells. Because of our pride in our work, we have records dating back many decades describing each piece and identifying the purchaser. We document items that are more recent in computer files as well as these books. We do have a project to computerize the older company sales records, but it is far from complete. With that as a preamble, would you please show me your item? I'm fairly confident that I'll be able to tell you whether it is a Tiffany design."

Irma retrieved a black velvet bag from her purse and withdrew a box from within it. That box had originally housed one of her bracelets, but she had needed a suitable container that was larger than her ring boxes. "Here you are, Mr. Carpenter."

He removed a jeweler's loupe magnifier from his pocket and studied the ring from all angles. Then he took a pad of paper from his inside jacket pocket and wrote a few notes on it.

"This is indeed a special piece. I can confirm that it is a Tiffany design. The central diamond is virtually perfect and quite large. It is the oldest ring I have seen that uses our six-point solitaire mounting. The smaller diamonds and other gems surround the central stone in the manner of bunches of grapes dangling from a fruit bowl. It is more ornate than modern designs, but it is definitely historically significant. This ring would have a very high value at auction today."

Irma said, "Do you think you will be able to identify the purchaser from your ledgers?"

"The ring is unique. It must have been custom made for a very wealthy individual. I suggest that you allow me to send for a tray of coffee and pastry. I will work on the search personally, along with our longest-serving jeweler, but it may take some time. Be assured that your ring will be safe in our hands, and now that we are working together on this project, please call me Selwyn." As he finished speaking, he returned the sample ledger book to the cabinet and withdrew a different volume.

Penny fished her credentials out of her purse. "That's fine, Selwyn. I'll be more open with you also, because it may assist your research. I represent a federal investigative agency. I won't be specific on how we obtained this ring, because I don't want to influence your search results, but I suggest you look at the period between 1920 and 1933."

Selwyn placed the ledger volume he had removed from the cabinet onto the table. The label on the cover read 1924 to 1928. "It does look like a Prohibition Era piece, and some Chicagoans of that period had plenty of money for jewelry."

He took the ring and the ledger and left the room. A few minutes later, a woman returned with a cart bearing a silver tray full of pastry and fruit and a silver coffee urn. After she left, they dove into the goodies with gusto.

Irma said, "This may not be the movie's version of *Breakfast at Tiffany's*, but it's pretty darned close to it. I'm going to take a few pictures with my phone camera to make the guys jealous."

"I'm betting Selwyn won't take very long to come up with something. He had the period pegged before I gave him the hint."

Ten minutes later, the door opened, and Selwyn entered, carrying the same ledger volume and the ring.

"First, I have to apologize to you, because I'm about to reveal a lapse in Tiffany's tradition of confidentiality with our clients. This ring was custom-made from an artist's sketch and sold on April 6, 1927. Because of our generous warranties, we always record purchaser information. That is, we always did except for the sale of this particular ring. Apparently, the customer was quite firm in stating that he didn't want it recorded, and that he would relieve us of our warranty obligation. However, contrary to our company policy of confidential dealings with our clients, some minor employee later wrote in the initials *A.C.*"

Penny said, "Alphonse Capone."

"I didn't say that, but you're free to reach your own conclusions. In any case, it's a spectacular ring. Tiffany's will not have any comment about the original customer if and when you choose to sell this piece."

Penny said, "Thank you very much, Selwyn; this ring is involved in an investigation, and won't be sold for quite a while, but this has been an enlightening visit in several respects. I'm sure Irma will join me in saying that if we can ever get our husbands to be enthusiastic about buying us jewelry, we'll be back to see you again."

"And please remember that Tiffany's has a federal history as well, designing such important items as the Medal of Honor and redesigning the Great Seal of the United States, as seen on the one-dollar bill."

CHAPTER 53 – THEORIES

This time, the Blakes' kitchen table had a decidedly different appearance. Irma had draped it with a fine white linen tablecloth and crowned it with a silver tray full of pastries and fruit plus a silver coffee pot. In the center of the table a framed picture displayed the similar arrangement Irma had photographed at Tiffany's. Irma had set four places for Joe, Penny, Arthur, and herself.

Arthur and Joe entered the kitchen and stood still, taking in the formality of the scene.

Joe said, "This place looks a lot different than it did for our all-guy meeting this morning. It looks as though your visit to Tiffany's changed your lifestyle, Irma."

"It's just a fun thing for today, Joe. The photograph shows how they treated us, using their extremely expensive serving pieces. I thought I'd emulate them a bit. Are you impressed, Arthur?"

"I'm impressed by the silver service, the goodies, and the tablecloth, but that fancy coffeepot can't possibly contain enough coffee for all of us."

"I realized that you're insatiable when it comes to coffee, so I prepare the regular coffee urn and left it in the pantry. You can bring it out and set it on the counter for your supply. The silver pot will probably be enough for the rest of us."

Arthur left to get the coffee urn, and Penny entered from the front room, where she had been talking on the telephone.

"I just spoke with Selwyn ..."

Joe interrupted her. "Who's Selwyn?"

"Selwyn is the helpful gentleman we met at Tiffany's."

"So you're on a first name basis with a man who gives out jewelry. Should I be jealous or worried?"

"He doesn't give it away; he sells it for a lot more money than we have. Stop being silly, and let me tell you about the useful information he gave me."

"Fair enough; I'm concentrating on Selwyn."

Arthur returned from the pantry carrying the heavy coffee urn. He placed it on the counter and plugged it into the wall socket to keep it warm, "Who is Selwyn?"

Penny said, "Enough! Everyone sit down, and we'll get this meeting started ... Selwyn is the Assistant Manager at Tiffany's, and he was very helpful. We showed him the ring, and he confirmed that it is a Tiffany design. Selwyn indicated that it would command a very high price at auction today. He said that someone who did not want his name recorded in the Tiffany records purchased that ring on April 6, 1927. A staff member, who abhorred the blank space in the ledger, penciled in the initials A.C. some years later."

Arthur said, "Presumably Al Capone ..."

"I just asked Selwyn to clarify something for me. In answer to my questions, he said that the individual referred to as A.C. had made other purchases of jewelry from time to time, and in all of those cases he had willingly let them record his name in their record books."

Joe asked, "Why don't you just say Al Capone?"

"Tiffany stresses confidentiality for their clients. I had to refer to the purchaser of this ring by the initials written in their ledger. Selwyn left things to our interpretation; he would not confirm the name that went with the initials."

"But it was obviously Al Capone."

"Yes, Joe, that's a very reasonable assumption."

Irma said, "I follow your line of thinking, Penny. Even though Al was a flashy dresser and was known to have had several mistresses, he treated this one as special, and he didn't want to take any chances that his wife would find out about the ring."

"That's it. This was a unique relationship.

167

Joe said, "At the gravesite, Irma said that this woman died from two small bullets to the back of her skull. The small caliber of the bullets could suggest the use of a concealable weapon typically carried by a woman."

Irma laughed. "You're conjuring up the image of a love triangle, Joe, but I doubt that we could build a strong case against any specific person after all these years. All the parties involved would be long gone by now."

"If you don't want to work in that period, I'll come back to the present, and I'll conclude that the person who burned down the Amboy Church was after the grave location information that led us to this ring. Do you agree, Arthur?"

"I'll at least give that a high probability. However, I have to ask who would have hidden that information in the subbasement warehouse, and who would have known about it? I assume that anyone connected with the woman, or her family, or the person who killed her, would have turned to the undertaker's records for the grave location information. Milton Jergens, as the undertaker, should have had it. Only an assistant or a hearse driver, someone who couldn't access Milton's records, would have made a separate record of the gravesite information and hidden it."

Penny said, "That's an important point. If Trina Jergens Danten had known about this burial and had been after the ring, she would have learned about it from her grandfather, and he would have told her the location of his records so that she could find the grave. She would not have needed to burn the church to find that information, so she is not the arsonist."

Joe nodded his head in agreement. "We need to find out who else went to the burial and then identify the descendants of that person – right, Arthur?

"That's the right direction of thinking, but it might be oversimplifying things. The person who hid the grave location or his descendant could have told someone else.

In that case, identifying the arsonist would become much more difficult."

Irma got up and placed her hand on Penny's shoulder. "Hold up a minute. We affirmed Penny's logic in eliminating Trina as an arson suspect, but we glossed over something important that Penny said. Trina may know the location of her Grandfather Milton's records, or at least have an idea where to find them. Those records would be our only chance to identify his helpers by name. If we don't know their names, we can't find their offspring."

Arthur said, "Irma's right. Our next step should be to question Trina about Milton Jergens' business records, but we'll have to be very focused and gentle about it. If we mention Trina's list of mob descendants or ask questions about the death of her husband and his girlfriend, Trina won't want to cooperate with us. She may hold the key to the arson mystery; we need her assistance."

CHAPTER 54 – MANDY

Mandy Miller had exited her plane at Yeager Airport in Charleston, West Virginia, and had started walking toward the baggage claim area when she heard the page. "Rome Passenger Mandy Miller, please report to the American Airlines Ticket Counter."

She made her way to that counter, thinking she must have left something behind on the plane. She approached a handsome, knowledgeable-looking agent and identified herself. He responded with a smile and indicated that an additional customs procedure would be required. After apologizing for any inconvenience, he escorted her into a windowless office, where a man and a woman sat at a table, viewing a computer screen. The agent nodded to them and left the room.

The woman rose and addressed her, "Ms. Miller, thank you for responding to the page so promptly. My name is Penny Gonzalez; this gentleman is Steve DuBois; and we're federal agents. We have to ask you a few questions about your activities in Rome before we can release you to leave the airport."

"I assure you, I'm not carrying anything illegal. You may search my bags and purse."

"We will do that, but we're more interested in your contacts while in Rome."

"I don't pal around with terrorists, if that's what you mean."

"We're more interested in your contacts with Americans there. First, please tell us the purpose of your trip."

Steve gave no indication of his making a video recording of Mandy's reactions to the questions and conversation.

Mandy relaxed slightly. "I travelled to Rome for vacation and to see Christian art in museums. I'm pastor of a small independent church here in Charleston."

Penny did her best to look and sound casual. "Did you meet with an American named Jerry Tackman while you were there?"

Mandy paled and touched the table for balance. "Of course I didn't meet with Jerry. He's dead." She wondered whether she should have said that, but she couldn't unsay it.

"Someone in Rome during the time of your visit has been using that name."

"It can't be the same person. I read in an obituary that Jerry died three years ago."

"You must be confused; there was no obituary for Jerry Tackman, formerly of Amboy, Illinois. He simply left that town and moved elsewhere. We have records of Jerry Tackman registering in a hotel in Rome. That happened three weeks before you flew from Charleston to Rome."

"It must have been someone pretending to be Jerry. It couldn't have been him."

"Did this *pretender* contact you, either before your trip or while you were in Rome?"

Mandy hesitated before responding, and Steve recorded uncertainty in her expression. "All right, someone claiming to be Jerry Tackman did leave a telephone message at my hotel, but I didn't return that person's call because I knew it had to be some kind of scam. Like I said, Jerry's dead."

"Tell me again how you know he's dead. How and where did he die?"

"I thought I had seen an obituary, but if there wasn't one, as you say, I must have heard it from some mutual friend. My recollection is that he died of some illness."

"And where was he living when he suffered this illness?"

171

"I'm not sure. It may have been Pennsylvania or Michigan. We knew each other in Amboy, Illinois, and then Jerry left town. I didn't follow his travels."

Penny jumped on her response. "You didn't follow his travels because you knew that he never left Amboy. We obtained a warrant and searched your house while you were in Rome. We found an old whiskey crate that matches those in a hidden chamber below your old church. You sold the bottles, but kept one of the old wooden crates. That was a big mistake, and it will cost you a long jail sentence."

Mandy sat down hard, and the remaining color drained from her face. Her dark hair appeared to lose its curl as sweat appeared on her forehead. Steve pivoted the camera to keep her image centered on the screen. Her body went limp, and she wiped her sweaty palms on her slacks. Then her face brightened, and she said, "My grandfather gave me that whisky case as a souvenir of his bootlegging days."

Penny made a *thumb down* gesture. "Good try, Mandy, but if you had checked the wooden case carefully, you would have seen the ink notation on it: 'rcvd. Amboy, SV'. After finding that crate, we contacted Ginger Tackman and discovered that she hasn't touched a thing of Jerry's since his disappearance. We were able to get samples of his DNA from his clothing and from hairs on his hairbrush. This allowed us to prove that the most recent body in that subbasement is that of Jerry Tackman. I'm sure you already know about the two older corpses there."

After several minutes of internal debate while the others waited silently, she nodded an affirmation.

"Jerry got greedy and wanted me to delay the re-carpeting of the main basement until we had cleared all the whiskey cases and beer barrels out of the lower room. I told him we had to play it cool and just take what we could sell within a reasonable time. We argued, and then he hit me twice in the face with the back of his hand. His attack scared me; I was sure he would keep hitting me if I didn't do something to stop him. I hit him with a crowbar that was next to one of the whiskey cases, but he took it away from me and chased me. Then I saw an old gun on a shelf down there. I grabbed it and shot him."

"I have two questions about that event. Weren't you disturbed at the sight of two dead people already occupying that chamber? Also, how did you learn about the entrance to that room to begin with?"

"The dead folks didn't bother me. My grandfather had worked for an undertaker in Chicago, and he once took me to a local funeral home to show me how they prepare bodies for burial. He also told me how, during Prohibition days, his boss would have him load cases of whiskey into coffins for transfer to Sammy Venta, the right-hand man for a bootlegging undertaker who used the Amboy church as a distribution center. Those initials you spotted on that crate were Sammy's. He told Grandpa about the hidden warehouse. I knew the entrance to the lower chamber had to be there, but I didn't know where to look. I used my position as seminarian to argue for re-carpeting the basement so that I would be able to study the flooring after they removed the old floor covering. Once I found the entrance, Jerry and I removed cases of whiskey while the floors were bare."

Penny nodded. "... which gets us back to Jerry's demand that you get them to delay the re-carpeting until you'd removed all the booze from the warehouse."

"Yes."

"And you rearranged the bodies around the table?"

"I couldn't resist that touch of humor."

Penny nodded once more and placed her hand on Mandy's shoulder. "Now that we've cleared up the matter of Jerry's body in the church subbasement, tell us how you reacted to that message from someone calling himself Jerry in Rome."

"I knew it had to be either a police trick or an attempt by Ken Cantini to get even with me. I doubted that Italian police would actively work on a minor murder case from Illinois, so I figured Ken had to be behind the attempt to scare me. He and Jerry Tackman had been close friends, and Ken never believed the cover story gossip that Jerry had left town to get away from both his wife Ginger and me."

"So you arranged to meet Ken."

"I suggested we meet as tourists in a shabby but historic section of Rome. I wanted to be able to melt into a crowd of tourists after I'd eliminated him."

"He was found shot to death. Where did you get the gun?"

"That wasn't hard. I'd noticed that the security guards at tourist hotels were careless with their weapons. I went to a different hotel and stole a guard's pistol while he was sneaking a nap. I figured he wouldn't report the theft because it would make him look bad for having slept on the job."

"Did you shoot Ken as soon as you saw him?"

"Of course not; do I look that crude? I told him his ruse of using Jerry's name to get my attention had been clever, and I suggested that we should forget past quarrels and start over as friends. I seduced him into that alley for some foreplay, and then I shot him. That's when I learned that Agatha Christie had been correct in her books."

"What do you mean?"

"She said that after you've killed the first time, additional killings get easier."

CHAPTER 55 – TRINA

Arthur had arranged for Pastor Lorna Dyner to introduce him to Trina Jergens in order to dissuade Trina from seeing anything related to law enforcement in his inquiries. They visited Trina at her single-story house near Amboy's business district. Lorna presented Arthur as the Bishop's representative who was interested in documenting the history of Amboy UMC for input to the debate over the merits of the Conference rebuilding the church. After making the initial introductions, Lorna left to prepare her sermon and to arrange for an ice cream social at a restaurant near the Railway Depot Museum.

Following Lorna's departure, Trina suggested to Arthur that they talk outside on her patio, where she had set out some homemade chocolate chip cookies and some lemonade. Arthur noted that Trina's initial comments and bearing did not agree with the descriptions he had previously received that had painted her as a cranky, irritable shrew. Her pleasant smile, round-lens wire-rimmed glasses, and short gray hair reminded him of his favorite eighth-grade teacher, Miss Newsome.

Once they had seated themselves on the patio, Arthur thanked Trina for making time for their visit. Then he said, "I'm very intrigued by the arrangement your grandfather had with the early church leaders to construct the Amboy Church building in exchange for using its basement as a funeral parlor for wakes. Can you tell me more about it? How did he explain it to you?"

Trina looked proud to discuss her grandfather's generosity. "Grandpa Milt was one of the dozen or so people who gathered to organize a Methodist Church for Amboy. They met in a restaurant near the railway depot. They had ambitious goals, but very little money, so

Grandpa suggested that they build a combination church and funeral home. If they handled it that way, he would be able to pick up most of the cost. Contrary to some of the legends of our church, he didn't pay for everything. He simply suggested that it would make good sense to build the dual-purpose church because memorial services would be held there anyway, and the basement could be used for church purposes when it wasn't needed for wakes."

"Nowadays, we would consider it creative thinking to combine projects for increased economy." Arthur could see that his compliment had pleased Trina. Then he asked, "Was Milton an undertaker or funeral home director for his entire career?"

"Actually, he later left that business and gave the church full control over the basement level that had been used for wakes. He went into the garbage removal business, which he described as an end-of-life service for things instead of people. He did very well at that, and his company ended up with contracts for quite a few villages and cities in this area."

Arthur finished writing in his notebook. "Do you remember when he switched from the funeral business to the disposal business?"

"That would have happened during the early 1930's, shortly before my father was born. The depression was in full swing, and he was able to hire many out-of-work men to help with trash pickups. Because of the depression, he had a dedicated crew that sorted the trash for items that he could sell for re-use. He was a recycler before they invented that term."

Arthur said, "You're obviously proud of your grandfather. Did he by any chance leave any records of his activities while he was in the funeral business at the church? I'd be very interested in them, because they would also document the passing of some of the earliest church members."

Trina hesitated noticeably. "I do have two old ledger books from his undertaking business. I don't advertise that they exist. He kept them under the floorboards of his office during the old days. They're in the basement. When my husband, Rob, was alive, he would look at them occasionally. I found them boring. You're welcome to borrow them, Pastor Blake, but you'll have to consider them confidential, and I don't want to part with them for very long. They're my only physical link to Grandpa Milt."

Arthur said, "I appreciate your willingness to let me study them. I promise that I won't make public anything that you might consider offensive, and I'll bring them back promptly."

Trina left and returned shortly with the books. She handed them to Arthur and said, "I mentioned Rob in connection with these ledgers. I rarely say his name any more. You have a reputation as a talented investigator. The police accused Rob of murdering his mistress, and then he died in a car accident, which they interpreted as a guilt-driven suicide. That was a terrible period in my life. If there's anything you could do to review the circumstances of her murder, and possibly clear Rob's name, I would greatly appreciate it. My husband was a gentle soul. I can't believe he was a murderer."

Arthur promised to look into Rob's alleged crime. As he left, he wondered about the contrast between the apparently docile Trina he had met, and her reputation as a bitter shrew. Which was correct?

CHAPTER 56 – ANALYSIS

Penny Gonzalez and Steve DuBois had not yet returned from West Virginia and their interception of Mandy Miller. They had arrested her for murders in Amboy, Illinois and Rome, and they were now meeting with state and federal attorneys to determine how to best proceed against her in the courts.

With Penny out of town, Joe Gonzalez had scheduled a meeting at their home in Parkville to discuss Milton Jergens' old ledgers with Arthur and Irma Blake plus Jeff Lee. They gathered around the dining room table, covered, per Penny's instructions, with the special foam-backed tablecloth they used for meetings. Joe had copied a few relevant pages from the ledgers and made sets for each of them. His preparations had also included placing the copier on a side table in case they needed it during the discussions.

As they prepared to start the meeting, Joe said, "I have coffee, but for snacks you'll have to settle for stale cookies. The baker is out of town."

Arthur smiled at Irma, and she reached into a cloth shopping bag near her feet. "We anticipated this situation. Here are a dozen doughnuts we bought on the way over here. Correction, there are only ten; we got hungry in the car."

Joe said, "That should be plenty for this meeting. Let's try to keep our doughnut-sticky fingers off the antique ledger pages. Thanks are due to Arthur for obtaining these books for us."

"I have them for a limited period, so let's get right to work. I was surprised to receive two books from Trina. I don't know whether they cover two different periods, or if one is for legitimate deals while the other is for criminal transactions. I delivered them here yesterday. What have you learned since then, Joe?"

"They're actually opposite sides of the same coin. I copied a few pages for each of you to illustrate the principle. One book records the accounting for each transaction, while the other records the names of the people assigned to the job and the details of their tasks. In the copied example, you see from Book #1 that Milt Jergens bought eight cases of whiskey for $15.00 each and transported them from Chicago to Amboy. From the corresponding pages in Book #2, we learn that Milt's people obtained the shipment at John Sbarboro's funeral home, where Gus Miller released it. He must be Mandy Miller's grandfather. The book shows that Sammy Venta and Mario Bitoli were the hearse drivers on that job and that Sammy supervised the loading of the booze into the warehouse."

Irma said, "Jergens certainly kept detailed records. Do those names show up on Trina's list, Jeff?"

"There are no people named Venta on the list; Either Sammy had no children or he had girls who changed their names after marriage. I assume that Trina would have known of him, as her grandfather's principal assistant. There are a couple of people named Bitoli. We'll see whether they get to be of interest as we continue the investigation."

Arthur said, "Jeff, I see that you're protecting the innocent by not discussing individual descendants until or unless we have a reason to focus on them. I think that's a good way to proceed. Some of these folks are well-established people who deserve their privacy. Mandy Miller's professor mother is a good example. Does anyone disagree with Jeff's cautious approach?"

Joe said, "Not hearing any objections, I'll proceed further into mentioning the names that show up in the ledger that deals with people. I notice that Sammy Venta's name shows up on many transactions at the beginning of the book, but that it disappears later. Mario Bitoli shows up rarely at the beginning but is quite frequent toward the end."

Irma said, "I have two questions for you, Joe. Did Mario's name appear more frequently at the same time that Sammy's name stopped appearing, and if so, what was that approximate date?"

Joe spent a few minutes examining the ledger entries. "The first answer is yes; It looks as though Sammy left, and then Mario took over some of his duties. I'd judge the transition date to be around March of 1928."

"That date fits with a possible date for the burial of the Lady of the Ring. Penny and I learned that the purchase date for the ring was April of 1927. The undertaker's staff shakeup was slightly less than one year after the ring purchase."

Arthur had sat making notes. He gestured with his hand for attention. "Joe, did you find a notation of the woman's grave location at Binghampton in the ledgers?"

"I'm glad you raised that question. There must have been something special about the burial of that woman. It doesn't have a detailed record similar to most of the other burials. I think Milt wanted to hide or disguise the event. In between two normal burials during March of 1928, I simply found a marginal notation of a gravesite location. I did a double-take when I saw it, because it doesn't match the actual location we found written on that piece of wood in the warehouse."

Irma asked, "What do you mean, Joe? How was it different?"

"The true location was Binghampton 13NW4SW. The marginal note in Milt's ledger is Binghampton 15NW2SW. I think Milt wanted to keep anyone from finding that woman's burial location. The only cryptic reference in his ledger increases one location coordinate number by two and decreases the other number by two."

Implications

Irma said, "Then it must have been Milt Jergens who hid the piece of wood with the correct grave location. He would have been the only one who would have known the ledger information was incorrect."

Arthur nodded his head. That's a reasonable conclusion, although it could have been hidden by someone who took part in the burial ... Joe, was there anyone else in Milt Jergen's organization whose name disappears from the records near the time of Sammy's leaving?"

Joe studied the pages for that period. "There was an embalmer named Louie – no last name given – who performed a bunch of body preparation jobs and just one interment. Then his name disappears from the book. This change came shortly after Sammy's name disappears, within a week, in fact."

"I suspect that the Louie may be the coffin-mate of the ring lady. Jergens would have been shorthanded after Sammy left, so he drafted his embalmer to fill in on the burial. Louie may have tried to steal the ring and paid for that action with his life. This group wasn't a bunch of choirboys. They hid behind a legitimate business façade, but they were mobsters."

Joe said, "That would set the date of the woman's burial as March, 1928."

Arthur consulted the notes he had made. "The timeline you've created intrigues me. Your interval of eleven months between the dates of the ring purchase and the burial, makes me wonder whether this woman had recently given birth."

"Why would that be important?"

"Burning the church to find the location of that ring would be a strong motive, but if it was your grandmother's ring, the motive would be even stronger."

181

CHAPTER 57 – MORE FROM TRINA

At two o'clock, in keeping with the schedule they had arranged by telephone, Arthur arrived at Trina Jergens Danten's house to return her grandfather's ledgers. Trina had prepared a tray of crackers and cheese slices, both to show her hospitality and to keep Pastor Blake from leaving too quickly. This unusual pastor had impressed her, and she hoped to engage him in a lengthy chat. This time she wouldn't have to guard her words. The pleasantness of her earlier discussions with Pastor Blake encouraged her to feel relaxed with him. Young Pastor Dyner was a bit too flippant and judgmental for Trina to feel the same way about having personal discussions with her.

They sat across a round coffee table from each other in her family room, encapsulated in air-conditioned comfort while viewing her neat back yard via a picture window.

Trina pushed the cheese and cracker tray toward Arthur. "Help yourself. I've become a fan of cheeses, so you have a wide variety to choose from."

"Thanks, Trina; your family appears to enjoy the details of life. You sample many types of cheeses, and your grandfather kept meticulous records of his work."

Trina relaxed against her seat back, feeling that she could share a good conversation with this man who represented the church, but was so down-to-earth in his outlook. "Thank you, Pastor. May I call you Arthur?"

"By all means, please do. Titles are for formal paperwork. I really don't care for labels; they oversimplify relationships. There's so much more to any person than his or her label."

"I so agree with you Arthur. When my late husband Rob had an affair with another faculty member at

Northern Illinois University, and people around here found out about it, I became *the cheated party* and received abundant sympathy. Then, after she died under suspicious circumstances, and people suspected him of killing her, I became *the murderer's wife*. The police never arrested him because there was no evidence linking him to the crime, but fellow church members and many people we had considered friends, shunned us and kept up a barrage of malicious gossip. Because of that, and because Rob needed to be taught a lesson about penalties for infidelity, I asked him to leave and take an apartment until they solved her murder. At that point, people began to call me *the self-righteous and vindictive bitch*. Later, I allowed him to move back here with me. He died in a car accident not long afterward."

"I've heard the story in general terms. Please refresh my memory as to how Rob's mistress died."

"The police said that Marie, his girlfriend, died from strangulation. That's a terrible way to go. I don't know why they thought Rob did it."

"Then you don't believe their theory that he killed her."

"Not for one minute, Arthur; Rob was a bastard for cheating on me, but he wasn't a violent man in any way. He was a kid in a candy shop who couldn't resist temptation."

"Did Rob ask for a divorce? Did his affair get that far?"

Trina hesitated and tightly gripped her left hand with her right. "He did request that I give him a divorce so that he could marry Marie, but I believe that she goaded him into it. He was the kind of guy who would have preferred to remain married to me, but look for occasional sex on the side. If he had left our marriage in order to marry her, that marriage would have failed also."

"Would you have been generous enough to remain married to Rob, but let him continue to have his outside flings?"

Trina examined her thoughts before speaking. "I probably would have granted him a few misbehaviors so long as they were not so serious as the relationship he had with Marie. I wouldn't call that attitude being generous, but more like being practical and giving up something small to save the larger relationship. I would have had to admit to myself that I couldn't provide him with the passion he occasionally needed."

Arthur realized that the subject of tolerated infidelity was stressful to Trina, so he moved away from that topic. "When Rob died in that one-car accident during the investigation, did you agree with the police that it had probably been a suicide due to his guilt feelings?"

"It was foggy that night, and I believe that it was a simple accident. He either strayed out of his lane due to the fog, or dodged another vehicle that he didn't see until the last instant. Either way, he went off the road and hit a tree."

"Do you think another vehicle may have forced him off the road deliberately?"

"I'd have no way of knowing, but if that had happened, his death would have been a murder, perhaps by the same person who murdered Marie."

"That's a definite possibility."

"Wow, Arthur; that gives me something to think about. If you can prove that someone murdered both Marie and Rob, then it would remove the cloud of suspicion that tainted Rob's reputation and still haunts me."

Arthur took another cracker with cheese and leaned forward toward Trina. "Getting away from Rob's outside relationship, I'd like to ask you a few questions raised by your grandfather's ledgers. Would that be all right?"

"Arthur, I'll be happy to discuss any topic. Your suggestion that someone unknown killed both Rob and Marie has given me new hope to clear the Danten and Jergens family names. What would you like to know?"

"What do you know about Milton's associates in the funeral business, Sammy Venta and Mario Bitoli?"

"I know Sammy by name only. He left Grandpa's company before I was born. Grandpa did make occasional kind comments about him. I've never heard of his having any children you could contact for more information, but he had a younger brother named Leo, who had a family. I met Leo's grandson once when I was younger. Mario Bitoli and Grandpa were friends and business associates until Grandpa died. I think he passed away before Mario. They worked together in the disposal business after Grandpa stopped doing funerals. They were so close, that I grew up thinking of Mario as part of the family. I always called him Uncle Mario. His wife's name was Sylvia, and they had a daughter and a son, Ruth and Anthony. Ruth now lives in Nevada, and she has two sons, William and John. Her married name is Fenton. Anthony married his high school sweetheart but left her a few years later to chase a Hollywood actress. Anthony and his wife Betty had only one son, Tony, Jr. before they split up. Tony and I played together when we were kids, and double-dated a few times during college. We never thought of each other in romantic terms. Anyway, nothing ever came of Anthony and the actress. He never married again, and died last year."

"I'm impressed, Trina. You certainly seem to remember the details of family trees."

"That talent stems from Grandpa Milt. He told me that whenever he held a funeral, he would get the names and addresses of all the relatives and draw up a family tree. Then he would send cards annually to the relatives in the hope of obtaining future business when someone else in the family died."

Arthur decided that he had to move beyond polite conversation. This would likely be his only chance to push Trina for information that only she had.

"Your grandfather must have been a good businessman and funeral director, but he and his colorful

185

friends involved themselves in other activities around the time of his building the church."

Trina sat silently for about ten seconds, and her hands visibly shook during her internal debate. "I never told anyone about that – not even Rob. How did you find out?"

"My associates and I have investigated the burning of your church, and all the background details that might lead us to identifying the arsonist. That led us to everything that went on during the earliest years of church operation. I'm also sure that even if you didn't say anything to Rob, he found out about it. Why else would he have studied and written about the Prohibition Era?"

"Grandpa Milt only gave country people a means to relieve their tensions while the temperance crusaders and the government had closed all of the normal outlets for drinking."

Arthur tried to reassure Trina in order to get additional information from her. He was not at all sure his tactic would work. "I'm not a policeman, Trina, and when I served at Parkville UMC, I taught the worshippers that they shouldn't be judgmental. Besides, all of that happened a long time ago. However, the people who were involved in bootlegging during Prohibition had families. You're a member of one of them. You described Mario Bitoli's family earlier, and you mentioned one of Sammy Venta's descendants. I'd like to know whether you know any other people who are members of such families."

"Not really, Arthur; about ten years ago, someone organized a reunion of people in northern Illinois whose families had once been involved in anti-prohibition activities. This happened shortly before I married Rob. I attended and met some interesting people, but I never stayed in contact with any of them afterward."

"Do you have any records of the people you met there?"

"That's an interesting question. At the time, I made some notes in a pocket notebook about people I hadn't met before, but I haven't seen that for many years. I either lost it or threw it out during one of my spring cleaning projects."

"Would it bother you if someone had found those notes and shared them with others?" He watched Trina carefully for her reaction to this question."

"Of course it wouldn't bother me. I'd never seen most of those people before or since. Occasionally, I'd run into someone from the Bitoli family – Tony lives on a farm south of Sterling with his dogs, and his mother occasionally visits him. The only reason I went to the reunion is that I enjoy studying history, and these people could tell eyewitness stories about what happened back then. Most of their tales contained exaggerations and distortions, but it was fun to hear them."

Arthur finished his glass of lemonade and stood. "Trina, I've thoroughly enjoyed this conversation, and I've learned from it as well. I'd appreciate your keeping your grandfather's record books handy in case I need to refer to them again."

"I enjoyed a chance to share my suppressed thoughts as well. When you feel that everyone is targeting you for criticism, you don't say much to anyone. Before you leave, I want to remind you that you promised to keep me informed about your findings on the deaths of Rob and his mistress."

"Consider that a pledge."

CHAPTER 58 – ARTHUR AND IRMA

On one of those lazy mornings you dream of fitting into your schedule, Irma raised herself up from her side of the bed and lowered her body onto that of her sleeping husband, who stirred and wrapped his arms around her.

"That's one of the best wakeup calls I've ever had."

She straightened her arms to push her upper body away from his. "What do you mean by one of the best? It had better be the best. Who else does it better?"

"Easy, Irma; your competition is you, when we were on our honeymoon. Anyway, I'm sure that I'll be able to show you my complete satisfaction this morning." He rolled over so that they were on their sides facing each other and began their favorite caressing ritual.

After a slow start, the ritual passionately accelerated to its highly satisfactory conclusion. Then they rested in an embrace. Irma reached up and pushed his straggly sandy hair curls back into place.

"If you don't get a haircut soon, I may have to tie your hair back in a ponytail."

"Thanks a lot; there's nothing like finishing up a sexy encounter with my wife by having her sound like my mother. She used to say things like that to me all the time. It's enough to make me want to get out of bed and face the day's problems."

"I apologize. Maybe I'm subconsciously training for when we have our own son someday. It's time for us to return to our adoption discussions."

He kissed her gently. "We'll get back to those discussions right after we complete this case. We've made a lot of progress. We now have a house that's suitable for children."

Irma frowned and slapped him on the back of his head.

"What was that for?"

"That was because you said we'd discuss children after we finish this case. Every time we have some important decision to make in our relationship, you defer it until the end of the current case. Are you afraid that we won't be able to raise children and investigate crimes too?"

"It's just that you usually come up with the key insight that solves the case. I wouldn't want you too distracted to clarify my thinking."

"I'm glad you appreciate my skills and genius, but you're not getting out of trouble that easily. Our discussions about children will continue on an irregular schedule regardless of the case's status. Can you accept that?"

"Fair enough; as long as we keep it *irregular* and don't push it to *top priority* right away."

"Agreed ... now let's get dressed and then adjourn to the porch where you can have a relaxed breakfast and tell me about your meeting with Trina Danten."

A short while later, Arthur sat on the porch, awaiting the arrival of Irma's new toy, a stainless steel restaurant cart that would convey their breakfast to this less formal location. As he sat, he pondered the possible effects of introducing one or two adopted children into their lives. He was in favor of that transition in theory, but he didn't feel prepared for its real-life unforeseen consequences.

The bumping of the cart's wheels over the threshold between the house and the porch pushed all thoughts of children from his mind.

After their breakfast, or more appropriately brunch, of vegetable omelettes, bran muffins, ham, and coffee, Irma rolled the cart with the dirty dishes into the kitchen for later cleanup and returned to the porch. In the meantime, Arthur moved to the soft cushions of the couch.

"Every time I let you interview a woman by yourself, you return saying that it was a satisfying encounter. Should I be jealous?"

"Only in the sense that I went there expecting a distantly polite and casual conversation, signifying little, and came through the process having a much greater understanding of our case and some of the people involved."

"That does sound like a successful encounter. Give me some of your spicy details."

Arthur turned to face Irma's chair, putting his back against the arm of his couch and his legs stretched out on its cushions. "My first and most important conclusion is that Trina Jergens Danten is a normal well-informed middle-aged woman and not the witch she was made out to be by others."

"She did have an impact on you. What are your reasons for that conclusion?"

"Trina gave me a very understandable summary of the changes in the ways people treated her as events transpired. The effects of gossip on her were profound, and they varied with time. At first, when people mainly discussed Rob Danten's affair with Marie Chance, they were sympathetic to Trina as the cheated party. Then, when the Police suspected Rob of murdering Marie, people shunned Trina as the murderer's wife. Finally, after Trina decided to teach Rob a lesson by making him live elsewhere, the gossip mill tagged her as a vindictive bitch. Unless we come up with a new understanding of what happened to Marie and Rob, Trina will probably retain that label from the gossipers."

Irma dunked half a muffin into her coffee and took a bite. "I never liked rumor-spreaders. As a scientist, I question the logical capabilities of anyone who jumps to a conclusion with insufficient information to justify it.

Gossipmongers are even worse. They broadcast theories and innuendos as facts without gathering any data at all. I can sympathize with Trina for the shifts in the ways some people looked at her. Did you get the impression that she thought her husband killed his girlfriend?"

"She said she always thought he was innocent. You could take her kicking him out of the house as her effort to avoid living with a possible murderer, or you could interpret it as punishment for his cheating on her. I think I'll go with the cheating version, because I think she would have been afraid to make him move if she thought he had murdered Marie."

"That's a reasonable assumption. Would she talk about her grandfather and his cronies?"

"She enjoyed talking about them, but she got a little defensive when I told her we knew they had been criminals. Even then, she answered all of my questions."

"That's interesting. Did she defend Milt's criminal activities?"

"I don't think she realized how brutal they were. I'm convinced she knows nothing about the church subbasement and the bodies in it. I came close to laughing out loud when she described the deeds of Milton and the other bootleggers as *being involved in anti-prohibition activities.*"

Irma smiled. "That is a classic euphemism. What about her list of gangster family members and their locations? Would she have been afraid of someone retaliating against her if she made that public?"

Arthur sat up and leaned toward Irma. "That was the biggest surprise of all. She voluntarily mentioned that list and did so in a way that made it appear completely inconsequential."

"How can it be trivial? Marie thought it was important, put it in her book, and thought it would force Trina to give Rob a divorce."

"Hold it. Now you're jumping to a conclusion. Marie did think it was important and put it in her book, but it's only a theory that she thought it would force Trina to give Rob a divorce."

"What about the importance of it to the mob? Why did they have Ken Cantini force the publisher to remove the book from retail outlets?"

"I have an alternate theory for that."

"Would you like to share it with me, or do I have to guess?"

Arthur tried to be cool and objective, seeing a touch of anger in Irma's words. "Try this as a possibility. We had guessed that the target of the mob was to keep people, and the press in particular, from seeing that list. The list appeared in an article from a phony Canadian newspaper, written by Sally Saunders. Sally Saunders is a transparent parody of Saul Sanders, the murdered Secret Service agent. Perhaps the mob suppressed the book's availability, not because of the list, but because it tied a list of mob family members to Saul Sanders. They may have been afraid the press would connect them to his killing and bring a new attack on their organization by several government agencies."

"That's a feasible argument. You're saying that they wanted to distance themselves from Saul Sanders' name. If that's the case, why isn't the list important?"

"You're going to love this one. It's not a list at all. About ten years ago, before she married Rob, Trina went to a reunion of families with ties to Prohibition Era bootlegging. As she met new acquaintances there, she made some rough notes in a pocket notebook, just to help her remember who was there. That notebook disappeared from her dresser drawer several years ago. Apparently, Rob took it and passed it to Marie. They both attributed more significance to it than the notebook deserved."

Irma made a few of her own notes. "That's very interesting. Presumably, the data in the published list is correct, but it's fragmentary at best. That also shoots down our theories that Trina would have acted against Rob and Marie to get the list back and that people on the list would have been angry at Trina for letting it get published."

Arthur stood and looked out over the hillside. "My visit to Trina gives us a whole new perspective, and it tells us to start all over again in investigating the deaths of Marie Chance, Rob Danten, and Saul Sanders."

CHAPTER 59 – AUTOPSY RESULTS

Three days later, Joe Gonzalez and Steve DuBois returned to the cemetery early in the morning for a second exhumation of the unknown woman's body. This time, they transferred her to a simple wooden coffin and transported it to a private autopsy facility in Chicago. By late afternoon, they had received their results from the pathologist and had returned to Binghampton Cemetery to replace her body in the original coffin and rebury her. The gravediggers, Lenny and Hank, promised to install a zipper on her grave to make it easier for Joe and Steve to remove the coffin for additional future exhumations.

Before leaving the cemetery, Joe called Arthur to suggest that they stop at his house to share the autopsy results, since they were already in the Amboy area. Arthur agreed and told Joe that he expected Penny and Irma to return from a shopping outing in about one hour. Joe indicated that he and Steve would stop for a quick supper along the way, in order to arrive at about the same time as the women.

Joe and Steve arrived at the Blakes' house just in time for Joe to watch Penny transfer four large bags from the Blakes' silver Saturn Vue to the trunk of her Ford Focus.

As Joe left his car and walked toward her, he called out, "You didn't have to buy so many presents for my birthday, Penny. You should have bought something for yourself."

"You'll be surprised to learn that there actually is something for you in one of those bags, but you'll have to wait for that birthday to find out what it is. Hi, Steve, has Joe behaved himself today?"

"He did have a date with another woman, but she occupied an autopsy table at the time, so there's no need for jealousy."

"There's an appetizing thought. Let's go inside and switch to cheerier subjects."

They entered the house to find Irma and Arthur loading snacks and drinks onto Irma's stainless steel cart.

She greeted them and said, "I thought we'd exchange our thoughts in the living room tonight. We need a change of scene from the kitchen, and mosquitoes would be a problem on the porch."

Her comment received a chorus of affirmations, so they headed for the front room, denuded of Midge's modern furniture and now graced by an antique couch, traditional wingback chairs, two of them recliners, and antique tables. Joe and Arthur each took a cup of coffee and a slice of apple pie and then outmaneuvered the others for the reclining chairs.

Joe leaned back in his chair and said, "This is ideal; it's at least one cut above your apartment for comfort and charm."

Irma smiled and said, "We had a different type of charm there, compact and conducive to sharing a couch together. Here, we can spread out and relax. Each living space has its own brand of charm. Right now, it's time for exchanging lively conversation. Start us off, Joe. I let you and Steve oversee the autopsy procedure today. What did you discover?"

"We confirmed once again that Arthur thinks a few steps further into the future than the rest of us. He suggested that if our unknown woman had given birth between the time of receiving her elegant ring and the time of her death, we might find that our arsonist was her descendant, trying to regain the family's treasured ring. I can't comment on the likelihood of that suggestion, but he may have been correct. The pathologist said it would be impossible to determine whether she had given birth within the few weeks prior to her death, but she had generous amounts of desiccated skin in the womb area. She may have been heavy, or she may have given birth. There's a fair probability that you were correct about a child, Arthur."

He responded with a curt nod. "The possibility of a child does complicate things. We may never even learn its family name or gender. Our arsonist is likely to be someone totally unrelated, but it's fascinating to consider the possibility that one of the descendants of this woman's child might be behind the fire."

Irma said, "If you feel my husband made us rethink things due to that childbirth question, you'll be completely shaken up by his new evidence from interviewing Trina Jergens Danten."

Penny asked, "Why be so formal with the two family names, Irma?"

"I did that deliberately because Trina confided many things to Arthur that gave him a new outlook on relationships and several aspects of our case. These new viewpoints involve both the Jergens and Danten families. Fill them in, Arthur."

"I'll summarize everything, but first, Steve, I'd like you to take notes for Jeff Lee. He's not here, and much of my story will be important to him."

"Will do, Arthur."

"I also want to congratulate Penny and Steve for the way they got Mandy Miller to confess to two murders. Her seminary training may have made those deeds a heavy burden for her to bear. How did you settle with the Italian police regarding her prosecution?"

Penny gestured to Steve that she would reply, and he nodded his agreement. "Mandy has confessed to both murders, so she'll be sentenced in an Illinois court, but we're negotiating with Italian officials to see whether she'll be allowed to serve a single consolidated sentence over here that will essentially be the sum of the two sentences.

That would allow us to eliminate any question of extradition later and the costs for sending her to Italy to stand trial again. She'll be behind bars for a very long time whether the Italians agree or not."

"Mandy's murder of Ken Cantini in Rome relates to the information I received from Trina that has altered my outlook with regard to the murders of Marie Chance, Rob Danten – I do consider that a murder rather than suicide or an accident – and Saul Sanders. I definitely think they are related."

Arthur went on to tell Penny, Joe, and Steve about Trina's reactions to the earlier gossip about her, including her punishing Rob for cheating on her by making him move out of their house to an apartment. He told them that Trina considered Rob to be a nonviolent person who wouldn't have strangled Marie under any circumstances. He also related that Trina had said that she would have wanted to avoid divorce, even if she would have had to allow Rob an occasional sexual fling with someone else. Finally, Arthur summarized Trina's knowledge of her grandfather Milton's associates and their families and detailed her tale that the list Marie published was simply her rough notes about people who attended a reunion with her before she married Rob.

When Arthur finished his summary, Penny asked, "Didn't she feel upset about her grandfather's criminal past?"

"I'm sure she feels bothered by it, but she told me that she considers him a good businessman and a member of an anti-prohibition group. That last term almost made me laugh. She also said that after Prohibition ended, Milton and his partner, Mario closed their funeral home and went into the waste disposal business. She said that they were quite successful at it."

Steve said, "I've taken notes as you suggested, Arthur. I gather that you believe Trina's story that our famous list was nothing but her notes from a mobster family reunion, filched by Rob, and Marie's over-valuing its importance."

"I do believe that story, Steve. It sounds real and makes sense to me. She said that she hasn't seen any of those people since the reunion, and she took notes because many of the people there were strangers to her. Trina claims she attended the reunion to gather interesting stories of events during Prohibition. She may have been thinking about writing a book about that period. The reunion took place before she met Rob, so she wasn't gathering information for him. She could relate to Prohibition events as an insider. Rob later had to study them from an academic viewpoint."

"That's all interesting, and could be true, but it sends us back to the starting line as far as solving the murders of Marie Chance, Rob Danten, and Saul Sanders. Jeff Lee won't be happy about your acceptance of Trina's story."

Penny studied Steve with a surprised expression. "Do you really mean what you just said, Steve? Jefferson Lee may be an important friend to you, but our job is to determine the truth about these murders, not to please someone in a cooperating agency."

"You're absolutely right, Penny. I phrased my comment poorly. Our theory was that the murder of Secret Service Agent Saul Sanders tied into the murders of Marie Chance and Rob Danten through the published list of mob family descendants and their locations. We're now suggesting that the descendants list was of no particular importance. If so, the murder of Saul Sanders could be a totally independent event, and there would be no reason for Jeff Lee and the Secret Service to assist us on this case."

Arthur said, "You're right, Steve; that's a better way of stating your concern. However, I made the point before I recited Trina's information, that I do believe that the three killings are related."

Joe said, "I'd like to believe that. It gives us a framework for continuing our investigations, but I have to agree with Steve that trivializing that list damages our theory of why things happened."

Irma shook her head. "I'll disagree with you on that point, Joe. Trina has told us the list had no special significance. If we accept her statement, it doesn't change anything, so long as Marie, Rob and Saul thought it was valuable and dangerous information. They didn't have to be correct. So long as they felt it was dangerous, it could have motivated someone to kill them. Arthur, what, if anything, should change in the way we look at these three murders?"

"That's a great question, and one I've been considering. There is something very important that should alter our outlook toward those three victims."

Penny asked, "How so?"

"We've been treating Rob and Marie as having had an affair because he had a dull marriage, and he couldn't resist the temptation of a pretty woman leading him on. We looked at the murder of Saul Sanders as a mob hit on an outstanding Secret Service agent. I suggest that we may have been wrong and that none of these three was innocent in any sense of the word."

Steve said, "There's a bombshell for me to drop on Jeff Lee. Why would you consider Saul Sanders to be anything but a good agent?"

"Who else having familiarity with underworld figures would have known about Marie Chance's book and could have arranged for Ken Cantini to pressure the publisher to withdraw it?"

CHAPTER 60 – THREE MURDERS

They took a break in their discussions for a light supper. Irma, Arthur, Joe, and Penny adjourned to the kitchen to make sandwiches, while Steve DuBois telephoned Jefferson Lee to fill him in on their latest discussion points.

"Hi, Jeff; this is Steve with your latest update on our investigation progress and how it might affect you."

"That sounds as though you're about to share some breaking news."

"Let's put it this way, I have at least two high-impact developments from discussions we've been having at the Blakes' house. Arthur, Irma, Joe, and Penny are here with me."

"I'm prepared for any bombshells you have to drop, Steve. My pad of paper and pen are at the ready. Enlighten me."

"The first development is that the list of mob family members that Marie Chance put in her book has very little significance. You were right in calling it Trina's list; it did originate with her, but it wasn't really a list at all. That document consisted of her random notes to help her remember people who attended a reunion of mobster families."

"I thought it lacked organization when I first saw it. I've done enough editing to have wondered why Marie passed it off as an article from the *Western Winnipeg Independent* without revising it. Even so, the list had impact. That Ken Cantini played the part of an attorney to convince the publisher to recall Marie's book."

"That's the other bombshell."

"What's the other bombshell?"

"Arthur pointed out that only one person who knew about Marie's book had contacts with mob people who could assign Ken Cantini to do that job."

"Who was that?"

"Saul Sanders was the only person who could have done that. Marie Chance and Rob Danten certainly wouldn't have had those connections, and the publisher wouldn't have put pressure on himself."

"In other words, you're suggesting that Saul sold out to the mob."

"He either sold out or became part of it."

"Let me think about that for a while. I'd better do a second inventory of his records with a different point of view."

"You surprise me, Jeff. I expected you to get upset by my new information, and you took it as just another step in the investigative process."

"That's because that's exactly what it is, Steve. As you know, I try not to say anything that would hurt a person's reputation or future opportunities unless it becomes important to the investigation. I didn't reveal that there has been adverse gossip in our offices for years about Saul Sanders. Some of my associates have long wondered aloud how Saul could have been so intimate with the details of the mob's organization without also having been close to some of its members."

"You continue to surprise me. Keep me informed if you find anything more about Saul."

"I'll do that, Steve. You've been a good friend as well as a competent colleague. Someday, we'll discuss investigating on multiple levels but restricting your reporting to the top one."

After Steve completed his conversation with Jeff, he went to join the sandwich makers. He entered the kitchen to find a large round tray full of assorted sandwiches on the table and Irma showing off a new lavender raincoat, bought during her earlier shopping spree with Penny.

"This thing is reversible, lavender on one side and black on the other, with a zip-in lining for colder weather when I wear it black-side out. Because it reverses, I can use the opposite side pockets for hiding items like forensic gadgets that I don't want to be obvious."

Steve announced his presence by saying, "Oh, I see that you bought the shoplifter special, with hidden pockets for stolen items."

They all laughed, and Joe asked, "How did Jeff Lee react to our surprises about Trina's list and Saul Sanders?"

"He essentially didn't react. He said that our new developments confirmed his reservations about the list and office gossip at Secret Service about Saul. Jeff is a card player. He shows one card but has others hidden; he analyzes on several levels, but only talks about the top one."

Irma said, "Thanks for the tip-off. I enjoy playing poker, but I'll avoid inviting Jeff if we hold a cards night here. I assume Jeff is going to do an internal investigation of Saul Sanders."

Arthur said, "I'll bet that he'll do that investigation without any of his colleagues being aware of it ... everyone grab one or more sandwiches, and we'll continue our discussions around the table here."

Penny said, "Creative sandwiches department; I have a BLT with sardines added. I must admit it's different but tasty. Where do we go with our discussion, now that we've decided that mob connections may have tainted Saul Sanders? Arthur, you brought up the point of re-examining Marie, Rob, and Saul. What more should we do there?"

"We have yet to determine whether Marie and Rob had something to hide, beyond their relationship, but first, I'd like to have a timeline of their deaths. We know that Marie died before Rob, because the police suspected him of killing her. When did Saul die, relative to the other two?"

Implications

Penny said, "I'm pretty sure he died after Marie, but before Rob. Marie would have been alive when her publisher removed her book from sales channels, because she vigorously complained to him afterwards. Our notes from interviewing him say that she complained so bitterly that he told her he would never again publish a book she wrote or edited. We now believe that Saul arranged for the pressure on the publisher to force the recall, so he would have been alive also. When we get back home, I'll check my computer files for the exact dates of their deaths, but I feel comfortable with saying that she died first. The point that interested me in researching their deaths was that the Chicago newspapers wrote long articles about her death but very little about his."

Irma said, that may have been because they had a juicy story about the presumed love triangle in Marie's death, and little information about Saul because he died in Indiana, and Secret Service may have suppressed a story about the killing of one of their agents.

CHAPTER 61 – MIDGE DRINKWATER

After Steve, Joe, and Penny departed, Arthur and Irma decided to treat themselves to ice cream sundaes at the kitchen table. Irma had added whipped cream and was about to top their creations with a cherry, when they heard a knock on the kitchen door. They opened it to find Midge Drinkwater there.

Irma held the door wide open for her. "Come on in, Midge. You usually retire to your apartment earlier than this. I hope we weren't so loud that you couldn't sleep."

"No, I'm not ready for sleep. I'm just in a lounging frame of mind. When you get to my age, you sometimes want to pack extra time into a day. Today has been a great success for me. I completed all the tasks on my list before I stopped for supper, and I've been doing extra things ever since. Once I heard your company leave, I thought I'd join you for a chat, if you're up to it."

Arthur smiled and held a chair away from the table for Midge. "You have more energy than we do sometimes; come and join us for an ice cream sundae."

"That sounds great, if you don't mind my interfering with your chit-chat."

Irma said, "We've been in meetings for hours. It's time for us to relax, and I can't think of anyone I'd rather have join us ... one more sundae coming up."

"Thank you, Irma. You've both been so good to me. I try to stay out of your hair, but sometimes an old lady gets curious and craves companionship."

"Just sit with us for a while and chat. I'm sure Arthur won't mind having two dates for ice cream."

Midge savored her first spoonful of the sundae. "Oh, that's good! "You two have been having frequent meetings lately. Are they all in connection with the church that burned down?"

Arthur buried his spoon into his sundae so that it stood upright. "That's it for the most part, plus a few incidental matters."

"I don't mean to be nosy, but be sure to let me know if my memories of the old days might be helpful."

He glanced at Irma. "Fine, Midge; you've already assisted us with your memories. If we have another specific question, we'll be sure to consult with you. Actually, I do have something for you. You had mentioned that as a child, you went to a wake in the basement of the Methodist Church with your father. Do you remember who was being waked?"

"I mentioned earlier that it was my friend Betsy's dad. I don't remember their last name, but he worked in the railroad yards. He was one of my dad's customers. Dad drove a taxi."

Irma said, "Amboy must have been a bigger city in those days, to support a taxi company."

Midge smiled. "It was a booming place. Everything centered on the railroads. We had the big Illinois Central Railroad freight terminal and maintenance facilities. Amboy was even the birthplace of the Carson Pirie Scott department store chain. Even today, the city brags that Abraham Lincoln stopped in Amboy long enough to get a haircut. That was way before my time, though."

Arthur asked, "Did your dad drive into Chicago, or limit himself to Amboy fares?"

"In those days, the taxi business was flexible. He drove all over the place. I doubt if he could have supported us on Amboy fares alone. There weren't many cars, so lots of people paid to have someone else drive them around."

Irma said, "I bet you miss those days and the excitement of being young during the Roaring Twenties."

"It was fun; I enjoyed wild dances and partied until the depression sobered us all up. It was pretty ironic that they imposed Prohibition on us when everyone had lots of money for partying, and then they repealed it during the depression years when no one could afford to buy a drink."

Irma asked, "Did you know anybody who worked for the bootleggers back then?"

Midge looked thoughtful for a few seconds. "Let's say that I knew more than a few of them, but that I can't remember any of their names. It was an unexpectedly wild period for people who would never have mingled with criminals under normal circumstances. Most of them turned to normal jobs after Prohibition ended – if they could get jobs at all during the depression. This conversation has taken an unexpected turn. Now that I've finished my sundae, I think I'll go upstairs to bed. All the talk of depression days has put a damper on my late evening energy."

They all stood, and Arthur said, "We don't want to stand in the way of your rest. Join us again for another evening chat. We'll try to select more cheerful topics."

Midge left the kitchen, and a few minutes later, they heard the elevator taking her to her second floor apartment.

Irma said, "I spotted your caution signal when you spiked your spoon into your ice cream like a flag on a mailbox."

"I wasn't sure whether you sensed it, but Midge wanted to pump us on the progress of our investigation. She knows more than she's telling about criminal elements in those past days. We'll have to be on guard to keep future case discussions private."

CHAPTER 62 – JEFFERSON LEE

There may have been something to the office gossip after all. Why didn't I reach the same conclusion as Arthur Blake? Unless some mob-type had come out of nowhere to put pressure on Marie Chance's publisher, it had to have been Saul Sanders behind it. What was that old saying? You lie down with dogs, and you get up with fleas. Secret Service management had appointed Saul to be our expert on the mob and its members, and now we discover that he got so close to them that he joined them.

When they first transferred me to Chicago, Saul delegated himself to be my informal mentor. He was easy to approach and fun to work with back then. Had he hoped to seduce me into working for the mob? If so, he learned that I wouldn't deviate from the guidance of my internal moral compass. I didn't realize it at the time, but my lack of corruptibility may have been what led to his distancing himself from me later. During the last few years before his death, Saul always turned me down when I suggested socializing after work.

Because of Saul's monitoring of organized crime information, management left his file cabinets intact after he died. I've looked through most of them before, but he had one locked file cabinet for which we had no key. I didn't give it much thought earlier and just bypassed it as not important. That cabinet may have been his Holy of Holies. Given our joint speculation about his corruption by mob contacts, it's time for me to open that treasure chest.

Jeff had brought the time-honored drive pin punch and hammer tool combination to Saul Sanders' old file alcove. He selected the third cabinet from the left, and centered the punch on the lock button. Two impacts of the hammer later, the lock button had disappeared into the innards of the steel enclosure, yielding him free access to the four drawers.

Top drawer – files, alphabetical by name – let's look for Ken Cantini. He has a sheet in the C folder. There's a notation on it – contact through Max Settlin. Max is one of the Las Vegas crowd, and that's where Ken Cantini was when they picked him to play the part of an attorney. It fits with the theory that Saul Sanders requested pressure on Marie's publisher. There's a sheet with contact information on Max Settlin in the S folder. It looks as though Sanders had contact info for virtually everyone in the Who's Who of Mobsters. Saul was a little old-fashioned, though, to use paper instead of computer files. Maybe he did it deliberately, so no one could hack his data mine.

Second drawer from top – city maps with annotations – we'll have to assign a team of agents to analyze these.

Third drawer from top – old newspaper articles and copies of same – these might be innocent, but I doubt it because of their location in this special file.

Bottom drawer – cell phones and pistols – I have a feeling we'll find that these are untraceable items for use on confidential jobs. Talk about hiding things in plain sight. Secret Service has more information on mob activities in its own Chicago office than agents would find in years of fieldwork. I'll request the assignment of a team of agents to analyze all of this stuff. It may also be time to remove Saul's picture from our gallery of honored agents killed in the line of duty.

CHAPTER 63 – BISHOP CHANDLER

Joe Gonzalez and Arthur Blake exited the Dirksen Federal Building in downtown Chicago after depositing the Tiffany diamond ring in the federal vault and formally registering that piece of jewelry to protect its chain of custody for future legal proceedings. They turned toward the old Dearborn Station to seek Joe's favorite pub for lunch, taking no more than a few steps, when Arthur's cell phone rang. Seeing that the caller was Irma, Arthur moved out of the flow of pedestrians to take it next to the wall of the nearest building.

"Hi, Irma. Mission accomplished. Joe and I are about to break for lunch before we head back."

"You may have to let Joe go by himself. Bishop Chandler just called, and he sounded very unhappy. He's at his office in the Chicago Temple Building; I calmed him down by saying that you were downtown and would visit him shortly. Sorry, but you'll have to delay lunch until later."

"Did he say what was bothering him?"

"No, he wanted to discuss something with you face-to-face."

"Good enough; I'll get over there right away. Thanks for the warning ... see you later."

Arthur shook his head as he walked over to where Joe stood. "It looks as though I won't be joining you for lunch. Irma says that I have to visit Bishop Chandler. He's upset about something, and he's only a few blocks from here."

"While you were on the phone, I bought a copy of the Tribune. It contains a good clue as to why he's upset. Look at this."

Methodist Bootleggers

AMBOY, Ill. – The Chicago Tribune has learned that the United Methodist Church that recently burned in Amboy, Illinois contained a subterranean chamber, used during Prohibition days as a warehouse for bootlegged whiskey. This facility appears to have been designed into the church's original blueprints. According to sources in the Division of Arson Investigation of the Office of the Illinois State Fire Marshal, that church originally housed a funeral director's business in its basement, and that operation masked bootleg liquor distribution from its subbasement. The Methodist Church, through its Board of Temperance, had been one of the primary advocates for the Prohibition Amendment to the U.S. Constitution. Tribune reporters will continue their research. Watch for future additional exclusives on this story.

Arthur said, "That's just about as bad a story leak as we could have. I can't believe that Dennis was the source, but someone else in his office has loose lips. Anyway, I'd better go face the music with the Bishop. Where will I meet you?"

"I have a few Chicago officials I should contact at the Daley Center, across the street from the Chicago Temple Building. Let's meet near the Picasso Statue on Daley Plaza. Then we can head for a late lunch together."

When Arthur arrived at the Episcopal Offices on the eighteenth floor, he told the receptionist that Bishop Chandler expected him and then took a seat. A few minutes later, the receptionist told him Bishop Chandler was ready to see him.

Arthur walked down the hallway, suspecting this conversation would differ from their cordial past meetings. As he entered the private office, the lack of any coffee or other signs of hospitality confirmed that assumption.

"Sit down please, Arthur. Have you seen today's Chicago Tribune?"

"I saw a copy ten minutes ago, after I received your message that you wanted to see me. I don't know who leaked the information for that article. The lead arson investigator is quite dependable and is just as interested in suppressing premature press stories as we are."

"That story is more than premature. It reveals damaging church history that I didn't even know until I read it. Why didn't you tell me about bootlegging out of that church?"

"I had hoped to keep that information completely secret, at least until we found and arrested the arsonist."

"You're not supposed to withhold damaging information from me. If I don't know about it, how can I set up a defense against it?"

Arthur shrugged. "If that's the way you want to handle information related to that church, Howard, I'll have to advise you that at one point, the arsonist returned to the church and locked Irma and me in that subbasement warehouse, hoping we wouldn't be found and would die there."

Bishop Chandler stood. "How did you get out? That's a terrible development."

"We had more resources than he or she expected. It did take significant effort by both of us."

"What else don't I know about that place?"

"Would it make you feel better to know about the two corpses that have been in there since Prohibition?"

"Do you mean that all of the services in that church since then took place with two unburied dead bodies beneath the sanctuary?"

"Yes, Sir – except that during the most recent three years, there were three bodies down there. We've arrested the murderer of the latest victim."

"This is all terrible publicity for the United Methodist Church as a whole, for the Northern Illinois Conference, and for the Amboy Church in particular. After learning all this, I don't know whether I'll be able to justify rebuilding that church."

Arthur stood and took a few steps to relieve the tension in his muscles. "That question about whether to rebuild that church might have something to do with my wanting to wait until we had more answers before I gave you a complete rundown on what we'd found. A church with an unsavory past can still offer a promising future."

"I'll continue to consider the question of rebuilding that church, because I don't want to be too judgmental. What are you going to do about limiting adverse publicity, Arthur?"

"There's an old saying that you can't push a genie back into its bottle. However, you may have more allies than you expect in your effort to minimize scandal. You and the Mayor are both in the same boat. It hurts Chicago tourism to keep bringing up the topic of Prohibition Era gangsters. The Tribune got its initial exclusive. If you promise them first access to official details once we arrest the arsonist, they might be satisfied."

"And are you close to making that arrest?"

"No, but we're unraveling the criminal tapestry strand, by strand."

"What's the criminal tapestry?"

"Actually, the arson investigation led to other crimes involving people in the Amboy Church, past and present. There was nothing evil about the church, only a few of the people in it."

"That's what bothers me about our arrangement, Arthur. I'm not sure how long I can have you be our Conference Troubleshooter. You're too good at what you do. You study a specific problem and spin off several others from it. I may not be able to keep you in a position where you might unravel our church's tapestry of human errors. We'll talk about this again."

CHAPTER 64 - LEAKS

Dennis Mikken picked up his office telephone after the first ring when he saw that the caller was Arthur Blake. "Hello, Arthur; I know why you're after me. I saw the Tribune article too, and I'm working on finding out how they got their information. I didn't give anything to the press, and Celia tells me that she didn't either. I didn't even put anything about that subbasement and its original use in any of my progress reports. So far, the source that leaked the story to them is a mystery."

"I hate to have to request an internal investigation, but Bishop Chandler has been all over me about the damage that story has done to our church."

"Fear not, Arthur; the investigation is under way, and it has a high priority. Mayor Emanuel called Governor Quinn, and he had our Director in for a personal discussion. The State of Illinois is in lousy financial shape, and its only bit of good news was that tourism has been increasing. Bringing up the bad old days and bootlegging mobsters can cost Illinois a ton of tourist dollars."

"It's comforting to know that I'm not the only one on the hot seat. If you didn't tell anyone, and Celia didn't either, who else had access to the information? Was it included in departmental reports that Celia wrote?"

"No, neither one of us had loose lips or a loose computer keyboard. It wasn't even contained in any emails."

"Do you have any theories about the source of the leak?"

"I'm afraid not, Arthur. I'm open to suggestions."

"I do have one that would be worth checking, Dennis."

"What's that?"

"After the arsonist trapped Irma and me in that warehouse room, you arranged for continuous State Police protection of the property. From a conversation with one of you or from poking around in the ruins, one of those troopers could have pieced the story together and shared it with a police reporter. How clear were you with them about the confidentiality of their assignment?"

Arthur heard a groan.

"That has to be it. We overlooked the weak link in the chain. We, or rather I, assumed they wouldn't hear or see enough for it to be a consideration. Those troopers aren't dummies; they train to observe everything and analyze each situation. They also probably compared notes with each other during shift changes."

"And State Police talk with reporters much more frequently than someone from your department or from our UMC Northern Illinois Conference. I suggest you work through their management to confirm whether they were the source of the leak. Then someone will have to inform the Governor."

"Hopefully, it won't have to be me. At least I had all the contents of the subbasement transferred to a secure warehouse after we exhumed that woman's body. We no longer need the State Police to protect the Amboy Church. Anything else we discover there will be confidential."

CHAPTER 65 – PENNY AND IRMA

Irma answered the insistent ringing of the doorbell to find Penny Gonzalez standing there holding a large bag of fried chicken.

"Hi, Irma; I brought lunch. It's time for us to have a girl-to-girl chat. Are we alone?"

"Come on in, Penny. Yes, I'm the only one here now. That's why it took me so long to get to the door. I was on the third floor. You certainly leaned on that bell enough. Do we have some kind of emergency?"

"Only that the chicken is getting cold. Let's head for the kitchen. I hope you have a couple of cold beers."

Penny went directly to the kitchen while Irma detoured to the basement refrigerator for the beer. By the time she went back up to the kitchen, Penny had the table set and the chicken on a large serving platter.

Irma opened the two bottles of Sam Adams Boston Lager and set them beside the plates. "Your chicken is most welcome, but I'm a little confused as to its purpose. I'd guess that it was a peace offering, but I can't remember our having a fight. Did I say something that offended you?"

"Not at all, Irma; this isn't that kind of chat."

"You'd better give me a hint. I'm not that good at guessing today."

"After the Bishop put Arthur through an inquisition over that Chicago Tribune article, Joe came home looking angry and upset. He thinks there's a fair chance that Bishop Chandler will fire or exile Arthur after this arson investigation is over. Arthur told Joe that the Bishop doesn't have the stomach for learning about the character flaws in people around him. He'd rather believe they're better than they really are, so that he'll feel comfortable working with them."

"Jesus said, 'Let him who is without sin cast the first stone,' and he had no takers. We're all bad in some way."

"Wow; you're starting to sound like a pastor too. I'm impressed."

"Don't be. I'm just saying that I understand your concern. There are a lot of people in this world, like Bishop Chandler, who want to believe the best of others, even when they see evidence to the contrary."

"I agree with your statement, Irma, but Arthur's boss goes beyond that. He's like an ostrich hiding its head in the sand. He doesn't even want to see that *evidence to the contrary*, and because of that attitude, Joe and I think he's going to distance himself from Arthur in some way."

"Well, if you're correct, you're not exactly the bearer of glad tidings."

"Ah, but I am, in an indirect sort of way. I'm here to let you know that if the Bishop acts against Arthur, we'll formalize the relationship between you two and our agency. You can continue as outside consultants, but with formal status and credentials, or you're both welcome to become government employees."

"So that's what this visit is all about. You and Joe have been great friends as well as colleagues over the years. I do appreciate what you're offering us, but I have to respond that I don't know how Arthur would react to the Bishop's firing him as the official investigator. He may not want to move in a direction that he would view as a separation from the church. I agree with you that we may be facing a fork in the road."

"Whichever direction he takes, Joe and I will support him and you."

"Thanks Penny; I'll, of course, guard his back too, even if we have to give up this wonderful house."

Penny raised her beer bottle. "Let's drink to supporting Arthur, but without losing the house."

CHAPTER 66 – *MARIE AND SAUL*

They had met at a small neighborhood tavern, known for its Polish food, its disregard for anti-smoking statutes, and its complete discretion regarding the identities of the couples who dined there. Marie arrived first, and Saul joined her ten minutes later.

"Thank you for coming, Mr. Sanders. I do believe that I have information that will interest the Secret Service."

"Call me Saul, and I'll call you Marie, if you don't mind. I prefer that we leave the name of my agency out of our conversations, especially in a public place like this."

"That's fine with me. Without getting into confidential background details, I wanted to let you know that I have a document that lists a large number of descendants of Prohibition Era gangsters, along with the current locations of many of these people. I'm on the faculty of Northern Illinois University, and I'm about to publish a compilation and analysis of newspaper accounts of Prohibition crimes and events."

"How do your list and your book relate to each other?"

"I plan to include the list within a supposedly-reprinted article from a fictitious newspaper. I'll give you the key information you'll need to find it in my book. If anything happens to me after the book appears for sale, I'd like you to publicize that list as punishment for the person who killed me."

Saul lit a cigarette and inhaled deeply before responding. "Are you really willing to risk your life this way? I take it that you feel my acceding to your wishes will act as insurance for you, perhaps keeping an assailant from acting against you. What do I get out of this arrangement?"

She fixed her stare on his greenish-brown eyes. "Saul, I understand from my newspaper connections that you're the organized crime researcher for your agency and that you maintain a database of specialized information about that period and its aftermath. The information in my list is available nowhere else. If you agree to work with me, you will be free to use that data for any purpose, regardless of whether anything happens to me or not. My list contains unique and valuable facts."

Saul inhaled smoke again before speaking. "I'll go this far. Upon the book's publication, we'll meet again in a more private place. At that time, with the help of your key to finding it, I'll review your list to see whether it indeed has value for me. If it does, I will agree to act as your insurance policy."

"You mean that you want the prize before you do anything to earn it. That's not acceptable."

"Take it or leave it; those are my terms."

Marie stood, preparing to leave. "I'll have to think about it. I may call you. If we do meet again, leave your cigarettes at home. I don't like smoke in my face."

After Marie left, Saul ordered his favorite Polish beer and lit another cigarette from the butt of his first one. A blond woman left a table in the back corner of the tavern and joined him.

CHAPTER 67 – TRINA

Arthur returned the kitchen telephone to its wall hook. "Irma, I have to visit Trina again after lunch. She says she remembered something important about Rob that she forgot to tell me last time."

"That's an excuse to get you over there. You have a new admirer. She could have given you the information over the telephone."

"You may be right, or she may have something to show me. Anyway, I'll head over there after dessert. I won't skip out on one of your apple squares."

"I have to give credit to Midge. I copied the recipe from one of her cards. She has an amazing collection of recipes for traditional specialties."

When Arthur arrived at Trina's house, he encountered two Amboy Police squad cars in the driveway, and an officer stringing up yellow crime scene tape around the premises. Before attempting to enter, he called Joe Gonzalez on his cell phone to request some official backup in case the police wouldn't let him enter the house. Joe told him that he was on his way to Northern Illinois University, but that he would cancel his appointment there and meet him at Trina's house in twenty-five minutes.

As expected, the Amboy Police officer outside Trina's house refused him entry until the crime scene investigators completed their initial survey. He did learn that a neighbor had called 911 after hearing shots. Trina had died from two gunshot wounds, one to the chest and one to the head. Arthur told the officer that the murder must have occurred within the previous hour, following his telephone conversation with Trina.

When Joe arrived, he showed the outside officer his federal credentials, identified Arthur as a consultant to his agency, and registered the two of them as having been at the crime scene. They entered the house and again identified themselves to the officers and evidence technicians inside.

Arthur said a silent prayer for Trina while he told the police how recently he had spoken with her. "I understand that she died from gunshot wounds."

Sergeant Kruger affirmed that the attacker had shot Trina in the chest and the head. He indicated that she must have tried to escape, because the chest shot entered from the front and exited her back, but that the head shot, presumably the second, entered from the back without an exit wound. They had found her body in the dining room, facing the sliding glass doors leading to the patio.

Joe stayed by the body to assist with the examination, but because of his familiarity with the house, Arthur chose to survey all the rooms to check for changes since he had last seen them. He entered the kitchen and found nothing out of place except for a pair of open cabinet doors. However, when he next checked Trina's den, he discovered that the large shallow drawer beneath the lowest bookshelf was open. He returned to the dining room to find Joe.

"Joe, this murder is part of our case."

"Why do you say that?"

"The assailant shot Trina as she prepared to meet with me and deliver new evidence concerning Rob. In addition, he or she stole Milt Jergens' old ledger books. She originally stored them in the basement, but when I returned the ledgers, she put them into a drawer beneath the bookshelves in the den. That drawer is now open and empty."

CHAPTER 68 – BINGHAMPTON

The ringing of the telephone interrupted Joe's briefing of Penny regarding the murder scene at Trina's house. He walked into his combination den and office to answer it. When he lifted the receiver, he heard a greeting from Gilbert Wilson, the manager of Binghampton Cemetery.

"Hello, Mr. Gonzalez; I have a development that will interest you. Do you remember what Lennie and Hank said to you the last time you were here?"

"Not exactly, but I do remember that they were in a very good mood."

"They told you and Mr. DuBois that they were going to install a zipper on that grave to make it easier to dig up the coffin inside it."

"Now that you mention it, I do remember that – why are you bringing it up now?"

"I thought you should know that when we arrived this morning, we found that someone had dug up a different unmarked grave close to the one you folks examined. We think they may have been looking for the one that interested you, but picked the wrong location. Until you came, we hadn't had an exhumation in that old section of the cemetery for decades. They did such a lousy job of reburying it, that the vandalism was obvious. I don't know whether they stole anything."

"Thanks for alerting me, Gilbert. Was the grave location they dug up 15NW2SW?"

"That's exactly where it was. How did you know that, Mr. Gonzalez?"

"Someone once made a mistake in recording the location of our victim, and that's the incorrect location he wrote. I'll send Steve over to photograph the vandalism before you do a proper job of reburial. Don't disturb any footprints or other items in the grave area. Send me a bill for your efforts in cleaning up the mess afterward. I'm sure this event relates to our investigation."

Joe walked back into the kitchen where Penny sat at the table with two fresh cups of coffee.

"Things are happening, Penny, and they're disturbing in several ways."

"What do you mean by disturbing?

"We did a good job of concealing the discovery of that woman's grave at Binghampton Cemetery and our removal of the ring from it. Apparently, the motive for Trina's murder was the theft of Milton Jergens' ledgers so that our arsonist could learn the location of that woman's grave. Last night, someone visited the cemetery and dug up the disguised grave location that Milt had written in his ledger's margin. If we had been more open about our efforts and their results, Trina Jergens Danten would still be alive."

"You're probably right, but at least we forced the arsonist into taking action. That dug-up gravesite is now a crime scene. We may learn more about our culprit by examining it."

"I already called Steve, and he's going to take care of evidence-gathering and photography there."

"I understand your feelings, Joe. This is the crummy side of our profession. Sometimes we have to put innocent people into dangerous situations while we're trying to track and trap criminals. If we had publicized our finding of the ring, we would have made identification of the church arsonist much more difficult."

"I know, Penny. We do our job well, but I still hate to see innocent casualties."

"Trina's death has changed our case. The grave dig-up ties her killing to our arsonist's motive – the ring. We can now be certain that our arsonist is also a murderer."

222

CHAPTER 69 – TRINA'S STUFF

Irma thumped down their wooden basement steps to find Arthur stretched out on the concrete floor next to the furnace.

"What happened? Did you fall, or do you just like lying there?"

"It's deliberate; I'm doing routine maintenance on the furnace and air conditioner and checking to see whether we'll need to replace anything soon. However, I am also enjoying lying on a cool concrete floor on a hot day. Feel free to join me."

"That sounds tempting, but I'll have to forego it, and so will you. Joe called and said that he's arranged with the Amboy police for us to have three hours of unsupervised access to Trina's house so that we can search for anything that might impact our case. The police only request that we list and photograph anything we remove. After our three-hour visit, they are going to seal the premises, and future searches will have to be done on a formal permission basis."

Arthur rolled over onto his knees and stood up. "Puttering around in your own house is fun, but I'd much rather search out something that will help solve Trina's murder."

"Oh, I almost forgot to relay what Joe said. It appears that solving Trina's murder will also mean that we solve the arson case. The murderer stole Milt's old ledgers to find the grave location at Binghampton, and dug up the incorrect grave per Milt's disguised location note. He or she didn't know that we'd already been there and had removed the ring. Our theory that the arsonist was after the ring seems to have been confirmed."

223

"Yes, but I'm having trouble getting inside the killer's head. I think the arsonist wanted to get into the church subbasement to look for the location of the ring down there. We found the scrap of wood with the grave coordinates without knowing what valuable thing might be in the warehouse chamber. Why did the arsonist decide to look for the location indicator for that grave in the subbasement, and why kill Trina instead of just breaking into the house and stealing the ledgers when she wasn't home?"

"You're right; those are troubling questions, but let's tackle those after we have our three hours of searching Trina's house. We have a deadline for today's work."

Arthur and Irma parked in Trina Danten's driveway and checked in with the officer guarding the premises. She provided them with a clipboard and a camera for them to use in identifying and photographing all items that they chose to remove. Then she gave them the front door key and returned to her squad car.

Arthur unlocked the door and entered, followed by Irma carrying her portable forensics kit. She knew that crime scene experts had already processed various areas of the house, but she wanted to have tools for handling any unexpected development.

Arthur said, "I'll start in the basement, because I've never been down there. You can join me downstairs or work independently on the main floor."

"The last time we searched a basement together, we got trapped down there. I think I'll stay on the main floor so that we'll be on both levels at the same time. I'll start in the kitchen; look for me there if you need me."

"Why search the kitchen?"

"Women feel most comfortable there, so they store important things in kitchen cabinets and drawers."

"That's good reasoning. Men feel most comfortable in a basement or garage, so that's where I'll look for items that belonged to Rob."

Arthur headed downstairs, and Irma started to scan the contents of every kitchen drawer and cabinet, working methodically from left to right and top to bottom, moving clockwise around the room. It didn't take her long to realize that Trina had been both neat and sparse in what she stored. Irma doubted that she would find anything unexpected, but she continued her deliberate, methodical search.

Upon arriving in the basement, Arthur turned on every light that he could locate and removed two flashlights from his backpack. Then he put on crime scene gloves and started rummaging at random. His search theory was that if he found one interesting item, other related things were likely to surround it. It took a packrat or an antiques dealer's son to sort through an untidy basement.

Arthur's first overall scan revealed that the front half of the basement was neat and utilitarian, with shelving bearing similar-sized items on each level and clotheslines for drying delicate items and special wash. He immediately bypassed the organized areas in favor of the dark corner by the furnace where items were stacked in a disorganized manner floor-to-ceiling or thrown into large plastic bins. This pile had to contain all that remained of Rob Danten's belongings and interests.

Given the neatness of the rest of the house, Arthur saw this collection of objects as Trina's way of separating herself from her dead disobedient husband. She hadn't even stacked his books neatly, showing a lack of respect for the academic life he had chosen. He found copies of Rob and Marie's recently published books and set them aside for removal and study. An old bucket from Kentucky Fried Chicken contained several pocket notebooks; a cigarette lighter; a multi-purpose hand tool; and two box-cutter knives. There were also many smaller miscellaneous items in the bucket, so Arthur decided to take the whole container and examine its contents later. The stack also contained a pair of heavy-duty bolt-cutting pliers. He started to throw a cracked baseball bat back onto the pile, but changed his mind when he saw a stain on it that appeared to be dried blood. As he continued to work through the assortment of items, Arthur scanned the book titles and neatened them up out of veneration for the knowledge they contained. When he came to a Bible that had been similarly mistreated, he set it aside to take, both to protect the sacred text and because people tended to make revealing notes and underlinings in their Bibles. When he had completed his basement search, Arthur carried a large heavy carton upstairs, swiveling his way through the upper doorway to clear the bottom end of the protruding baseball bat.

Irma came out of the kitchen as he placed his carton on the floor by the front door.

"You have a lot more stuff than I do. I'll bring mine out, and then we'll go through the rest of the house together."

"That sounds good to me. Let's wait until we get our goodies home before we discuss them."

"That suggests that you feel you found something significant. I may have a useful thing or two also."

Irma and Arthur worked together in surveying the rest of the house's contents. They enjoyed the joint search process, but found little more of any significance. The one exception was the large envelope that Arthur discovered taped to the bottom of Trina's center desk drawer.

CHAPTER 70 – SAUL'S STUFF

Jefferson Lee locked his office door after packing some seminar notes and memos into his briefcase for homework. His wife, Helen, had gone to spend a week with her parents in Salt Lake City, leaving him a Chicago bachelor. She had encouraged him to go out and do things with his friends, but he felt he'd rather catch up with the tedious side of government work. As Jeff waited for the elevator, Wanda Williams approached him.

"Jeff, are you in a rush? If not, I'd like to fill you in on our findings regarding the items retrieved from Saul Sanders' locked filing cabinet. He had some unexpected things in there."

"Sure, Wanda; I can hang around for a while. Helen's out of town, and I was just planning to spend the evening on paperwork. What's the most unexpected item you found?"

"You won't believe this, but he had a man's below-the-knee prosthetic leg in there. I hope he didn't steal it from someone who needed it." She led him toward the conference room that she and two others had used for examining Saul's archives.

Jeff trailed behind her. "The guy who belongs to that leg must be hopping mad."

"Ooh; bad joke!"

"I realize that, but it was the best I could do on short notice. Who knows? That prosthesis might be significant."

They entered the conference room, and Wanda closed the door.

"We'd better keep our analysis to ourselves. Anything overheard might affect Saul's reputation around here. We owe him that much."

Jeff raised a quizzical eyebrow over her remark. "Meaning that we don't owe him much more than that?"

Wanda's own reputation was that of a brilliant analyst who lived by rules that sometimes coincided with those of the rest of society and sometimes didn't. Her clothes were frequently unique personal innovations, and she had enjoyed living with a long chain of male companions over the years, usually one at a time, but not always.

Jeff scanned Wanda's current attire. She had combined large, round, black-framed glasses with a blue denim work shirt topped by a red patterned silk scarf and paired that upper-body clothing with a wrap-around brown plaid skirt and black penny loafer shoes. He said, "Wanda, would you mind answering a couple of personal questions?"

"Sure, Jeff, ask anything you want."

"Are those glasses strictly for effect? I don't remember ever having seen you wear glasses in the past.

"You caught me; I plead guilty. They're glasses I once wore in a school play – just window glass. It was too many years ago. Do you like the style?"

"They're a little out of date, but they look good on you. My other personal question concerns your relationship with Saul Sanders. Were you two ever an item?"

"That is a bit personal, but I don't mind. Saul moved in with me from July of 2003 until May of 2004. We had some fun, but he was too secretive about what he did when he was away from me. I understood what *need-to-know* meant. We both worked for Secret Service. I just wondered whether he went off to have kinky sex with someone else, or if he robbed banks in his spare time. I couldn't be comfortable with him. On the other hand, I could enjoy time with you, Jeff, if you wanted a fling."

"Sorry, Wanda; I'm married to both my wife and the job; I couldn't handle anything else right now."

"You can handle me whenever you're ready, Jeff."

"That's tempting. Right now, let's get back to Saul's behavior. Did he mention anyone he was meeting when he wasn't with you?"

"You have to be kidding. That was a long time ago. Why don't you come out and say what you really mean? Are you looking for his sex contacts or the gangsters he knew?"

"Did you know his gangster contacts?"

"I knew a few, like Manny Roder, Howie Schultz, and Vito Marino."

"Was he friends with them?"

"I guess he must have been. They played poker at least once a month. I could tell how he did at the game by his disposition with me the next day. Saul was a moody guy when he didn't have to hide behind the cautious investigator mask he wore at work. You probably didn't ever notice his moods; he could be mean."

"That's useful information, Wanda."

"I could give you more useful information if you came home with me."

Jeff stared at her. After a pause, he said, "Tell me about the interesting things Saul had locked up."

"Whatever you like, Jeff; I already mentioned the artificial leg."

"Speaking of that, doesn't Manny Roder wear one of them?"

"Past tense, please, Jeff; Manny died before Saul did. I'd heard that he had a leg replacement due to a war injury, but I never saw it. We weren't that close."

"That's interesting; I mean Manny's leg and time of death, not that you weren't sleeping with him."

Wanda pouted. "I don't sleep with everyone who comes along."

"I didn't mean it that way. I'm sorry.'

"You're forgiven. Getting back to work, I also found the silk scarf I'm wearing. It was too high a quality to throw away with his other junk. He had books written by Rob

229

Danten and Marie Chance, and a box of twenty-dollar bills that turned out to be counterfeit. Based on their poor quality, I think he stole those bills from the inventory you recovered from that print shop in Maine."

"That's an interesting development. Did you find anything else that might tie Sanders to the mob?"

"I always looked at Saul as a paper-pusher and not a field agent. In all the months he lived with me, I never saw him go out on a risky assignment, undercover or otherwise. Yet, he had six pistols of different types and matching ammunition in his file drawers. None of those weapons was official issue. They were all street types. My guess is that he took guns from the evidence locker. Either that, or he bought them on the black market."

"Saul didn't confide in anyone. I wonder what he planned to do with those weapons."

"There are some old photographs you can study. They didn't mean anything to me."

"I'll do that. Thanks for all the help."

Wanda repeated her pouting expression. "Will you at least say thanks by buying a girl a beer?"

"That's only fair. Where would you like to go?"

"Let's try Shorty's; it's one of my favorite bars."

"Great; we'll both drive. I'll follow you. In case we get separated in traffic, where is it located?

"You can't miss it. Shorty's is a big place in Wrigleyville. It's a block and a half from my apartment."

CHAPTER 71 – DISCOVERIES

Arthur rose from the kitchen table and made a circular massage motion over his stomach. "That was exceptional pizza, Irma. You make it better than any of the restaurants around here."

"Thank you, food fan. I use a secret ingredient in a crust recipe given to me by my father. He swore me to secrecy about it, so don't try to make me tell you."

"I won't, but I'll comment that your father must have had some Irish ancestors."

"That's enough of your shrewdness. Let's apply your insights to the collection of items we brought back from Trina's house. Some of them roused my curiosity. You probably found some surprises too."

"I did, and I have to admit that some of the objects proved my shrewdness needs a tune-up. I was wrong earlier, in accepting too many of the things that Trina told me as being correct."

"Before you judge yourself, let's clear the table and lay out all of our scavenged items for discussion."

They removed all of the dinner residuals, wiped down the rugged wooden tabletop, and brought in the cartons of items they had retrieved from Trina's house. Then they spread out the various objects to cover the entire table. The finished result resembled a booth display at a flea market.

On Arthur's side was the old Kentucky Fried Chicken bucket, now sitting empty, surrounded by all the things that had been inside it. He also had the cracked baseball bat, a Bible, Rob's and Marie's published books, some tools, and a photograph album.

On Irma's side of the table, she had laid out several wall calendars for different years, three photograph albums, a Jerbit Disposal Company keychain, and a green address book.

In the middle of the table sat the large envelope Arthur had found taped to the bottom of Trina's center desk drawer.

Arthur smiled at Irma and bowed. "Just to show you that chivalry isn't completely dead, I'll let you open the envelope that has intrigued both of us since we found it."

"I'll acknowledge that you found it. I'll also graciously accept your offer and will take the first view of its contents."

Irma slit open the flap of the envelope and peeked inside. Then she slid something out and stared at it intently.

"Are you planning on sharing your prize with me, or do I have to wait for a complete laboratory analysis?"

"Sorry, Arthur, the object took me by surprise, and I felt the need to study it." She rotated the object she had removed from the envelope so that Arthur could see it.

"I see what you mean. Milton Jergens took a photograph of the ring lady before he had her buried. She looks beautiful, and she's laid out in the coffin with her hands crossed so that the ring is centered in the picture."

"Even though it's a picture of her after death, I feel better for having seen her in her original condition, rather than just the version of her body I saw many decades later."

"I have to agree with you, Irma, even though I believe and teach that after death, the physical body loses its importance. The eternal soul is what's essential."

"Someday, we'll have to analyze and debate the eternal characteristics of the soul, but not right now. We have a case to solve – pragmatism trumps philosophy."

"It does in most instances. Turning to the practical aspect of the ring lady's photograph, I wonder who taped it to the bottom side of that drawer, and whether Trina knew about it."

Implications

"I'll add the question of whether Rob knew about it before he died. The answers to these questions may alter the way we regard several people."

"As one who grew up surrounded by antiques, I'm sure that Trina's desk is old enough to have been inherited from her grandfather. Milt Jergens could have placed the envelope there and forgotten about it. Either that, or he may have wanted to hide the photograph, the way he hid her body in an unmarked grave."

Irma examined the envelope. "From a forensics point of view, I'd say that this envelope is old enough for it to have belonged to Milt. The more interesting question concerns the nature of the tape used to fasten the envelope to the bottom of the drawer. Tape has changed greatly over the years, and some adhesives fail after a relatively short time."

"Believe it or not, I have an answer for you. You probably noticed that there is no adhesive residue on the envelope. That's because the person who did the taping job wanted to protect the envelope and photograph. The tape used was cotton-backed military-grade duct tape from sometime during or slightly after the Second World War. They changed the manufacturing materials and techniques for duct tape shortly after that period. The person who mounted the envelope under the drawer used duct tape in a Tic-Tac-Toe pattern. The portions of the tape that touched the envelope were not adhesive, because he or she stuck two lengths of tape together, face-to-face in the envelope area, so that only the tape backing touched the envelope, cradling it, while the tape extending beyond the envelope in each direction had adhesive facing the metal drawer bottom."

Irma nodded. "That's a pretty strong case for Milt being the person who hid the envelope there. He would have been active in the middle of the twentieth century, and Trina and Rob had not yet been born."

"When I found the envelope, I checked for stray adhesive on the drawer. If someone had removed the envelope and remounted it, the alignment would probably have been slightly different. I didn't see any misalignment marks, so I think that we're the first two people to see this picture since Milton Jergens hid it under his office desk drawer. Trina saved her grandfather's desk because he was her hero."

"In other words, we've opened a time capsule. That's awesome, to use a modern expression."

"If our conclusions are correct, it also says that neither Trina nor Rob knew about this photograph. Let's look at some of the other items we retrieved from Trina's house."

Irma took one final look at the woman's picture before returning it to the envelope. "I'm putting her away, but I have a feeling that she resembles someone I've seen. I'll give her face some more thought later."

Arthur took a piece of clothesline rope from a drawer in one of the counters, and looped it in an irregular pattern to enclose the Kentucky Fried Chicken bucket and the objects that had been stored inside it. "Let's look at Rob's bucket of goodies. They may reveal something useful."

Arthur picked up one of the pocket notebooks and started flipping through it. He paused at three widely separated pages. Then he flipped through the second and third volumes.

Irma asked, "Are you going to share the contents of those notebooks with me?"

"I am, indeed. These little notebooks are not what they seem. They resemble academic composition books, but they're actually full of love letters and photographs exchanged between Marie and Rob. He has one book given to him by Marie, one that he had prepared to give her, and one in which he had written his speculations about her death."

"The one from her must be the oldest, since she would have had to be alive to give it to him. He would have completed the one he prepared for her at about the time of her murder. Presumably, she died before he could deliver it to her. The final one suggests that he didn't kill her, because he was trying to figure out who did."

"I agree. Rob had to have some detective skills because of the way he developed his book. He managed to trace the growth of hidden amateur distilling groups during Prohibition and learned about the bootleggers' smuggling techniques."

"Let me see that notebook that Marie assembled."

Arthur flipped through it briefly before handing it to her.

"Marie was quite attractive and dressed stylishly without being formal or showy. I can see how Rob would have taken to her as they worked together at Northern Illinois University."

"Take a look at the back end of that notebook. I didn't read everything, but I glimpsed a passage where she indicated that she felt uncomfortable about someone she had met."

Irma searched through the notebook. "I have it. She doesn't include a name. 'I don't know how to take him. When I offered him something to help his group, he wanted to know what was in it for him. Maybe he only pretends to like his job. He wants a personal pay-off. I hope he's not holding out for sex. I couldn't take that. Rob, you're the only man for me.' She wouldn't be the first woman to worry whether working with a male stranger would lead to forced sex."

Arthur picked up the notebook that Rob had created for Marie, and turned to its final entries. "Let's see what Rob was thinking as he finished his notebook and prepared to give it to Marie. Listen to this. 'I hate to see you being so tense and upset. I'll help you through any difficult situations. We could even leave town and live together someplace else.'"

"Marie definitely thought she faced problems."

He nodded agreement. "She did. Somebody murdered her."

"Arthur, did you notice the writing underneath the rim of that chicken bucket?"

"It says 'stuff from Marie's place'. We're not the only ones looking for clues from items found at a murder scene."

Irma frowned. "I'm surprised the police let Rob gather up this stuff, especially if they thought he had murdered Marie."

"He may have scooped it up before the police arrived, but that would place him at the crime scene immediately after the murder, which sounds incriminating."

The telephone rang, and Irma left to answer it in the front room. Arthur could hear only muffled bits of the conversation, but it was enough to convince him that something significant had happened.

Irma returned to the kitchen three minutes later. "We'll have to finish sifting through our trophies later. That was Lorna Dyner on the phone. She said she went back to the Amboy church to scavenge any remaining useful items, and she found Dennis Mikken lying in the basement, unconscious. She also said the subbasement entrance was open, but that she hadn't gone down there. She's waiting for the paramedics now. We'd better get over there."

CHAPTER 72 – AMBOY UMC

By the time the Blakes arrived at the burned-out church, the paramedics had already taken Dennis Mikken to the hospital for treatment of the gash in his head. They found Lorna Dyner leaning against her car's right front fender in the church parking lot when they arrived.

Arthur approached Lorna. "How's Dennis? Was he able to give you any details about what happened to him?"

"He said that when he went into the main basement to take some additional photographs for his final report, he found the entrance to the subbasement open. He had previously moved most of the contents of that room to a warehouse, but he found the little that remained ransacked and scattered all over the place. He said he took a few pictures down there and then came back up to the main level. As soon as he reached the upper basement, someone hit him from behind. I discovered him lying unconscious near the access panel to the lower chamber."

Irma asked, "What prompted you to come here today, Lorna?"

"I stop by about once a week to search for items we'll be able to use in the rebuilt church and just because I feel responsible for this place. They're still paying me to take care of our members, and I'm nominally in charge of what remains of the building."

Arthur said, "It was lucky for Dennis that you chose today to come. I wish I had definite news as to whether the Conference will fund the rebuilding of this church, but the Bishop and his Cabinet members haven't reached a decision. You and the Amboy Church members will have to remain in limbo for a while longer."

"We can handle that, Arthur. Thanks for your help in promoting our cause. I'm glad I was here to call the paramedics, but I didn't see anyone other than Dennis."

"We'll look around the place for evidence, and then we'll check in with Dennis to see how he is. Thanks for calling us."

Lorna picked up a cardboard box half-filled with small objects. She shook hands with them and climbed into her car with her box.

After Lorna left, Irma approached Arthur so that he would be able to hear her when she spoke softly. "What do you think about Lorna's happening to come here right after someone attacked Dennis?"

"I get your point, and I agree with you. Neither one of us is comfortable with coincidences."

"I'll also point out that she and her youth group were in this church just before the fire started, and that she returned here to witness the fire before we arrived following the Bishop's summons."

"I'll add to that the standard police mantra that the culprit will be someone who had means, motive, and opportunity. She definitely had the opportunity because she was here. Almost anyone would have the means, because the arsonist set the fire with gasoline. What was her motive?"

"Do you remember that when we studied that photograph of the ring lady in her coffin before burial, I said that she had a slight resemblance to someone I had seen?"

"Yes."

"I've now sorted my memories, and I'm convinced that Lorna Dyner is one of the two people I've seen who remind me of the ring lady."

"One of the two people ...?"

"Yup."

CHAPTER 73 – PENNY AND JOE

Steve DuBois had returned to Washington to take charge of a new case. It had stemmed from a White House staffer's need for confidential background information on potential appointees. The Agency run by Penny and Joe was ideal for handling such politically sensitive matters because it didn't have an official name and didn't appear on any government organization chart. Steve had been more than happy to take on this Washington assignment because he would be able to spend time with his family. Ellen and Eric had left for their new DC apartment one week after the Blakes' housewarming party, and their absence had begun to burden Steve as he continued to work on the Amboy Church arson case.

Steve's departure gave Penny and Joe the opportunity to spend more time together. They took the day off and went to Starved Rock State Park for sightseeing and horseback riding on wilderness trails. When they returned home to Parkville in the early evening, their muscles ached, but their brains operated at peak efficiency, freed by intense physical activity from the cobwebs associated with long meetings and paperwork. They fired up the barbecue and lounged on their backyard deck with beers and hot dogs.

Penny leaned back in her chair and raised her legs to exercise them with scissor-kicks. "This day has been special. We need more active breaks."

"It was unique because we've been sedentary lately. Our current case hasn't had us traveling as much as usual."

"Speaking of our cases, have you noticed that when Arthur involves us in a seemingly straightforward assignment, it always leads to complications and spinoff investigations?"

"Our friend is talented that way."

"In our present case, we signed on to see whether the church arson had interstate connections. We're still working to solve that crime, but in the meantime, we've arrested Mandy Miller for murders in both Illinois and Italy. We also have to investigate the murders of Marie Chance, Rob Danten, and Saul Sanders because they connect to the Amboy Church and its burning."

"Don't forget the ring lady and the guy who ended up sharing her coffin."

"Do we have to solve those too? They died in 1928."

"There's no statute of limitations for murder, but they're only peripherally connected to the church and its arson demise. We could get lucky and solve those crimes for extra credit, but they're not part of our main assignment."

"You could say the same for those two Prohibition Era skeletons in that subbasement warehouse."

"Affirmative ... and we can add the attack on Dennis Mikken yesterday."

"I almost forgot about that one. That's a direct consequence of the arson investigation. At least he's still alive."

"I checked, and he's doing well at the hospital. You're correct, Penny. We have a messy case involving more than one killer and other kinds of criminals as well. Let's get everyone together and see whether we can solve one or more of these crimes by comparing our individual findings. I'll make some calls and send out emails while you relax and enjoy lounging out here."

"How come I get a free pass, Joe?"

"You earned that pass when you and Steve got Mandy Miller to confess to her two murders."

CHAPTER 74 – CONFERENCE PART 1

They had decided to hold the results-sharing conference at Secret Service headquarters in Chicago. Jefferson Lee, as host, would act as the moderator. To keep logistics simple, Jeff requested that those attending bring documents and photographs of physical objects, but not the objects themselves.

The group assembled at 9:00 a.m. in the main Secret Service conference room. Joe and Penny Gonzalez arrived first, followed by Arthur and Irma Blake, and then Celia Masters, taking the place of the injured Dennis Mikken. Jeff Lee introduced the visitors to Wanda Williams whom he had invited to represent the in-house team investigating aspects of Saul Sanders' work.

After everyone had taken drinks and selected their seats around the table, Jeff reviewed the agenda of the meeting.

"Whenever you try to solve a murder or other crime that occurred in the past, you have to work from fragmentary circumstantial evidence and documents left behind by those who are no longer available for interviews. Because we represent different agencies and points of view, Joe Gonzalez and I thought that it would be useful to compare the evidence that we have individually uncovered up to this point. We'll concentrate on the murders of Marie Chance, Rob Danten, and Saul Sanders, but we'll allow the discussion to expand to other topics and crimes whenever it appears valuable to do so. Who would like to volunteer to speak first?"

Irma gestured with a slight wave of her right hand; Jeff nodded and took his seat.

"As most of you know, my specializations are forensics and pathology. Because of that, I tend to notice details of

241

interest, even when they seem to be irrelevant. Jeff asked us to bring documents and photographs to enhance our oral accounts of our investigations." She withdrew something from a large shoulder-carried fabric bag. "We found this notebook, which resembles a miniature school composition book, in a pile of Rob Danten's things that had been shoved into a corner of Trina's basement. Trina probably would have discarded it if she had read it and discovered that its author had been Rob's mistress, Marie Chance. The notebook contains love messages and diary notes that Marie wanted to share with Rob. It also contains several photographs of Marie wearing some of her favorite outfits. Two of those pictures show Marie wearing the same red accent scarf that our colleague, Wanda Williams, is wearing today. I'd like to ask Wanda where she obtained that."

Irma passed the notebook around the table and listened to the resulting murmured comments.

Joe asked, "How do you know that's the same scarf, Irma? It could just be a duplicate of it."

"Men absorb the overall impression of a woman's outfit without examining it in detail. If you look closely at the photograph of Marie, you'll see that she cut off most of the label because it stuck out and ruined the soft lines of the scarf. Wanda's scarf has that same cut-off label. Only a quarter-inch of the label remains attached to it. The scarf is very stylish."

Wanda stood and pivoted so that everyone could see the scarf and its stubby label. "I'm impressed by your observation capabilities, Irma, and I thank you for your compliment on my outfit. I found this silk scarf in a locked cabinet containing Saul Sanders' belongings. I borrowed it because it appealed to my sense of fashion. I admit that I technically tampered with evidence, but I didn't expect it to be an important item."

Penny stood and walked over to examine the scarf, which Wanda had untied and removed from around her neck.

"Wanda, I'll agree that it's stylish, but it may have less appeal for you when you consider that this scarf may have been the weapon that killed Marie. She was strangled, and the scarf shows signs of having been stretched to the point that the weave is not even in both directions, and there is a slight tear along one edge."

Wanda took the scarf from Penny and held it gingerly as she peered at it. "If that's the case, how did it get into Saul's locked file?"

Jeff said, "I can only suggest that he kept it as a trophy. He was a womanizer, but until now, I thought he was a harmless one."

Arthur gestured for attention. "My first instinct as a pastor is to caution you that the scarf could have been a romantic trophy without being the murder weapon. However, I'll have to bear witness against my own cautionary statement. Now that Irma has identified that scarf as Marie's, I'll add that Rob Danten had retrieved a fried chicken bucket full of miscellaneous items taken from Marie's house shortly after her murder. One of those items was a cigarette lighter with the inscription SAS."

Wanda said, "I don't think that was Saul's. His middle initial was M. Isn't that right, Jeff?"

"His middle initial was M, but he was born in England, and he served in the Special Air Service, SAS, over there – he was an air commando - before he came to America. When you get home and have that lighter, Arthur, turn it over to see whether the SAS Sword and wings insignia is engraved on the other side of it."

"That's not a problem, Jeff. The lighter is so small that I disobeyed your documents-only instructions and dropped it into my pocket." He reached into his left pants pocket and retrieved a silver object. "It does have the sword and wings emblem, but it's almost worn off. I'd say that Saul considered this his special charm and rubbed it for good luck on a regular basis."

Arthur passed the lighter around the table for all to see.

When it reached him, Jeff examined the lighter and then said, "We're making progress. We'll never know exactly what happened, but in summary of our findings so far, we know that Saul had Marie's red silk scarf, the probable murder weapon, and that he lost his favorite cigarette lighter at her house around the time of her death. Rob retrieved a group of items from Marie's house, including Saul's lighter, right after she died, but before the police could isolate Marie's house as a crime scene. These facts suggest that Saul murdered Marie shortly before Rob arrived."

Joe waved his hand for attention. "I see some ambiguity in that summary. Rob and Saul could have worked together to kill Marie, since they were both at her house at about the same time."

Jeff said, "Repeating my earlier comment, we'll never know what happened there."

CHAPTER 75 – *MARIE'S HOUSE*

Marie heard a knock on the front door and paused at her full-length mirror for a final inspection before answering it. She straightened her skirt and adjusted the way the ends of her favorite scarf draped down from her neck. Smiling because Rob's early arrival meant he was anxious to see her, she hastened to the front door.

When she opened the door, she discovered Saul Sanders instead of Rob standing there and recoiled slightly.

"Mr. Sanders, what are you doing here?"

"When we met earlier, I said that we should meet again in a more private location to discuss your offer. Your house will give us that privacy."

Marie didn't like his aggressive tone. "I don't use my home as a meeting place for business matters, and this isn't a convenient time anyway. I'm expecting company."

Saul said, "This won't take long." He sneered as he prepared to light a cigarette.

Marie's right hand lashed out and batted Saul's lighter across the floor and through the railing surrounding the basement staircase. "I told you no cigarettes if we met another time. You'll never blow smoke in my face again."

"I admire spunkiness in a woman. I decided our meeting should be at your house because I'm willing to do as you requested in exchange for some bedroom time with you. I'm here to collect my price."

Marie would not be a pushover for this beast. "That's it; you get the hell out of here and out of my life right now, or I'll sic my dog on you."

Saul moved toward her, but turned his head to look for a dog. He heard noises on the basement stairs and pivoted to face a large golden retriever that had sensed the anger in his master's voice.

She meant what she had said. "Rex, attack him! Attack!"

Saul sidestepped as the dog charged. He delivered a vicious karate blow to the side of the dog's neck and followed it rapidly with a second blow to the back of the neck. The dog faltered and collapsed. A moment later, Saul collapsed alongside Rex. Marie stood over the two of them holding a bloody and cracked baseball bat that she had retrieved from its hiding place behind the couch. The bat had been a gift from Rob to serve as emergency protection. Marie dropped the bat and knelt beside her loyal Rex to comfort him as he fought to move. She disregarded her unwelcome visitor and wept.

A few minutes later, she felt pressure around her throat and grabbed her scarf to prevent it from cutting into her windpipe. Saul's bloody face appeared as she turned her head to see what was happening to her. He had pulled himself up to a kneeling position and had grabbed her scarf. She felt him place his knee against her back for additional leverage as he pulled hard on the scarf. She felt a snap as something in her spine shifted. She gagged and fell forward as the decorative knot in the scarf came untied. The shuddering Rex licked her face twice.

Marie's back hurt, and she despite several tries, she couldn't raise her body off the floor. She felt the scarf encircle her neck once more. This time there was no release, only a transition to black as she prayed that Rex would survive.

Sanders struggled to his feet, stuffed the scarf into his back pocket, kicked the dog twice, and headed for the door. She had said something about expecting company. He'd nurse his head wound somewhere else.

CHAPTER 76 – CONFERENCE PART 2

After a coffee break, Jeff Lee called the conference back into session. "Before the break, we reached a tentative conclusion that Saul Sanders probably murdered Marie Chance, although we didn't get too far on pinning down his motive. Let's continue now by asking who killed Saul and Rob. Irma, you did a great job of starting the discussion of Marie's murder. How about starting us off again?"

"I'll be happy to do so, Jeff. My initial question concerns the timeline. Who died first, Rob or Saul?"

Penny turned several pages in her notebook. "My records show that they died only about three months apart, but that Saul died before Rob."

Arthur said, "Then we have to conclude that Rob could have killed Saul, but that Saul could not be Rob's murderer."

Jeff turned toward Arthur. "Why should we consider Rob as possibly behind Saul's death? Your earlier notes indicated that Trina refused to believe that her husband Rob could be a violent person."

"Rob would have looked for revenge if he knew or suspected that Saul had killed Marie. We don't have any evidence to confirm what Rob knew. He did have a bloody, cracked baseball bat among his possessions. Regardless of who wielded that bat, we should check the blood DNA to see whether it matches Saul's."

Jeff said, "Let me remind you that someone beat Saul to death, apparently without using a weapon of any kind. Do we have any evidence that Rob had fitness or martial arts training?"

Penny consulted her notebook again. "Our background notes indicate that Rob Danten served in the

Army for two years in the Judge Advocate General's Corps as a Paralegal Specialist. He wouldn't have served in a hand-to-hand combat assignment, but he would have had the training to defend himself."

Jeff nodded. "I won't debate the point further. With that background, he had the capability to slug it out with an enemy, even if he wouldn't normally have expected a physical confrontation. Is his possession of Saul's lighter enough evidence to conclude that Rob believed Saul had killed Marie? Don't forget that the police suspected Rob of Marie's murder, and they were monitoring his activities."

Arthur said, "I'll respond to that one. Remember that the organization keeping track of Rob's movements was a small-town police force with a limited number of officers. He could have evaded their eyes easily. They certainly wouldn't have followed him to Indiana where Saul died."

Wanda jumped up from her seat and raised her hand. "Saul knew all about Rob, even if the reverse wasn't true. His records show that he assigned two agents to learn all they could about Marie Chance and her associates. They even had pictures of Rob and Marie making out in his car in a Northern Illinois University parking lot."

Joe Gonzalez asked, "Why was Saul in Indiana at the time of his death anyway? Was he on assignment there?"

Wanda stood again to respond. "I'll take that question. Saul's long-term job was tracking organized crime people and their activities. At the time of his death, he had initiated a study to determine whether gambling interests had infiltrated auto racing and might be rigging races. He was in Indiana to study aspects of the Indianapolis 500 organization and race. He didn't come up with anything conclusive, but he told me that he got to know several drivers and mechanics."

Arthur asked, "Would Rob Danten have known of Saul Sanders' location in Indiana at that time? It would be more likely that Sanders angered a gambler by asking too many pointed questions. If Rob wanted to kill Saul, why would he do it in Indiana?"

Jeff said, "Lack of communication among small town police departments so that they wouldn't know his whereabouts is one possible answer. Does someone have an additional thought on that subject? Yes, Celia; we haven't heard from you until now."

"You haven't heard from me because I've been wondering why I'm even here. My department is working to solve the arson destruction of the Amboy Church, and you folks are working on three unrelated murders. Even so, I may have something to contribute. There are some bad dudes living across the line in northwest Indiana, and they'll act against your enemy for a lot less than a hired gun in the Chicago area. They're also harder for the police to track. This Rob guy could have been watching Sanders travel back and forth to Indiana, and could have arranged for a hit on him while he was there. It wouldn't have been hard to have someone track Sanders' car from the border."

"That's a good point Celia. Whether it was the mob or a hit man hired by Rob, Saul Sanders' killer could have been someone paid to do the job. There's no indication in the case file that Saul fought his attacker. His death may have been an execution."

"Jeff, in our earlier discussions, there was some speculation that Saul's monitoring of the mob's activities may have led him to get close to some of its members and collude with them on criminal projects. How does Secret Service respond to that line of thinking?"

"We hadn't planned to discuss that, Joe, but this conference is aimed at revealing everything. We've had the same suspicions, and perhaps some evidence, that Saul wasn't clean. We don't think that the mob paid him to do its bidding, but rather that Saul paid a few of his gangster contacts to do his own dirty work. Sanders may have run a mini-mob of his own."

Arthur leaned forward. "If that was the situation, one of Sanders' thugs may have turned on him or may have had orders to do so from a mob boss. There's a good probability that Saul's death had nothing to do with Marie's murder or Rob Danten."

Jeff said, "Unless we get an unexpected clue or confession from someone arrested for a different crime, we won't know for sure. We have enough evidence to consider Saul Sanders' career with Secret Service a dishonorable one. You may be right in your suggestions of a paid or professional murderer, but my gut tells me that Rob Danten had a major motive if he knew that Saul killed Marie, and I'll wager that he acted upon it."

CHAPTER 77 – *ROB DANTEN*

I'm in real trouble. Somebody strangled Marie to death, and the police think I did it. Why would I kill her? I loved Marie, and even if we had broken up, there wouldn't have been a need for murder; we would have just gone our separate ways. This is crazy.

What's even worse than crazy is that I'm all alone now. I can't talk to Trina about Marie and her death. I hope that Trina believes me when I tell her and the police I didn't do it. Maybe she'll be afraid of me and will think I might kill her. How did I get into this mess?

Marie said that she was going to publish that list I found about mob descendants and where they live. She said that for insurance, she would give a reliable person the key to finding the list in her book. Why didn't I ask who that was? She mentioned Secret Service, so it could have been someone there. If I knew that person's name, I'd have someone to talk with about Marie's murder. I'll miss her, but even more, I'll miss being able to do what I want without people suspecting me of being a murderer. I can't even buy things at a hardware store without other shoppers suspecting me of buying weapons of some sort. Some of those mean folks are church people too. They're not supposed to judge others, but they do turn against you at the first hint of suspicion. I'm tainted, bad news for anyone who talks to me. People will think anyone who associates with me is guilty of something. Are all of us that stupid? Yes, there have been times when I subscribed to unproven nasty rumors. I'm getting what I deserve, but that doesn't make me feel any better.

How can I convince the police I'm innocent? Maybe I should try investigating the case myself. I doubt that I have any special talent as a private eye, but at least it would give me something to do while others shun me. The bloody bat and other things I found at Marie's house might help. Marie hadn't been hit with a bat, so she must have used it to fight back against her killer. I should look for someone who knows how to find someone from DNA evidence – if I can do that without facing an evidence tampering charge.

Trina says she believes me, but she wants me to move out of our house anyway. She says my moving out is punishment for taking up with Marie in the first place. Life would have been so much simpler if I hadn't touched the forbidden fruit. Please, let me back into Eden, God.

If I'm going to be a detective, where do I start? Marie gave me a copy of her book. I could search it for where she inserted that list of names and places. Maybe she left a clue in there regarding the identity of her reliable person. Maybe I'll still be able to make that connection. I'll try. That makes me feel better already. I have something useful to do. I wonder whether her friend is a guy or a girl.

CHAPTER 78 – CONFERENCE PART 3

Jeff Lee reconvened the meeting after the second coffee and restroom break. "We all now realize how difficult it is to reconstruct past events based on fragmentary evidence. We are confident about the correctness of our conclusion that Saul Sanders murdered Marie Chance. We are not as certain regarding the manner in which Saul Sanders died. We have questions as to whether Sanders died at the hands of Rob Danten, seeking revenge for Marie, or whether a mob hit man or a paid street thug killed him. For now, we'll have to live with that ambiguity. Our third and final case study for today concerns the death of Rob Danten, three months after Saul Sanders died. At the time, local police assumed that Rob had killed Marie and that his one-car accident was actually a suicide provoked by his guilt feelings. We are now sure Rob didn't kill Marie. Was his death an accident, suicide, or murder? Start us off, Arthur."

"If Rob Danten believed that Saul had killed Marie, he would have felt relieved after Saul died, regardless of the identity of the perpetrator. Rob had also moved back into his home with Trina, so he would have felt good about that. I see no reason for him to have committed suicide."

Irma said, "It could have been a simple accident. Your notes indicate that Trina said it was a foggy night. My problem with the accident theory is that his death so soon after that of Saul Sanders suggests a coincidence, and I don't like coincidences."

Arthur said, "Let's try a totally different theory. Rob and Trina had Milt Jergens' photograph that he took of the dead ring lady prior to her burial. Irma and I earlier assumed that they didn't realize it was there because of the neatness of the tape that secured it to the bottom of

Milt's old desk drawer. Suppose Rob had discovered and studied it, but then returned it to its hiding place with careful tape repositioning. He might have shown that picture to someone, and that person might have decided to go after the ring shown in the picture."

Celia said, "You mean he may have shown it to the arsonist. At last, we're discussing something that gives me a reason for being here. If the arsonist burned the church to find the ring location information stored in the bootlegging warehouse, he or she would have needed to know about that subbasement and the fact that it contained the gravesite data."

Penny stood to get attention. "Hold it. If the arsonist knew the warehouse chamber contained grave location information, he or she already knew about the ring and wouldn't have had to see the photograph."

Arthur said, "Good point, Penny; perhaps the arsonist knew about the ring but didn't realize how spectacular it was before seeing the picture."

Jeff Lee interrupted. "I'm supposed to be coordinating our discussions, so I have to point out that we've gone away from our assigned topic of Rob Danten's death. If we can get back to that issue, I promise I'll extend the meeting to continue these arsonist discussions later. Who has something to contribute pertinent to Rob's death?"

Jeff received nothing but silence for a few minutes. Then Wanda stood up and started to walk down her side of the table.

"Forgive my pacing, but it helps me think. I didn't know much about Rob Danten prior to this meeting, but if his death was a murder, the killer had to have a motive. From what I've heard today, Rob had interpersonal connections with only two of the people we've discussed after Marie and Saul had died. He was married to Trina, and he may have shown the ring lady's death picture to the arsonist. Unless we introduce other connections for Rob, Trina and the unidentified arsonist would be our prime suspects for his killing." Wanda made a hand gesture to indicate she had made her point, and sat down.

Irma was the first to react. "I like your thinking, Wanda. I see no immediate reason for Trina to have killed the husband she had campaigned to get back. She had even gained stature in the community by defending him against police suspicions that he had murdered Marie."

Jeff said, "Then by Wanda's logic, the arsonist would by the most likely person to have killed Rob. What's the motive there?"

Joe stood up. "I like this idea of standing to speak; we've sat for most of the day. Let's backtrack a bit. Arthur gave us the *what-if* of Rob having shown the arsonist the ring lady's photograph. I know how Arthur thinks, and I'll suggest that he did that to expand the possibilities that we're considering. We have absolutely no evidence of a connection between Rob Danten and the arsonist. Therefore, I would like you to consider the theory that Rob's one-car crash was an accident and nothing more." He sat down, pleased by the amount of murmuring he'd stimulated.

Arthur raised his hand for attention, "I'm not sure I agree that Joe knows how I think, but I do agree with him that we don't have a strong case for ruling Rob's death a homicide."

Jeff said, "Fair enough; unless someone wants to continue the argument that Rob's death was a murder, I'll drop that subject and return to the question of the arsonist's identity. I haven't been as close to the Amboy Church case as some sitting here. Who will summarize the status of the arson case?"

Celia said, "That would be my ball of wax. We know that the arsonist burned the Amboy church using gasoline as an accelerant and setting fires in the sanctuary by the altar and in the basement below the rear of the sanctuary. We discovered the bootlegging warehouse chamber in the subbasement after removal of the burnt basement carpeting. You are all aware of the bodies found in the warehouse chamber. I won't discuss them at this time because I doubt that they will help us identify the arsonist. To date, our most likely scenario is that the perpetrator burned the church to gain access to the warehouse chamber in order to find gravesite location information hidden there. That information would allow him or her to unearth the coffin of a woman buried in 1928 with an extremely expensive ring on her finger. That ring was the arsonist's pot of gold at the end of the rainbow."

Penny said, "We should add that the perpetrator is dangerous and far more than an arsonist, having tried to kill Irma and Arthur Blake by imprisoning them in the subbasement warehouse, probably having murdered Trina Danten, and having assaulted Fire Inspector Dennis Mikken. This is a vicious person who needs to be identified and stopped as soon as possible."

Arthur stood, following Joe's earlier example. "I'm not sure I know how Joe thinks, but I'll follow his style and stand to make my point. The murder of Trina Jergens bothers me. I think it may be the key to identifying the arsonist. The person who killed Trina took Milt Jergens' ledgers and used their grave location information to dig up an incorrect grave in Binghampton Cemetery. That suggests that Trina's killer either didn't know about the hidden location information in the warehouse chamber, or couldn't find it."

Penny said, "I'll modify your last alternative and say that the arsonist killed Trina to get Milt's books because the warehouse information was no longer available. The arsonist couldn't get into the subbasement of the church during the days immediately following the fire because outsiders of various sorts occupied the premises continuously. Once the state fire investigators left, after Celia discovered the subbasement entrance, the arsonist tried again, only to find you and Irma exploring the chamber. That's when he or she locked you beneath the hatch, hoping that no one would find you until you'd become additional corpses down there. After you escaped, Dennis Mikken arranged for continuous State Police guarding of the church ruins. Then we found the block of wood with the grave location coordinates, and we took it away with us. The only remaining clue to the ring lady's grave location was in Milt Jergens' old ledgers, so the arsonist had to go after those books."

Irma shook her head. "Penny, I agree with most of your comments, but I have two questions that bother me. First, wouldn't the arsonist have figured out that we had already exhumed the woman's body after we removed the wooden block with her grave location from the warehouse chamber? My second question is even more basic. Why burn the church at all, if Trina had Milt's ledgers with the information? Nobody knew that Milt had encoded that information so that it would lead to an incorrect gravesite."

"Penny, would you mind if I answered Irma's questions?"

"Go ahead Arthur."

"In response to your first question, my guess is that the arsonist didn't expect us to realize the significance of the block of wood from the subbasement. Don't forget that it took us a while to figure out what the markings on the wood meant. Dennis Mikken figured out that the word Binghampton referred to a local cemetery and that the numbers and letters had to be coordinates for the location of a grave there. Going on to your second question, no one except Trina knew that Milt Jergens' ledgers had survived to the present. She knew that her grandfather had wanted to hide them because he kept them under floorboards in his office. She told me that she had never told people that they existed. I asked the right question when I inquired about them, and by that time, I had gained her confidence, so she let me borrow them. My guess is that she would have told a stranger that there were no ledgers."

Irma said, "He did it again. My husband has a way with words. Arthur has just brought us to the conclusion that Trina was murdered by someone she knew. Otherwise, she would have claimed she didn't have any ledgers."

CHAPTER 79 – *RECONCILIATION*

Trina and Rob Danten sat on the patio behind their house trying to decide whether they had a future together. Although she had consigned Rob to a remote apartment, Trina yearned for him to realize that he needed her strength and common sense to regain stability in his life.

"Rob, Marie is gone now. I cursed her many times in the past, even before I learned her name, for stealing your affections from me, but I won't say anything bad about her now that she's dead. The police suspect that you killed her, but I know that you don't have that kind of violence in you. I'll stand by you and accept you back home if you'll promise that you won't dishonor me by taking up with a mistress again. If I'm going to support your innocence with my loyalty, you'll have to swear your fidelity to me, even if you don't love me anymore."

"I do love you, Trina. You give my life stability and direction. I turned to Marie for sexual passion and a different perspective on life, but I know now that passion is dangerous. It can burn everyone it touches and hurt those forced to witness it from the sidelines. I'll come home if you'll have me. Just realize that I'm damaged goods right now. I don't know how long it will take for me to regain my drive, but if you'll settle for a temporary lack of purpose and a drifting outlook, I'm yours again."

"I'm not sure that's enough for me, Rob. We need to be a family again, and not just two individuals living together."

"I do have a suggestion to bring us closer to each other, but I'm not sure you'll go for it; you might even refuse to let me come home for suggesting it."

"Try me."

"Marie's dog, Rex, survived the attack, but just barely. He'll need a lot of care to recover his strength and overcome the trauma of his injuries. If we adopted him, he could bring us closer together, if you wouldn't resent him too much for having belonged to her."

"I'm a sucker for taking in straying husbands and injured animals, but I'll have to give a definite 'yes' to your suggestion. Rex will change the nature of our relationship in ways that neither one of us can predict."

Four months later, Rex had regained his physical skills and stamina and had become an equal partner in the Danten household. Rob had trouble comprehending how close Trina had become to the beautiful golden retriever. On many occasions, he heard her talking to Rex in lengthy one-sided conversations. He had to admit that his own feelings of friendship for the dog had grown, and that it had very little to do with his feelings for Marie.

One Friday, Trina announced that she would be gone for the weekend and that he would have charge of Rex. She told him that she was going off for a *family* gathering. She and Mario Bitoli's grandson, Tony, had plans for an outing to reacquaint themselves with each other and to compare a few of their grandfathers' antique possessions. On Saturday morning, Trina spent several minutes talking to Rex before she left. Rob was pleased to see Trina's enthusiasm about the outing, and he walked with her to Tony's truck. As they walked, he asked where she and Tony would be going. Trina responded that they would be visiting several animal welfare organizations and rural spots in Indiana. She added that Tony had become quite active in the American Society for the Prevention of Cruelty to Animals and that she would soon give Rex to Tony so that Rex would have the companionship of Tony's two other dogs.

CHAPTER 80 – RECOLLECTIONS

During the drive home from the Secret Service conference, Arthur and Irma exchanged comments on everything from their dinner menu to the possibility of a three-day trip to New York City. As frequently happens during such more-or-less-continuous conversations, they suddenly came to a lengthy pause while each digested past comments. Arthur used the pause to express something that had bothered him subconsciously.

"This isn't a double-take, because I've had it in the back of my mind for so long, but I remember your saying that the photograph of the ring lady in her coffin prior to her burial reminded you of two people. You said that one of them was Pastor Lorna Dyner. Who was the other one?"

"I don't really know, but it's time for us to find out. The second person with a resemblance to the ring lady was a young man wearing a baseball uniform in one of Midge Drinkwater's photograph albums. It wasn't a recent picture, so he's probably quite a bit older now."

"Are you saying that you think Midge is involved with the arson and the other crimes?"

"No, Arthur, she's probably completely innocent. This is a rural area with comparatively low population. Midge has ten children, personally and through marriage. Midge is more than ninety years old, so her children and her children's children have their own offspring. With that size family, she may have ties to half the people in the county. When we get home, we'll have to sit down with her and learn more about her family tree."

"From what we've seen so far concerning the descendants of Prohibition Era gangsters and their associates, a lot of the family trees in this area are gnarled and distorted. The biblical quotation about the sins of the fathers being passed down to multiple additional generations definitely applies to the people we've encountered during this investigation."

CHAPTER 81 – FAMILY TREES

Upon their arrival home, Arthur and Irma decided to sit on the porch to enjoy the early evening and the light breeze. After ten minutes of basking in nature, they heard a vehicle coming up the driveway. At first, they thought the white Ford pickup truck belonged to someone making a sales call, but after two minutes of idling, the passenger door opened, and Midge Drinkwater climbed down. She reached back inside to retrieve her cane. Then she used that support to wave goodbye to the driver, a rugged-looking bearded man, as he turned his truck to descend the driveway and depart.

When Midge approached the house, Irma called out, "Midge, we're on the porch. Come sit with us and enjoy this beautiful evening."

Midge used her cane to wave once more and then ascended to the porch using the ramp at its left end instead of the front stairs.

"Hello, you two; I see you're inseparable as always. You're still in the newlywed category. I didn't check with you before, but I'll bet you haven't celebrated your first anniversary yet."

Arthur had stood and pulled a chair over so that they would have a triangular conversation arrangement. He said, "As always, you're right on target, Midge. We have a couple of months to go before our first anniversary."

"Remember to make that date very special, Arthur. I had so many anniversaries with my three husbands that they began to lose their significance."

Irma poured a glass of iced tea for Midge. "If you don't mind, I'd like to hear more about your three husbands and all of your offspring. I'll bet your family reunions are huge."

"We haven't dared to have a complete reunion. There's no place big enough to hold it. Fortunately, some of my kids and their branches of the family have moved to other parts of the country. I hope you two won't brand me a terrible matriarch of my clan, but I don't even try to keep track of the names of my great-grandchildren and their kids. That would be asking a lot of someone my age."

Arthur asked, "Are there any other Drinkwaters around?"

"I'm sure there are, but don't ask me where. My two brothers, Fred and Daniel, have both passed away, but they had two sons each to continue the name. I was the only girl in our family, and my brothers didn't have any girls. Our family genes are definitely biased toward males."

Irma put a yellow legal pad and a pen on the glass-topped coffee table. "Do you think you could draw up at least a partial family tree for us so that we'd have a better understanding of the size and scope of your clan, Midge?"

"I can do better than that, Irma. I have a *cheat sheet* chart down to the level of my grandchildren that I use whenever I have to keep them straight for some event. I let my kids and grandkids remind me of the names of people in the following generations. I have ten children, twenty-eight grandchildren, and God only knows how many great-grandchildren and great-great-grandchildren. It's a very prolific family. Give me a few minutes to find my chart, and I'll bring it back here. While I'm gone, you could hustle up some ice cream for all of us."

Midge headed for the elevator to go upstairs to her apartment, while Irma went to the kitchen to dish out the ice cream as requested. Arthur remained on the porch and pondered what would come of this discussion of Midge's family.

We were hoping to find some connections between members of her family and our investigation, but it appears that any useful information will have to lie among the names of her children and grandchildren, because she claims that she doesn't even know the names of the younger family members. Midge has definitely tried to monitor our discussions about the case; she has a purpose behind her curiosity that must have some connection to our interwoven tapestry of crimes. I hope that her chart will reveal something useful.

Irma returned first with her serving cart bearing three bulk containers of ice cream, dishes, and assorted toppings. Midge entered a few minutes later, carrying a large framed chart.

"Here it is in all its glory. I drew it out by hand with my pen, but I framed it to make it a handy reference."

Arthur said, "You did a great job on it. It's both attractive and useful. Tell us about your three husbands, Midge. I understand you outlived them all."

"That's your pastor side, trying to find a delicate way of putting things. When each of them died, I was a frantic basket case over his passing. My first husband, Bill Picoli, had been my high school sweetheart. We were happy, young, and I was popping out a kid every year. Then World War II started, and Bill decided that he had to get into the action. He was patriotism personified. Anyway, he joined the Marines and served in the Pacific until he died during the assault on Iwo Jima. That chunk of rock in the ocean turned many thousands of loving wives into widows; I guess that was true on the Japanese side too. I was left alone to raise two daughters and a son."

"How long did you remain alone before you remarried?"

"It was just a couple of years, but it felt as though it was much longer. I married Ronald Stacek late in 1946. He had been in the Army in Europe, and one of my friends who worked at the USO in Chicago introduced him to me. Once Jill learned that Ronald was going to study at Northern Illinois University on the G.I. Bill, she figured it would be perfect to pair him up with me. She was right of course. We were married for thirty-one years, and most of them were great. After he finished his business courses, he opened up the only hardware store in Amboy and was very successful. Many of the customers became our friends, and we never lacked for social events to attend. Ron died from a heart attack when he tried to be an over-achiever and open two more stores in nearby towns. He was on the go all the time and couldn't cope with the pace of it. I never did understand why he felt that one store wasn't enough of a challenge."

Irma asked, "How did you meet your third husband?"

"That was really strange. After Ron died, I had to borrow money from the bank to pay off debts on the two new stores that would have to close soon after they had opened. Then I tried running the original store by myself. I could have kept that one going if I didn't have the burden of repaying the loans for the other two places. The bank foreclosed on me and put me out of business. I tried to negotiate my way out of the mess with the bank president. I lost the negotiation, but I ended up marrying the guy who had foreclosed me. Albert Detwiler was a mean bargaining opponent, but he turned out to be a loving husband. He insisted we buy this house and fix it up as our retirement dream home."

"That is a wild set of circumstances, but somehow I feel that it's a match for your adventurous life, Midge."

"Thanks, Irma; my husbands were all special, each in his own way. Our kids all showed character as they grew up, and the same applies to the younger generations. I'm proud of my family, even if I don't brag about them. By now, we include a whole bunch of background nationalities."

Arthur asked, "Would you mind filling us in on your children and their spouses, so that we get a feeling for at least the top level of your clan?"

"With pleasure; I don't get many requests like that. Bill Picoli and I had Edward, who never married. He's the one who'll end up with your Mustang instead of the

Corvette. We also had Sarah, who married George Kubich, and Nancy, who married Walter Himes. My second husband, Ronald Stacek, and I had John, who married Judith Sweeney; Andrew, who married April Warren; and Sylvia, who married Jon Pumphrey. My third husband, Albert Detwiler, brought his own children into the mix. I was way too old to have children by then. The Detwiler brood includes Barbara, who married Frank Blanding; Oscar, who married Esther Perkins; Paul, who married Ruth Wong; and Phyllis, who married Rodney Burns. Barbara's marriage to Frank Blanding was her second marriage. Earlier, she had married Marc Venta. He died in the Vietnam War."

Arthur dropped the pen he had been using to make notes. He tried to cover that sudden action by leaning back and crossing his legs to look casual. He hoped he would sound casual too. "So, Barbara had two husbands; did she have any children with Marc?"

"Marc and Barbara had one son, Newt. He's the man who drove me home tonight. If his schedule hadn't been so tight, I would have invited him to come in, and he would have met you, here on the porch."

Irma placed her pad of paper on the cart. "I'm impressed that you remembered all of those people without even looking at the chart."

"If I try hard, I can remember the twenty-eight grandchildren too, but I probably wouldn't get all the spouses matched correctly without consulting the chart. As I said before, I don't even try to extend my family listings beyond the grandchildren. With few exceptions, I have them clue me in on the younger folks' names at each family gathering."

"I have a question for you, Midge. When we looked over your photograph albums, I noticed some pictures of baseball players. Who were they? They looked athletic and capable."

"I know just the ones you mean, Irma. Our one set of family twins, Larry and Lance Pumphrey, are former professional players. They're identical twins, but they grew up to look quite different. They made it to the Cubs' Iowa farm team, but they never got called up to the Big League team. Even so, they're both proud of their baseball careers. Nowadays, Larry teaches high school physics somewhere in Michigan, and Lance is a cop in Chicago. They both still share similar personalities."

Midge was surprised to see Arthur hold up three fingers for Irma to see.

"Is that a Scout salute, Arthur?"

"I didn't mean to distract you. It's just a private joke. Let's have our ice cream before it melts. Irma brought out lots of goodies for toppings and sauces. After that, we should probably call it an evening. Irma and I have a busy schedule tomorrow."

"I knew that I could still outlast you young people. Make mine two scoops of strawberry with chocolate sprinkles on top."

CHAPTER 82 – SIMILARITIES

As they prepared for bed, Irma gave Arthur a shrewd look. "I caught your three-fingered signal. You were signaling that we have three people who could be related to the ring lady, since the ballplayer whose photo I remembered turns out to be an identical twin. Larry and Lance Pumphrey plus Lorna Dyner are all possible descendants from the ring lady, at least based on the similar facial features of one of the twins."

"I could invite Lorna here for coffee, and you could test the DNA on her coffee cup against the sample you took from the exhumed body. How would we get DNA samples from Larry and Lance for you to test? Larry lives in Michigan."

"Sherlock, you're forgetting your biology. Identical twins have identical DNA. We would only have to test one of them. Lance works as a Chicago cop. It shouldn't be hard to convince his superiors that his DNA test would be relevant to our investigation."

"That would work as long as we didn't have to pronounce him a suspect, because we really don't have anything to connect either twin to the church fire or any of the other crimes we need to solve. I'm sure there are thousands of people who somewhat resemble the pre-burial photograph of our ring lady."

"I'll have to agree with you that testing of the twins should await some significant evidence that they are likely to be involved. However, Lorna Dyner has direct connections to the church fire and other events. She should get a DNA test as soon as possible."

"Agreed, Irma; I'll get her to stop by to discuss our progress on the case tomorrow. Then I'll save her cup with its residuals so that you can test the DNA on and in it."

"You're very cooperative tonight. I think you're hiding something from me."

"Irma, I'm always cooperative with you at bedtime. It's just that I'm beginning to wonder whether the motive for the arson, assaults, and murders was an attempt to get that fancy ring or if it was something else."

"Apparently I missed something during our session with Midge that changed the direction of your thinking. What's the new motive that has grabbed your attention?"

"Revenge is probably the oldest motive there is."

CHAPTER 83 – REVENGE

Irma propped herself up with an extra pillow. "Why is it that our best investigative conversations transpire in bed? Married and dating sleuths are supposed to attend to other things in bed, just as normal people do. Lay your new theory on me, and if it's a good one, we might get normal in a while."

"Let's start back in that subbasement bootlegging warehouse. You'll remember that we searched out that scrap of wood from a liquor crate that had the grave location coordinates on it."

"Sure."

"That piece of cloth wrapping the wood came from the shirt of the male skeletal corpse."

"That's right. I matched it to a photograph I took of his remains."

"And what did you say about the condition of that piece of cloth?"

"I can't remember exactly what I said."

Arthur leaned toward her and gave her a short but loving kiss.

"That was nice. What did I do to deserve it?"

"You may have pointed us in the right direction to finally solve this case. When we discovered that cloth-wrapped piece of wood, you stated that the piece of cloth hadn't deteriorated from contact with the decomposing corpse, so someone must have torn it from his shirt and used it to wrap the wood scrap shortly after he died. I'll guess that someone was his murderer."

"Let me get in on this game. If the murderer tore the shirt from the dead man in order to wrap the grave location scrap, then the male victim died on or very close to the day of the ring lady's burial."

"I'll suggest that both the male and female victims died at the same time because the killer shot them both from the same angle."

Irma showed her excitement by getting off the bed and starting to pace around the room. "They may have been a couple."

"I'll agree with that suggestion. Now, what did we learn from Milton Jergens' ledgers about his staff at that time?"

"His assistant, Sammy, quit, and he had to use his embalmer as the second person to work with his partner, Mario, for the ring lady's burial."

"Bingo! What if Sammy didn't quit, but instead became a permanent resident of the subbasement warehouse?"

Irma stopped pacing and sat on the edge of their bed. "If that's true, and his killer had to know the location of the unmarked grave, the gunman had to be either Milton Jergens or Mario Bitoli. The embalmer probably didn't know much, if anything, about the bootlegging business."

"Milt encoded a slightly disguised version of the grave location into his ledger, so he wouldn't have had to mark it on a piece of wood in the warehouse."

"Our obvious conclusion should be that Mario killed Sammy and his girlfriend and then tore his shirt to get a wrapping cloth for his wooden grave location record."

"I think it all sounds reasonable, but what's your logic for linking these deaths to Midge's family tree and revenge as the motive for the church arson and a bunch of other crimes, including imprisoning us in that warehouse?"

"Do you remember Sammy's last name?"

"I'm afraid it never registered with me."

"It was Venta, the same family name as Newt Venta, who drove Midge home tonight, and Newt is the son of Midge's stepdaughter Barbara Detwiler Blanding, from an earlier marriage."

"I understand now. If Sammy died in that subbasement and he had a family, they would be out for revenge."

"Trina told me that Sammy had no children, but that he had a brother, Leo. Leo would be the father of Marc, who married Barbara Detwiler, and Newt is their son."

"Why would they be so patient seeking revenge? Generations have passed since Mario killed Sammy."

"Don't leave Milt out of that equation. He probably ordered Sammy's killing. I'll guess that there was something the Ventas didn't know about until Newt talked with Trina at that reunion where she took the notes that we later called Trina's List."

"Vengeance also had to skip a generation because Mark died young in Vietnam."

Arthur showed Irma what he had written in his night table notebook. "I'm sure it's a coincidence, but the name Venta could almost be considered a short form of *vendetta*, meaning a blood feud in which the family of a murdered person seeks vengeance on the murderer or the murderer's family."

"I'll raise you one on name curiosities. Newt's real name would be Newton, after Sir Isaac Newton, whose Laws of Motion include the third law: *Every action produces an equal and opposite reaction.* It suggests that Newt's father might have planned his son's destiny as an avenger from the day he named him."

CHAPTER 84 – PERSPECTIVES

Dennis Mikken welcomed the Gonzalezes and the Blakes to his fire investigation conference room. "I'm pleased that you folks continued to make progress on the church arson case while I recovered from that attack at the Amboy Church. I'm back in good shape and ready to go now. Where do we stand?"

Irma opened a file folder. "I'll lead off, if no one else minds. Arthur and I have two suspects under investigation. The first is Pastor Lorna Dyner, who always seems to be on the scene when something bad happens at the Amboy Church. She was there just before the fire started, was there to witness the blaze, and showed up right after someone attacked you, Dennis, in the basement. Lorna also resembles a photograph we found that Milt Jergens took of the lady with the expensive ring lying in her coffin prior to burial. That resemblance would fit with the theory that a descendant of the ring lady initiated the fire and other crimes in order to reclaim the ring as a family treasure."

Penny said, "It wouldn't be the first time a pastor incinerated his or her own church. Our arson searches revealed a pastor who burned his church to hide his theft of funds from the treasury there."

Irma said, "I have to keep a close eye on my pastor friend all the time ... Seriously, I'm about to test the *family treasure* theory, thanks to a DNA sample from Lorna's coffee cup that Arthur obtained for me. I'll compare that to the DNA sample I took from the ring lady's body when we exhumed it. If the result shows they are relatives, we'll focus in on Lorna as a strong suspect; if the test result is negative, the argument for Lorna's involvement gets weaker, but she's still a potential suspect because of her proximity to the crimes."

Dennis said, "You mentioned two suspects; who is the other one?"

"Arthur and I have reached tentative conclusions about the two unidentified older corpses in the warehouse chamber. We believe that the male was Milton Jergens' assistant, Sammy Venta, and the female was his girlfriend. Arthur will summarize the rest of our analysis."

"We have concluded that Milt's other assistant and later partner, Mario Bitoli, killed Sammy Venta and his girlfriend on Milt's orders, on or just before the day of the ring lady's burial. Mario later returned to the subbasement warehouse and hid the scrap of wood with the location information for the unmarked grave. He wrapped that piece of wood in cloth he tore from Sammy's shirt prior to the onset of his body's decomposition."

Joe said, "So the cloth-wrapped scrap of wood had to be hidden between the time when Sammy was said to have quit, per Milt's ledger, and the day of the burial, because Mario had to record the location coordinates before he forgot them."

"That's right. It's a very short time window, perhaps only one day."

Penny said, "I follow your logic this far, Arthur, but how does it point to a suspect?"

"Sammy had a much younger brother, Leo, who would have known about Sammy's activities and the hidden bootlegging warehouse. Leo may have suspected foul play when Sammy suddenly disappeared, but he couldn't prove what happened. He would have been too young to get involved with all the active Prohibition Era gangs fighting each other. Leo knew that Sammy had been in a dangerous line of work, so he couldn't do anything about his brother's disappearance at the time. Many of the police were on mobster payrolls, so he wouldn't have felt safe discussing his suspicions with them. Leo grew up to be a family man. He had a son named Marc who got married just before he went off to serve with the Army in Vietnam. Marc and his wife, Barbara, had one child, a son they named Newton, and Marc wrote a family history for Newt to read when he grew older. Marc didn't live to share that history with his son. He died during the Tet Offensive of 1969."

Dennis asked, "What happened to Newt?"

"Newt is still in the area. He drives a white pickup truck and assists some of his relatives on his mother's side. Midge Drinkwater's third husband was Barbara's father. I'm sure that Newt is very aware that he is the last of the Ventas. I haven't seen the family history that Marc left for his son, but I'm sure that it contains expressions of family pride and resentment that Sammy had been taken away from them so suddenly."

Irma scanned the faces of Penny, Joe, and Dennis. "I'll anticipate your questions. Midge and I play cat and mouse during our conversations. She tries to find out details about the progress of our investigation, and I try to learn why she is so curious. Once we discovered her family connection to Newt Venta, Midge's curiosity began to make sense. Without revealing any special interest in that branch of the family, I led her into discussions of Marc's wartime accomplishments, and she volunteered his close family ties and his journaling to create a Venta family history for his son."

Joe said, "It sounds as though we are making good progress. We're focusing on one suspect, Lorna, who has been on the scene and had the opportunity to commit these crimes, but if the DNA tests show she isn't a relative of the ring lady, she has no obvious motive. These crimes would destroy her career as a pastor, so she would have a disincentive to have committed them. We're also looking at Newt Venta as an alternate suspect. He has a strong motive for the arson-related crimes and the murder of Trina Jergens as well, but we don't even have evidence of his ever having been at the Amboy Church. Where should our investigation go next?"

Arthur had walked over to the side table for a coffee refill. He turned to face those around the table. "I suggest we wait for Irma's DNA test results to determine whether Lorna remains a prime suspect with a significant motive. If she and the ring lady aren't related, we should focus on Newt Venta. In the meantime, I'll see whether Midge Drinkwater will contribute more insights into Newt's background and character. I'd like to know whether his personality profile matches our suspicions.

CHAPTER 85 – DNA TEST RESULTS

Arthur had taken a day off from investigations to visit with some of his friends at Parkville UMC and with Bobby Andrews at the Parkville Police Department. By the time he reached the outskirts of Amboy on his way home, it was late afternoon. He called Irma's cell phone and suggested that he stop on the way to buy a pizza to take home.

Irma applauded his thought. "Great idea; I've been working with the lab on the DNA tests and a few other things, so dinner planning has been a low priority item. You bring the dinner, and I'll bring a bottle of wine and some news. How's that for a deal?

"It sounds good to me. I'll see you soon."

Irma arrived home first, but Arthur pulled into the driveway before she finished changing into a more casual outfit. As Arthur entered the kitchen, he heard Irma's distant yell that she would be down in a few minutes.

He had the table set and coffee brewed by the time she arrived. A hug and a kiss later, they sat down to enjoy their oversized dish. Arthur always insisted on buying the largest pizza available, because he looked forward to having leftovers for snacks.

Irma said, "I have news. The DNA tests showed that Lorna Dyner is not a descendant of the ring lady, despite her resemblance to that pre-burial photo we found."

"Are you suggesting that we should no longer consider Lorna a suspect?"

"Not in the slightest – I had the lab run a second set of tests, just to be thorough. It turns out that Lorna is related to the second person we found in that coffin with the ring lady."

"Now that's an interesting development. I've nominated the embalmer, Louie, to be that extra person in the coffin. Milt's ledgers didn't indicate Louie's last name."

"Based on the DNA results, you may be able to determine it by tracing Lorna Dyner's family tree."

"I don't think his family name is as important as the fact that we now know that Lorna had a motive for burning down the church and trying to find the unmarked grave. It's not the quest for the ring that we thought would be her goal, but it's still a motive."

"I don't know how strong a motive that would be, Arthur. To take such determined actions based on a murder almost ninety years ago, might require some hope for a payoff. Louie's family wouldn't have known about that expensive ring, and Lorna is only a distant relative, according to the test results. She may be so distant that she doesn't even know about Louie or the family connection."

"Our other current suspect is Newton Venta. Would Sammy Venta's family have known about the ring?"

"If the two skeletal corpses in that subbasement chamber were Sammy and his girlfriend as previously speculated, then the Venta family probably knew about the ring."

"Why do you say that, Irma?"

"I didn't mention it before, because I didn't think it was significant, but the female corpse's ring finger had a slight fracture. That would suggest that she had a ring pulled violently from her finger."

"So, you're concluding that Sammy snatched the ring for his girlfriend, and the two of them paid the penalty of death for his having done so."

"I can't be sure because it happened so long ago, but that explanation makes sense."

"It makes a lot of sense.

"What did you learn in Parkville, Arthur?"

279

"It was mostly a social trip and a chance to let our old friends and associates know more about our case. They've felt left out of the process. After having assisted with so many of our older investigations, they wanted to feel involved. I did learn one interesting thing, though."

"What's that?"

"At our housewarming party, Lorna told me an unlikely story about listening in on conversations because she thought she had heard a voice that matched a telephone call asking her for a date."

"I remember your telling me that."

"It turns out that it actually happened. Jeremy Hadley wanted to find some way to contribute to our efforts, so he called Lorna and claimed that a mutual friend had suggested they meet each other."

"Did they?"

"No; Jeremy said that he called her again after the party, but she wouldn't talk with him. She told him she already had a boyfriend and wasn't interested. He's not sure whether she identified him during her party snooping or not. Either way, he gave up and resigned himself to sitting on the sidelines for this case."

"That showed initiative. If we need an unknown agent before we wrap this thing up, we should call on Jeremy."

"Agreed."

CHAPTER 86 – JOE GONZALEZ

The excitement in Joe's voice over the telephone jarred Arthur. Joe had never been this emotional before. "I know it's early, Arthur, but get over to Newt Venta's Automotive Passion Service Center. We've come up with enough evidence to arrest him."

"You have him for arson plus all the later attacks?"

"We're going after him for the murders of Rob and Trina Danten, and I'm pretty sure we'll get him to confess to the church arson during the interrogation process."

"Pretty sure?"

"Don't quibble, Arthur. Get over to that garage so that you'll be in on the action."

"I'll meet you there in thirty minutes."

Arthur woke Irma to give her the news, filled his travel mug with coffee, and drove toward Newt's Automotive Passion Service Center on the road to DeKalb. On the way, he reminded himself that this would be Joe's show, and that he would play the part of an objective observer.

When Arthur arrived, he parked alongside Joe's black government-issued SUV and two Illinois State Police cars. As he got out of his car, Joe motioned for him to follow behind the group as they entered the building.

Once inside, Arthur watched as Joe approached Newt, standing next to a blue Ford Mustang with its hood open. Joe spoke quietly to Newt, and then the two of them walked toward the private office. Arthur followed them inside, while one trooper stopped by the office door, and the other took up a position where he could watch both the front and the back entrances. Two mechanics glanced at the activity with minor curiosity but continued working on their assigned cars.

Newt filled his mug with coffee and sat down at his old oak desk, surmounted with catalogs and piles of seemingly unsorted work order forms. His face showed little concern. "What can I do for you folks? I assume this is some kind of official visit."

Joe showed his identification. "Newton Venta, we're here to arrest you for the murder of Rob Danten two years ago, and the recent murder of Rob's wife, Trina."

Newt sipped his coffee. "I assume, Mr. Gonzalez, that you have some evidence to back up these serious charges."

"Among other items, we have documents from Trina's files showing that she had work on her car done here, two days before Rob's fatal accident. He drove her car that evening, and that car remains in the State Police car pound because the case is still open. We examined the car and found the brake line cut. You probably expected to kill Trina in the crash, but you killed Rob instead because he drove her car; and you had to return later to murder Trina after enough time had passed so that people wouldn't connect the two crimes."

Newt leaned back, scratched his graying beard, and looked up at Joe. "Would you mind telling me why you think I murdered these people? Isn't there supposed to be a motive?"

Arthur sensed a slight degree of uncertainty in Joe's voice as he responded to Newt's unexpected calmness. "We believe that you sought revenge for the murder of your grandfather's brother, Sammy Venta, by the hands or direction of Trina's grandfather."

"That happened a very long time ago, many years before I was born. I don't carry grudges that long. I'd also like to point out that anyone can cut a brake line; it doesn't require the expertise of a service center."

"The State Police lifted fingerprints from the car at the time of the supposed accident. Some of them were yours."

"Didn't you say that Trina Danten had the car in here for service just before that event? If so, you should expect to find my fingerprints on it, even though I try to be neat and wipe the things I touch. Mr. Gonzalez, I'll be happy to accompany you and the troopers if you wish, but I don't think you have much of a case against me. I haven't committed any kind of a crime; I certainly haven't killed anyone."

Arthur decided to take a more active role. "Joe, may I see the papers for that last job Trina had done on her car here?"

Joe removed them from his jacket pocket and handed them over. After a short period of studying them, Arthur handed them back to Joe and questioned Newt.

"Do you remember Trina Danten and her cars?"

"Sure; she's been a regular customer for a long time. We did work on the car that her husband smashed up and on its replacement too."

"Describe the condition of the car that she had you service just prior to the crash."

"In those days, she kept her cars very neat and clean. Maybe it was her husband's influence, but they never had any food wrappers, junk, or anything inside the cabin. She even had us service the spare tire regularly. We had it out for balancing on the date of the crash. Her replacement car was a different story. I think she lost her drive for neatness after Rob died."

"Did Rob service his car here too?"

"No, now that you mention it, I don't know where he took his car for repairs and service. It wasn't here."

"I have just one more question, Newt. Would you mind comparing Trina to your other customers? What do you remember about dealing with her?"

"You asked two questions; but your answer is that I had to be on my toes with her. If we discovered something extra that needed servicing while we worked on her car, she wouldn't pay for it. She always held me to my original estimate, even if we performed extra work. I had to build a slight cushion into my estimates for her in order to cover my costs. She was a no-nonsense woman."

Arthur turned to Joe. "Those are all the questions I have for Newt."

He wasn't sure what Arthur had gained from his questioning except time, but Joe knew he had to make a quick decision. He realized that his logic for arresting Newt had been faulty. How could he make a graceful retreat? He turned back to Newt.

"You've done a reasonable job of explaining your actions. I'm not going to arrest you at this time, but we'll have people watching you. Don't decide to leave town."

"That's fine with me, Joe Gonzalez. I've been in this area for most of my life, and I doubt that I'll get a sudden urge to go elsewhere. You just go find the person who really did those killings so that I won't have to worry about anyone framing me for them in the future. In the meantime, both of you bring in your cars for service, and I'll throw in a free oil change. That deal goes for the troopers on their personal cars too."

As they walked back to their cars, Joe whispered to Arthur, "That was embarrassing."

Arthur whispered back, "...embarrassing but useful."

CHAPTER 87 – INKLINGS OF CLARITY

Joe and Penny Gonzalez drove up to the Blakes' house unannounced at slightly before noon, carrying a basket. Joe rang the doorbell and counted the seconds until a response. At the seventeen-second mark, Irma answered the door.

"Hello, you two. This is a pleasant surprise."

Penny said, "Have you eaten yet? We hoped you'd be available for a picnic on your porch or in a park."

"The porch will work well. Set your basket on my food cart out there while I get Arthur."

Irma went inside and found Arthur mounting new handles on the kitchen cabinets.

"Penny and Joe are here with a basket of food. They want to have a picnic with us on our porch."

"As they said in connection with the Trojan horse: 'Beware of Greeks bearing gifts.'"

"You think they want something from us?"

"I do; let's join them and find out what it is."

Arthur and Irma went out to the porch and selected the couch so that they could sit side-by-side. They left the individual chairs for Penny and Joe. Then Arthur said, "Apparently, you are going to wine and dine us; do we get a serenade from you too?"

Joe said, "You're enjoying this too much. Believe me; you don't want me to vocalize a serenade."

Irma said, "It might be fun to hear you sing in Spanish. Is this picnic a spontaneous outpouring of affection for us, Joe, or is there a reason behind this exuberance?"

"It's a form of penance for me. I muffed that plan to arrest Newt Venta so badly. I felt sure that he was our culprit, but his explanations for his actions were so plausible that I had to back off and retreat from the scene. At this point, I don't know whom to nominate as our killer and arsonist. That's why we're here to sit at the feet of Arthur the oracle. Maybe he can do another one of his magic tricks and guide us."

Penny said, "Joe's the one feeling miserable; I'm here to serve the food and humor him. Even so, I'll also welcome a miraculous breakthrough from you."

Everyone looked at Arthur; their facial expressions conveyed a mixture of expectation and doubt.

In response, Arthur stood, walked over to the picnic basket, removed an apple, and showed it to the others. "The problem with an apple is that it looks so solid and simple. It's difficult to see what's going on inside. A single apple can cause damage when someone throws it at another person or thing, but plant the seeds inside that apple, and you can produce trees full of new apples that someone can throw at multiple targets to cause more trouble than was possible with just the original piece of fruit. That's the nature of our current case."

Joe said, "I knew he'd have something mystical to say to us. Please elucidate, Oh Sage."

Penny said, "Using his chosen symbol, he's saying that the apple doesn't fall far from the tree, and that we're dealing with a bunch of evil children of Prohibition Era gangsters."

Irma nodded. "Note the plurality in Penny's comment. We've been looking for one arsonist who assaults and murders people, when he or she doesn't exist. We've had multiple nasty events perpetrated by several different people. Isn't that right, Arthur?"

"You're all doing very well, class. We've already arrested Mandy Miller for the murders of Jerry Tackman in the warehouse chamber beneath the church and Ken Cantini in Rome. We've concluded that Saul Sanders probably murdered Marie Chance, but there'll never be a trial because he's dead too. We need to determine the arsonist behind the Amboy Church fire, the person who trapped Irma and me in the church subbasement, the killer of Rob Danten, the killer of Saul Sanders, the killer of Trina Jergens, and the person who attacked Dennis Mikken. I'm quite sure that we'll find that we're looking for more than one person."

Joe asked, "Are you suggesting that these were all independent events, each having a different perpetrator?"

"No, it's likely that we're talking about two people working together, at least on some occasions."

Penny said, "You were right, Joe; He does like to speak in mystical terms. Do you know the identities of your two villains, Arthur?"

"Have you ever done a Sudoku puzzle, Penny?"

"Sure; that's the one with the nine by nine grid squares, divided off into nine subsets of three by three grid squares."

"Right; the rule underlying Sudoku is that each line of nine squares and each small grid with nine squares has to contain every digit from one through nine."

"So?"

"One of the tricks you use to solve the puzzle is that if only two squares in a set of nine digits remain open, and you can use logic to figure out one of them, the number in the final empty square becomes obvious, because it is the only digit left in the one-to-nine sequence."

Irma said, "That's all very interesting, but we don't have nine suspects for the current arson and violent attacks."

"That's true, but if we include other crimes involving members of Amboy UMC, we have nine suspects and have eliminated seven of them."

Joe said, "I told you Arthur would do a magic trick. Who are the seven people with connections to the church and other suspects that we've eliminated?"

"We've arrested Mandy Miller for other crimes; eliminated Marie Chance, Rob Danten, and Jerry

Tackman because they died before the church fire; Ken Cantini because he was in Las Vegas at the time of the fire and died later; and we've decided that Pastor Lorna Dyner and Newton Venta are probably innocent."

"Thanks for the reminder on that last one."

"There's no blame due in connection with suspecting Newt Venta, Joe. At one point, he was a likely villain for me too."

Irma said, "One of the two remaining people has to be Trina Jergens Danten. How does she fit into these events, Arthur?"

"She had me fooled for a while. Prior to the two times I interviewed her about her grandfather's role in building the church and his business activities, I had heard several other people call Trina a witch and a malicious person. Yet, I found her to be relaxed and charming. I had to ask myself which Trina was the genuine person."

Joe reached over and took a bite out of Arthur's demonstration apple. "That's why you asked Newt Venta those questions about her. Our visit to his garage wasn't a total fiasco after all."

"That visit turned out to be the key to seeing the truth about this case. After Trina's murder, Irma and I searched her house and took away some of her belongings. We found that she kept many apparently useless things and hated to discard anything. Newt Venta said that Trina's car had absolutely nothing in it when it left his shop a few days before Rob Danten's supposed accident. Trina even had Newt remove the spare tire for her to pick up later after he serviced it."

Joe nodded. "She planned to make the car crash, so she removed everything beforehand. She valued those miscellaneous items more than she valued her husband."

"She couldn't even bring herself to part with the murder weapon. One of the items I removed from a pile of Rob's belongings in the basement was a pair of heavy-duty bolt-cutting pliers. Irma, if you have the lab test them, I suspect you'll find traces of brake fluid on the cutter blades."

Penny said, "So Trina murdered Rob. Despite her statements to the contrary, she never forgave him for having an affair with Marie."

"Nope; as you suggested earlier, Penny, the apple doesn't fall far from the tree. Milt Jergens couldn't tolerate Sammy Venta's grabbing of that fancy ring for his girlfriend, and Trina couldn't accept Rob's having a mistress."

Irma looked up from the notes she had been taking. "Getting back to your Sudoku puzzle, you're saying that Trina is one of the villains in the two open spaces. Who is the other one?"

"History again leads us to that answer. Milt Jergens and Mario Bitoli became partners in everything they did, after Mario removed the problems of Sammy Venta, Sammy's girlfriend, and, later, Louie the embalmer. Milt was the brains of their partnership, and Mario was the muscle. Trina's partner in crime was her childhood playmate and lifelong friend, Tony Bitoli."

Penny leaned back and nodded. "That's a neat and plausible story, but how can we prove that Tony was involved?"

Irma said, "I'll guess that the proof will lie in forensics. Tony is a dog-lover, and he now owns Marie Chance's golden retriever, Rex, as well as two other dogs. Marie's murderer injured Rex badly that evening. Trina told Arthur that she and Rob first cared for Rex and then gave him to Tony for long-term care. We can recheck the crime scenes and evidence already in our lockers for dog hairs. If we can find hairs from Rex at a crime scene, we'll have proof that Tony was there."

Joe said, "I suggest that the first item to be checked should be the clothing that Saul Sanders wore on the day of his murder. I know Secret Service has that in their evidence storage."

Irma said, "I'll also check the coveralls that Dennis Mikken wore when someone attacked him in the basement of the Amboy Church. We'll come up with some other places to check, along with evidence already stored to recheck. If dog hair evidence exists, we'll find it."

CHAPTER 88 – BUILDING THE CASE

The Gonzalez home in Parkville had become Case Headquarters following the group's decision to focus on Trina Jergens and Tony Bitoli as the people behind the arson at Amboy UMC and the other outstanding crimes. Penny took the lead in compiling and cataloging the evidence as it arrived. The first positive development came from Jefferson Lee at Secret Service when she took his phone call.

"Hi, Jeff; do you have something interesting for us?"

"I definitely do, Penny, and I want to thank you for pointing us in the right direction. We had the FBI Lab check out the clothing that Saul Sanders wore the day someone beat him to death, and they did find dog hairs on it. They identified golden retriever hairs and hairs from two mixed breed dogs. They also cautioned us that a smart lawyer would claim the hairs came from dogs sniffing the body as it lay undiscovered by the side of the road."

"To counter that argument, have the lab document their findings and guard those hairs against contamination. We'll have to compare them against fresh hairs taken from Mr. Bitoli's dogs when we get a search warrant. That's a great contribution, Jeff. We'll keep you advised on our other evidence."

Penny announced Jeff's report to Joe, Irma, and Arthur as they continued to work on their own segments of the evidence-gathering operation.

Arthur said, "If all the hairs came from Tony's dogs, we have him for Saul's murder, but if the mixed breed hairs came from strays and the golden retriever hairs came from Rex, we won't be able to prove that he did it, because Rex was still Trina's dog at the time of Saul's death."

Irma said, "Even so, if they were both at the murder scene, they're accomplices and equally guilty."

Joe completed a telephone conversation and announced his findings. "Dennis says that the State Police Crime Lab has identified dog hairs on the coveralls he wore when someone assaulted him from behind. It will be very interesting to compare them with those found on Saul's clothing much earlier."

Arthur said, "I doubt that dog hairs would remain at Trina's house from the day when Tony killed her, but it would be worth rechecking. What do you think, Irma?"

"I'm afraid that would be a lost cause, because of the passage of time, the presence of various crime scene investigators, and the fact that Rex once lived there. In addition, Tony undoubtedly visited her from time to time. It would be difficult to isolate hairs unique to the murderer. However, I do have some good news. The private lab I use has identified brake fluid on the cutting jaws of the bolt-cutting pliers from Trina's house. She cut her own brake line and then gave her car to Rob to drive on that foggy evening."

Penny said, "Why would Tony kill Trina? She had been his partner in all of this mayhem, and their grandfathers had been partners too."

Arthur nodded. "That was exactly the problem for Tony. In the old days, Milt Jergens was the brains, and Mario Bitoli was the muscle. No matter how long they worked together, Mario was the junior partner. Flash forward to the present; and it's not surprising that Tony got very upset when Trina started treating him as less important than she was. He killed her from behind as she walked away from him."

Joe asked, "Who instigated this whole series of events, Arthur? Was it Trina or Tony?"

"That's an easy one to answer. It would have been Tony. Mario Bitoli hid that scrap of wood with the grave location information for a reason. He planned to tell his children about it so that they could dig up the coffin and claim the ring as their inheritance. It was only after we found and removed that key to buried riches that Tony had to rely on Milt's notes in his ledger. The fact that Milt encoded his notes to give the incorrect grave location says that he didn't really trust Mario."

Irma added, "And Trina shouldn't have trusted Tony."

Penny said, "The Lord visits the iniquity of the fathers upon the children unto the third and the fourth generation. Isn't that right, Arthur?"

"Absolutely, Penny, but you stole my line. You could train for clergy work."

"Actually, I quoted it from one of your sermons at Parkville UMC. Do I get extra credit for having remembered it?"

Irma said, "This case has shown us the truth of that biblical quotation. How did Trina and Tony divide up their violent acts? What's your guess, Arthur?"

"I don't like that word *guess*. I'm sure that Trina would have been the arsonist. She was familiar with Amboy UMC as a member there, and witnesses wouldn't have suspected her evil intent if they had seen her there before the blaze started. Bystanders would have considered Tony a suspicious stranger. I think that Trina watched the church from a hiding place and waited until Lorna Dyner and her youth group left before she prepared to start the fire in its two hot spot locations. The dog hair evidence suggests that they worked together to kill Saul Sanders, and Trina alone used the bolt-cutting pliers to cut the brake line in the car that Rob drove to his death."

Irma added, "And Tony shot Trina. I wonder whether they had been in the midst of an argument or if he simply surprised her. Either way, the evidence says that he shot her in the chest as she faced him and then finished her off with a shot to the back of her head as she tried to run away."

Joe gestured to Arthur. "Let me take this one. I think that Tony arrived after Arthur talked with Trina on the phone. She may have been planning to accuse Tony of having been behind everything. Tony wanted the ledgers because we had removed the grave location information from the church subbasement. Trina probably tried to stall him until Arthur arrived, but Tony got suspicious and impatient. I won't speculate whether she told him where the ledgers were or if he found them by searching her house."

Arthur said, "She must have told him. The house was too neat for him to have done a determined search. There was only a short interval between Trina's phone call and my arrival anyway. If I had jumped into my car right after talking with her, Trina might be alive today."

Penny said, "There's no reason to feel guilty, Arthur. Trina didn't express any urgency about your coming."

"You're right, of course, but we always have choices to make, and we wonder if we might have done something better."

Irma said, "Changing the subject away from my husband's feelings of imperfection, I'll complete our discussion allocating their misdeeds by saying that Tony would have been the person who attacked Dennis Mikken in the church basement and that he must have been the one who imprisoned Arthur and me in that warehouse chamber. I don't think Trina had the strength and speed to lock us in that subbasement without our realizing we were under attack, and Dennis found dog hairs on the coveralls he wore the day he was assaulted there."

Penny made several notes. "I'll accept your interpretation. I could argue that Trina had sufficient strength to imprison you, but it really doesn't matter because she's dead. What's more important is deciding how to confront and convict Tony. He's the only evildoer who's still alive. We've had far too many deaths connected to this case."

CHAPTER 89 – TONY

Throughout his formative years, Tony had heard about people working to give Chicago a new image, free from the taints of Al Capone and Prohibition Era gangsters. He couldn't endorse those efforts because he idolized Grandpa Mario and his tales of poor, unknown immigrants who became important and wealthy by catering to the nation's love for alcohol. Nobody blamed the people who had shelled out lots of cash to buy illegal booze – only those who procured and sold it.

Grandpa Mario had leveled with him about the rough side of the Prohibition Era organizations too, but that had seemed so far in the past that it had merged with legends and fairy tales. Mario and his friends represented a lifestyle that had dwarfed today's politically correct normalcy, and Tony had subconsciously craved a taste of it, even as he studied to be an accountant. Perhaps that was part of the legendary attraction; why keep track of other people's money when you could grab some and invest your own?

Grandpa had insisted that he had been a businessman rather than a gangster but that he had been willing to use any means necessary to overcome barriers to his success. He had told Tony that it was a dog-eat-dog world and that the timid ended up in the gutter. He had also preached the gospel of opportunity through unfailing loyalty to a superior and an organization. Mario had believed in hitching his wagon to a star. This philosophy had served him well as he had grown from an underling to a trusted associate and then to a partner, first in the mortuary business and later in waste disposal.

Tony had enjoyed his many discussions with Grandpa Mario, but he had never gone along with Mario's loyalty principle. Tony didn't want to be dedicated to following a superior; he wanted to be that leader and have others be loyal to him.

Despite his respect for his grandfather's lifestyle and accomplishments, Tony did not want to be perceived as a tough guy, beyond the degree to which his slight build and small stature required it in order to earn the respect of others. His regimens of exercise, martial arts training, and nutrition had made him significantly stronger than his appearance suggested. He could hold his own in a fight, but swagger was not his style; alert caution was. He deliberately cultivated a reputation of harmlessness through his love of dogs and his proclaimed desire for eternal bachelorhood. The reverse psychology of this stance made him a magnet for single women who enjoyed pets. He especially enjoyed the recent attentions of Trina Jergens Danten, his childhood friend who had become more than that after her husband, Rob, died in a car accident.

He had tried to keep his relationship with Trina on the former playmate level because the ghost of her grandfather Milt kept reminding him that Grandpa Mario had been the junior partner in their businesses. As time passed, and Trina continued to let him take the lead in all of their activities, he had relaxed and let their friendship develop into something much more intense.

CHAPTER 90 – SEARCH WARRANT

Tony Bitoli's farm on Hickory Hills Road, south of Sterling, Illinois had been the fruition of Mario Bitoli's successive partnerships with Milt Jergens. Mario didn't know the first thing about farming, but he had enjoyed spending his final years in bucolic surroundings. Tony knew little more than his grandfather had about agriculture, but he did understand the value of real estate. He had created a steady income stream by contracting with a neighboring farmer to allow him to expand his cultivated acreage onto Tony's land for an annual fee plus a share of the harvest revenue. Tony spent most of his resulting free time searching the stock market for potentially lucrative investments, training his dogs, and wondering whether he would have done as well as Grandpa Mario in Prohibition Era Chicago. He knew he wouldn't have been a good underling within a large bootlegging organization; but he thought he could have been a big success as a crooked elected official within that wide-open political setting.

Tony and his dogs had just returned from a long walk when three State Police cars and a pair of unmarked black SUV's drove into his driveway. He tied his barking comrades to fence posts and approached the man in civilian clothes who had driven one of the SUV's and appeared to be in charge.

"Hello; I'm Tony Bitoli. May I help you? Are you in the right place?"

"My name is Joe Gonzalez, and I represent a federal agency that is investigating church arson cases, including the burning of the Amboy United Methodist Church. We have a warrant to search these premises for evidence in connection with that investigation." He handed Tony a copy of the warrant.

Tony accepted the document and scanned the uniformed and plainclothes officials. Then he took a ceremonial step backward. "Go right ahead. I don't know what you expect to find on my little farm."

As they talked, a tall blond woman wearing light green coveralls emerged from the second SUV and approached them.

Joe said, "Mr. Bitoli, this is Doctor Jennifer Billingsley from the University of Illinois, College of Veterinary Medicine. She will need to get hair samples from your dogs."

Jennifer shook hands with Tony. "I won't be hurting the dogs in any way, but I'd appreciate your accompanying me to assure that they will feel comfortable during the process."

"I don't understand why you need hair from my dogs. They're healthy and well treated. What are you going to do with the hair samples?"

"I'm not at liberty to tell you that at this time, but the sampling is covered by that document you're holding."

Tony glanced at the warrant as they walked toward the fence and the three dogs tied to it. As they walked, he noticed that Joe Gonzalez and two State Troopers had entered his house through the unlocked kitchen door, while another Trooper had entered his barn. He would have preferred to be in the house watching what those searchers did, but he knew he'd have to accompany the veterinarian first.

"How much hair will you have to take? It won't be traumatic for the dogs, will it?"

"No; I'll only take about eight hairs from each dog. I'll have my samples before they realize their loss."

Tony had to admit that Dr. Billingsley was adept at her task. She walked up to each dog, petted it, and then pinched a fold of loose skin behind its shoulder as though she were about to administer an injection. Instead, she withdrew her hair sample with gripping tweezers and then released the dog. Jennifer inserted each sample into an individual plastic test tube, sealed it, and then labeled it with the dog's rabies tag number and description. Tony volunteered each dog's name, and she added that to the label as well. Following the hair sampling procedure, Tony headed for the house to observe the interior search, but the State Trooper who had come out of the barn stopped him and told him he would have to wait outside. Dr. Billingsley took her dog hair samples to her car, where she stored them in a special case with multiple compartments. Then she drove away, having completed her portion of the search.

About forty-five minutes later, the State Troopers and Joe Gonzalez came out of the house carrying several wrapped items and packages. Joe gave Tony a sheet of paper listing in general terms the items authorized by the warrant for removal and certifying that the objects they had taken complied with the warrant's list. Tony played it cool and didn't express any emotion, but he was surprised that they hadn't arrested him for anything after this elaborate search. He knew the lapse might be only temporary and that he'd have to schedule an immediate conference with his lawyer.

After the search party left, Tony entered the house and scanned each room to identify the missing items. He was not at all surprised to find his laptop computer gone, but the absence of another object shook his confidence.

CHAPTER 91 – ANALYSIS

Jeff Lee and Dennis Mikken had couriered their hair sample evidence to Dr. Jennifer Billingsley at the University of Illinois for comparison with the samples she had taken from Tony's dogs. Penny and Joe Gonzalez had opted to analyze the contents of Tony's computer. That left Arthur and Irma Blake to organize and analyze the other objects removed from the farmhouse during the search.

The first two items they examined encouraged Arthur to proclaim a successful first step in building a case against Tony. He felt that Milt Jergens' two ledger books that sat on their table would be the centerpiece of their evidence. When he and Irma had arrived at Trina's house immediately after her murder, Arthur had looked for the ledgers, and when he couldn't find them, he had concluded that Trina's killer had taken them. He voiced this conviction to Irma and was surprised when she shook her head.

"Sorry, Pastor, you'd never convince a jury with that logic. A good defense attorney would point out that Tony and Trina were friends and that he could have borrowed the ledgers at any time between your return of them and Trina's murder. You have no evidence that the murderer took the ledgers; it's only a theory. Why should Tony murder her to get the ledgers, when he could simply ask her for them?"

"Touché on that one. I'll admit to seeing what I wanted to see. I'll try to be more objective from here forward. What's the next item to evaluate?"

"You'll like this one, Arthur. It turns out that Tony Bitoli had the twin to the cigarette lighter that Saul Sanders lost at Marie's house when he murdered her. It has the initials SAS on one side and the Special Air

Service, SAS, sword and wings insignia on the other side of it. Good luck rubbing hadn't diminished the insignia clarity yet."

"That suggests that Saul Sanders carried a spare SAS lighter after he lost the original one at Marie Chance's house. Then Tony took it as a trophy when he killed Saul alongside that Indiana road."

"Details again – I'm not sure whether Saul died next to that road, or died elsewhere, with his killer dumping the body where they found it."

"Either way, the lighter plus a confirmation of the hairs on Saul's clothes coming from Tony's dogs should yield a conviction of Mr. Bitoli for Sanders' murder."

"Perhaps with Trina's assistance, but no court will try Trina posthumously."

"Hopefully, Tony will cooperate by revealing Trina's crimes in the hope of negotiating a lighter sentence."

"Again, the court may not allow his evidence against Trina, because she is dead and can't defend herself, and because he might lie to get a better deal for himself."

"You are being rigorous today. What else do we have from Tony's farmhouse?"

"I hope you're ready for this, Arthur. We have a surprise. Joe found Tony's file of receipts for maintenance of his pickup truck. It includes several receipts from the Automotive Passion Service Center. Those receipts tell us that Tony and Newt Venta knew each other, or at least dealt with each other on a business level."

"More than that, they say that Tony had his truck serviced in Amboy, even though it isn't close to his farm south of Sterling, and they give us a list of dates when Tony was in Amboy."

"Those dates may coincide with visits to Trina, but he probably visited Trina on additional dates when his truck didn't need service." Arthur had been looking through the file; he returned it to Irma.

Implications

"This file is interesting, but it doesn't give us any real insights into Tony's activities. Did the search crew find any other surprises?"

"It's what they didn't find that surprised me, Arthur. There was no indication that Tony owned or had ever owned a gun. Trina died from two well-placed shots, one to the center of her chest, and one to the back of her head as she tried to flee. The person who fired those shots must have had experience with weapons and practice. Tony didn't serve in the military, and he didn't have a hunting weapon in the house or barn."

"You're saying that while we have good evidence against Tony for beating Saul to death, we would have a questionable case against him for Trina's murder. If he didn't kill her, Tony might be very angry with the person who did. Hopefully, the examination of his computer files will clarify things."

CHAPTER 92 – EMAILS

Penny and Joe sat side-by-side looking at the list of emails on a single screen. They had opened and examined about thirty of them when they found one that piqued their interest and relieved the boredom of the process.

Penny said, "This is the smoking gun. It's the one that underlies several of our crimes."

"It's also a connection that I wouldn't have suspected, but it makes a lot of sense."

"The problem, Joe, is that we have to work backwards from each crime, and that process encourages us to examine the overt suspects in the foreground, while discouraging us from looking for covert participants in the background."

"You're right, of course, but this time we have enough of an overlap between foreground and background to make arrests and see the overall picture. You call the Blakes to inform them, while I arrange for the necessary personnel."

CHAPTER 93 – UNRAVELING

When the official cars re-entered his driveway, Tony knew it would be the end of the road for him and that he needed to make the best deal he could. He watched as Joe Gonzalez and an Illinois State Trooper approached him as he sat on the steps to the kitchen door with Rex.

Joe said, "Tony Bitoli, based on our review of the evidence removed from these premises under our search warrant, you are under arrest for the murder of U.S. Secret Service Agent Saul Sanders. Trooper Colvin will read you your rights."

After the completion of the formal rights declaration, Joe said, "You don't have to say anything without representation, but you may chose to do so if you wish."

Tony shrugged his shoulders. "Will I get a better deal if I cooperate and give you information that may lead to other arrests?"

"I can't promise you anything, but we can recommend leniency if the circumstances warrant it."

"That's good enough for me. I'll admit to beating that Sanders guy, but I didn't expect him to die so easily. We decided that he needed punishment for having killed a woman named Marie Chance." He gave his golden retriever a hug. "Rex, here, was her dog originally, but Sanders tried to kill him too as Rex attempted to protect Marie. It took a long time for him to recover and get healthy again."

"You said 'we' when you spoke about punishing Saul Sanders. Who else participated?"

"Trina Danten was with me, but she didn't touch Sanders; she acted only as a cheerleader."

"If she were still alive, that would be enough to get her prosecuted as an accessory. Did you kill Trina?"

"No way, Mr. Gonzalez; Trina was my friend, and eventually more than that. I wouldn't hurt her."

"Do you know who did kill her?"

"No, but I have my suspicions."

"It's time for us to go. You can continue your story at State Police Headquarters where we'll video record everything."

"What about my dogs? If you arrest me, who'll you get to take care of them?"

"We'll drop them off at a shelter for temporary housing and make long-term arrangements later."

"I knew this wacky scheme wouldn't end well."

CHAPTER 94 – BANK BUSINESS

Barbara Detwiler Blanding enjoyed being President of Detwiler Community Bank in DeKalb, both because she genuinely enjoyed working with people on financial matters, and because her position gave her social status and power. As a young adult, she had desired to study law, but events changed her outlook. Following her father's death from pneumonia after an unwise fishing outing during a storm, she discovered that neither her two brothers nor her sister would consider picking up the reins of the bank and guiding it forward. Oscar and Paul had careers they wouldn't abandon in the insurance business, and Phyllis had no choice but to be a stay-at-home mom with her five young children. At least, becoming a banker had helped to fill the void after her first husband, Marc, had died in Vietnam.

Her secretary, William, knocked twice and then opened her door, draining the family memories from her consciousness.

"I have Mr. and Mrs. Gonzalez waiting to see you. They indicate that it's in regard to a confidential and important matter."

"Are you sure they're not fund-raisers or politicians?"

"They appear to be quite reputable, and the kind of people you don't want to offend. They're quiet, but very assertive."

"Thanks for your evaluation, William. You'd better bring them in here."

William left briefly and returned escorting and announcing Mr. and Mrs. Gonzalez, before deferentially departing and closing the door behind him.

Barbara stood to greet them. "Good morning; William tells me that you are here in connection with a confidential matter. How may I assist you?"

Penny stepped forward to assure that Barbara focused on her. "We represent a federal investigative agency. We indicated that our business with you is confidential, because we didn't want to make our purpose obvious to your customers and employees. We're here to arrest you for conspiracy, murder, and being an accessory to the arson burning of a church. Joe will inform you of your legal rights."

Following Joe's announcement of the legalities, Barbara sat and said, "These are very serious charges. You will have difficulties making them stick in a court of law. I have an excellent team of attorneys representing me and this bank."

Joe said, "We would definitely want you to have the best representation possible, because you'll need it."

"I've never even been in Amboy or near that church."

Penny said, "We'll get into the details after you've formally checked into our federal facilities, but we've already taken note of the fact that you've focused on the burning of the Amboy United Methodist Church, when we hadn't indicated which church is involved in your charges."

"I said that because it's the only church I know about that burned down."

Joe said, "The jury will decide whether that slip is important. Now, it's time for us to leave. You may make any necessary arrangements with the bank staff."

Barbara nodded, picked up the intercom phone, and pressed a button. "William, I'll be going out with Mr. and Mrs. Gonzalez. Please tell Charles Zoring that he'll be in charge while I'm gone, and route anything important to him."

As they left the office and walked through the bank lobby, Barbara Blanding smiled and greeted various clients and staff members, minimizing the chance that anyone would attribute anything serious or significant to her departure with the Gonzalez couple.

As they drove away, Penny said, "I've already requested that federal bank examiners perform an expedited audit of your bank for any unusual transactions and activities."

Barbara slumped in her seat.

CHAPTER 95 – BARBECUE

The barbecue party started at four o'clock in the afternoon, but the invitations had specified that it would not break up until midnight. Arthur and Irma had invited Jeremy Hadley, Wally Sanborn, plus Bobby and Renee Andrews from Parkville. In addition, they had included all of the investigators who had worked on the case that had started with the burning of Amboy UMC. Penny and Joe had volunteered to be co-hosts. Jefferson Lee was doing his best to convince people that he and Wanda Williams were independent guests, rather than a couple. Steve DuBois had flown in from DC without his family, but he continuously talked about them, convincing everyone that Ellen and Eric were with him in spirit. Dennis Mikken and Celia Masters had driven together to attend their first social gathering since they had become coworkers. As they all shared their first round of drinks and appetizers on the long porch, Irma took center stage to announce a couple of modifications to the original list of invitees.

"I want to welcome you all to our end-of-case party. We'll collectively share what happened along the way, to guide us to its conclusion. First, I'll head off any questions about the absence of Midge Drinkwater today. As you know, Arthur and I were thrilled that Midge chose to sell us this house, and we were more than happy to have her continue to live with us in a second floor apartment. However, after we discovered the involvement of one of her family members in our case, Midge decided that it would be more appropriate for her to reside with her eldest son, Edward Picoli. Midge will still visit us from time to time, and we'll continue to be close friends. The other change in the party roster involves my dream for Arthur and me to adopt a son."

Implications

Renee Andrews jumped up from her seat. "Have you gone ahead and adopted? Oh, I'm so happy for you."

"Thanks for your endorsement, Renee, but I was going to add that Arthur hadn't shared my enthusiasm. I'll admit that this bothered me for some time. We did discuss several possibilities and, yes, finally went ahead with it. Arthur will introduce our son to you."

The door to the house swung open, and a blond blur ran out.

Joe said, "It's Rex. You adopted Rex."

Arthur gave a thumbs-up sign. "Yes, this house will be his fourth home. Rex played several key roles in the course of solving our case, and we felt he had earned a home where he could count on long-term love. Irma would have preferred a son to a golden retriever, but we agreed that Rex needed our love and that he wasn't likely to give us the problems that come with a teen-ager. We didn't preclude a possible future human adoption, but Rex is the perfect addition to our family right now."

Everyone applauded, and several surrounded Rex.

Steve said, "You two had a brilliant idea. I think there might be a canine adoption in the future for our family too. The new baby should grow up with a puppy friend."

Joe walked over to shake Steve's hand. "Congratulations to you and Ellen. You've proved that family life is compatible with your career as an investigator." Joe heard someone applauding behind him and turned around to see Penny standing up and clapping with a big smile on her face.

"You finally said the magic words, and I have a whole bunch of witnesses. We're going to have a long-delayed discussion about adoption tomorrow ... and don't even think about settling for a dog."

Joe's smile matched that of his wife. "Your wish is my command. Put it on the agenda for right after breakfast."

The assembled group responded with a chorus of cheers, accompanied by some applause.

Richard Davidson

Arthur invited everyone to freshen up their drinks and then gather their chairs into an elongated circle on the porch in order to discuss the results of their combined investigations. Jeremy Hadley pulled a notebook from his back pocket and prepared to take notes.

Once they had all settled into their seats, Arthur said, "The best way to summarize our case is to work backward from its conclusion. I'll let Penny lead us into the story."

"Thanks, Arthur; as we investigated various aspects of this case, it began to look like anarchy, with many different people doing bad things to each other. Then, when Joe questioned Tony Bitoli, we started to see the puppeteer behind the screen.

"A long time ago, in 1927, Al Capone bought one of his mistresses a very fancy ring. When someone murdered her, Al had her buried away from Chicago, in Amboy, still wearing the ring he had given her. Sammy Venta, Milt Jergens' assistant, thought no one would miss the ring, so he took it for his girlfriend. That cost both of them their lives, and they became the two skeletal corpses we found in the bootlegging warehouse beneath the church. Sammy had told his brother, Leo, about the ring by telephone, but didn't live long enough to show it to him. Leo passed that knowledge on to his son Marc, who died during the Vietnam war, but not before he told his wife, Barbara Detwiler Venta, about it.

"Barbara remarried to become Barbara Detwiler Blanding, and she took over the presidency of her father's bank after he died. She enjoyed the respect that accompanied that position, but she had a weakness for using some of the bank's money to finance her gambling habit. She knew that she would have to come up with replacement funds soon, or the bank examiners would discover the shortfall, and she would end up in prison for a long time."

Arthur said, "I'll take it from there, Penny. Barbara remembered the story of the ring, and decided that she could more than get out of debt if she could locate that woman's grave and remove the treasure from her bony finger. She had met Trina Jergens Danten at a reunion of bootlegger descendants, when she attended with her son Newt Venta. Trina had met Newt as a child and didn't feel she needed to take notes on him or his mother. That's why there was no one named Venta on Trina's list of new acquaintances she met there. Barbara befriended Trina, who had heard a little about a special ring, but didn't know very much. Trina, in turn, introduced Barbara to her childhood friend, Tony Bitoli. Barbara discovered that Tony knew the whole story about the ring, including information about a key to the location of the woman's grave that his grandfather, Mario, had hidden in the underground warehouse.

"Barbara asked Trina and Tony to assist her in getting the ring, in exchange for a share of the proceeds. She also told them that as a member of the Venta family, she would forgive them for the sins of their grandfathers having killed Sammy and his girlfriend, and would guarantee that there wouldn't be a Venta family vendetta against them."

Joe said, "My turn Arthur. According to Tony, the first step in the scheme was for Trina to set the fire to destroy her church. She would set one of the two fires in the basement, so that the people cleaning up the ruins would have to remove the lower level carpeting. Trina was careful to wait until all the people meeting at the church that evening had been gone for several hours, so that no one would get hurt in the fire, and none of the meeting people would become suspects. Even as she torched the church her grandfather had built, she respected its history and members. Tony's assignment was to wait until the firefighters fenced off the church ruins. At that point, he would locate the entrance to the subbasement. Then he would enter the warehouse and find the piece of wood on which his grandfather had written the grave location. No one was supposed to get hurt.

Richard Davidson

"The obstacles to success in their scheme came when we paid more attention to this particular church fire than they expected. Bishop Chandler put Arthur on the case during the fire; Arthur convinced us to give it federal attention; and Dennis Mikken representing the Illinois Fire Marshal, joined the investigative team. Thanks to his partner, Celia Masters, we discovered the entrance to the subbasement warehouse, and then we kept that chamber under our control until after we found the grave location scrap of wood."

Irma gestured that she wanted to speak, and Joe nodded his agreement.

"This case became complicated as we investigated its loose ends, most of which had nothing to do with the main arson scheme. We saw how descendants of Prohibition Era mobsters tended to get into trouble themselves, but their crimes went in so many directions that for a long time, we failed to see the pattern behind the arson. Because Milt Jergens had built the church and the underground warehouse, we devoted substantial efforts toward discovering who killed Trina Jergens' husband, Rob, and his mistress, Marie Chance. The most recent corpse in the subbasement triggered an investigation that led to arresting Mandy Miller for that murder plus a second one in Rome. We even solved the murder of Secret Service Agent Saul Sanders before we learned the identity of our arsonist."

Arthur said, "We did keep returning to that expensive ring as being the target and motive for what went on at Amboy UMC. In that, we were correct. However, we concentrated too long on who wanted to steal it, before we got to the critical question of how they would be able to sell it and convert it into cash. Once we turned the corner toward disposition of the ring once stolen, the banker widow of Sammy Venta's nephew became a logical suspect."

Implications

Joe shook his head and raised his hand for attention. "You're a little out of sequence, Arthur. We didn't know about Barbara's involvement until we studied Tony Bitoli's emails, following which, he confessed to his part in the plan and her instigation of it. Once we zeroed in on her, we realized that she would have the legitimacy to move the ring through one of the main auction houses. It would be worth millions of dollars today because of its gems, its design, and its connection to Al Capone."

Arthur said, "I stand corrected. Tony's confession was the key to finding that Barbara was the hidden conspirator, but Rex's hair, transferred from Tony to Saul Sanders' clothes when Tony beat him to death, was the key to getting Tony to confess. Revenge for Saul's cruelty to Rex was the motive for Tony's attack on Saul."

Penny said, "I still have one question. Why did Barbara murder Trina?"

Arthur said, "She wanted Milt's ledgers to find the ring lady's gravesite, but Trina had already given those books to Tony, and since Trina and Tony had become lovers, Trina wouldn't turn Barbara loose on him. Instead, she insisted that the ledgers didn't exist, and that brave decision cost Trina her life. Barbara also wanted revenge for Milt and Mario killing Sammy Venta. She probably would have killed Tony too, if she had seen an opportunity."

"Who dug up the incorrect grave at the cemetery? We had thought it was Trina's murderer, but the ledgers and the location information in them were gone by the time Barbara killed Trina."

"Tony had the ledgers, Penny. Consequently, Tony dug up the grave, using the disguised information from Milt's ledgers that gave him the incorrect location. That's essentially the whole story. Now we can relax and enjoy our barbecue."

Irma said, "I have one more question for my husband. Arthur, how do you think Bishop Chandler will react to all

315

of these crimes involving members of Amboy UMC and a supposedly respectable banker?"

"I suspect that he won't be especially happy with either the conclusions from our investigation or with me. Once the media start reporting our findings, he'll be happy to have both the news reports and me just fade away."

"And will you fade away?"

"I may find myself out of his sight, but I doubt that he'll be able to get me out of his mind."

-END-

ABOUT THE AUTHOR

Richard Davidson is the author of the self-help guidebook: *DECISION TIME! Better Decisions for a Better Life*. He has written the five-novel Lord's Prayer Mystery Series: *Lead Us Not into Temptation, Give Us this Day our Daily Bread, Forgive Us Our Trespasses, Thy Will Be Done,* and *Deliver Us from Evil*. He has edited an anthology, *Overcoming: An Anthology by the Writers of* OCWW. His latest novel, *Implications*, continues to chronicle the exploits of Arthur Blake and the investigative associates who aided him in the earlier mystery series. Mr. Davidson is Past President of Off-Campus Writers' Workshop, the oldest ongoing group of its kind in the U.S. and is the founder of the ReadWorthy Books Book Review Blog. He is the founder of the Independent Mystery Publishing Society (IMPS). Mr. Davidson is a Certified Lay Servant Speaker and a former Lay Leader in the United Methodist Church. He is also an aeronautical & astronautical engineer and a businessman.

WORKS BY THIS AUTHOR

NONFICTION:

DECISION TIME! Better Decisions for a Better Life, VBW Publishing, Inc.
ISBN 978-1-60264-063-4 (paperback)
ISBN 978-1-60264-064-1 (hard cover)

Richard Davidson

ISBN 978-1-4581-8395-8 (Smashwords Edition eBook)

ASIN B0052GOZEO (Kindle Edition eBook)

Where you are in life today is the result of all of the past decisions you have made or which have been made for you in response to the various situations and events that have impacted your life. The decisions that you will make from this point forward will determine the degree to which your future will be positive or negative. *DECISION TIME!* gives you insight into the subjective decision-making process as applied to both small and large choices you will face. It includes dynamic aspects, cultural effects, and morality as applied to decision-making for individuals, teams, corporations, and societies. *DECISION TIME!* prepares you to face the continuous impacts of decision situations confidently and without hesitation.

FICTION:

Lead Us Not into Temptation (The Lord's Prayer Mystery Series, Volume I),
VBW Publishing, Inc.
ISBN 978-1-60264-407-6 (paperback)
ISBN 978-1-4581-7381-2 (Smashwords Edition eBook)
ASIN B0052MGI6Q (Kindle Edition eBook)

Arthur Blake, former NASA engineer turned minister, receives an emergency appointment to be pastor of the United Methodist Church in Parkville, a distant suburb of Chicago, following the bizarre sudden death of the church's unusual former pastor. Pastor Blake's attempts to unravel the mystery that shrouds his predecessor become involved with tracking the child of a possibly bigamous soldier in World War II England, art and jewelry treasures plundered by the Nazis and their sympathizers,

Implications

and the eventual results of childhood sibling conflicts in combined families. Arthur's allies in his investigation include Parkville Police Chief Bobby Andrews, County Medical Examiner Irma Custis, and the married team of Penny and Joe Gonzalez who work for a clandestine government agency. During the course of *Lead Us Not into Temptation,* the reader discovers how seemingly minor historical events lead to major present-day dislocations in church, village, and family relationships.

Give Us this Day Our Daily Bread (The Lord's Prayer Mystery Series, Volume II)
RADMAR Publishing Group
ISBN 978-0-9829160-0-1 (paperback)
ISBN 978-1-4580-6717-3 (Smashwords Edition eBook)
ASIN B0052MQI66 (Kindle Edition eBook)

Arthur Blake, Pastor of Parkville United Methodist Church, has to deal with the aftereffects of a traumatic communion incident. He works to assist the authorities in investigating the cause while doing his best to convince members of his congregation that it is safe to return to church. Working with the police and federal agencies, he discovers that the terror of the initial event is minor compared with the potential chaotic impact of future disasters being planned by the perpetrator. The investigation is interwoven with several relationship situations that affect the final outcome.

Forgive Us Our Trespasses (The Lord's Prayer Mystery Series, Volume III)
RADMAR Publishing Group
ISBN 978-0-9829160-1-8 (paperback)
ISBN 978-1-4657-3739-7 (Smashwords Edition eBook)
ASIN B005SULQ6Y (Kindle Edition eBook)

Richard Davidson

Arthur Blake, Pastor of Parkville United Methodist Church, tries to assist his father to resolve his trauma after learning that his best friend, recently killed in a car accident, may have been an imposter with a heinous background. The investigation reveals that the presumed accident was but one link in a chain of murders. Blake works to determine the true identity of his father's friend, while also discovering the man's past activities and affiliations. Arthur works to solve the murders in conjunction with his colleagues at ABC Consultants. He also draws on assistance from associates at a covert government agency with which he has worked before. The coordinated effort to solve the puzzle examines incidents that span the period between World War II and the present in order to defuse the personal, national, and international dangers resulting from them.

Thy Will Be Done (The Lord's Prayer Mystery Series, Volume IV)
RADMAR Publishing
ISBN 978-0-9829160-2-5 (paperback)
ISBN 978-1-3013-4293-8 (Smashwords Edition eBook)
ASIN B009JU6EZM (Kindle Edition eBook)

The sudden death of a young woman attending Parkville United Methodist Church infuriates her brother and leads to congregational outrage over his outburst and subsequent murder. The investigation of that slaying by Pastor Arthur Blake and his associates leads to revelations of a previously undetected criminal organization operating in the area. Unraveling the mystery and scope of this group entangles Arthur and his associated investigators in a web of conspiracies extending from Illinois to both U.S. coasts and through Mexico to Guatemala.

Implications

Deliver Us from Evil (The Lord's Prayer Mystery Series, Volume V)
RADMAR Publishing
ISBN 978-0-9829160-3-2 (paperback)
ASIN: B00EBDUXFY (Kindle Edition eBook)

Arthur and Irma's wedding day has finally arrived, but an unexpected interruption leads to their need to investigate a possible murder committed by someone close to them. With the aid of friends and federal agents Penny and Joe Gonzalez, they follow a series of clues, crisscrossing the United States to learn more about the murder, related subsequent events, and the significance of a rare object brought home by a veteran of the Iraq War. A second murder close to Pastor Arthur Blake's church involves them in a new investigation, assisting Parkville Police Chief Bobby Andrews. Are these murders and the tracking of that strange object connected? Will marriage deteriorate or improve the relationship between Arthur and Irma? Character flaws in many relationships color the outcome.

Overcoming: An Anthology by the Writers of OCWW
Edited and with an Introduction by Richard Davidson
RADMAR Publishing
ISBN 978-9829160-4-9 (paperback)
ASIN B00E80NN4I (Kindle Edition eBook)

This anthology covers many aspects of overcoming life's problems, obstacles, and challenging developments. The contributing writers have used fiction, non-fiction, memoir, poetry, historical chronicle, and drama to highlight our continuing need to overcome our problems, rather than dwell on them. The reader will learn from many talented writers the skills needed to respond constructively, energetically, and sometimes humorously

Richard Davidson

to whatever obstacle bars one's path. Apply their lessons to your own needs and to those of others you cherish.

Implications: An Arthur Blake Mystery Novel
RADMAR Publishing
ISBN 978-0-9829160-6-3

Bishop Howard Chandler has assigned Pastor Arthur Blake to investigate the burning of a church in the small city of Amboy, Illinois. He learns from that church's pastor that she had to overcome past improprieties by former members. During the investigation of the fire's cause, Arthur and the other state fire investigators uncover disturbing aspects of the ninety-year-old church's design and history. Arthur calls on his federal associates for assistance, as the investigation of a local church fire expands to seeking solutions to related crimes occurring from the present to recent years and back to the Prohibition Era. Progress in the investigation intertwines with new developments in Arthur's family life.

Learn more about the writings and random thoughts of Richard Davidson at: davidsonbooks.blogspot.com davidsonbookshelf.com betterlifedecisions.blogspot.com and at the Independent Mystery Publishing Society (IMPS) https://www.mysteryimps.com
Richard Davidson's author page is on Amazon at https://www.amazon.com/author/richarddavidson and on Facebook at https://www.facebook.com/richarddavidsonauthor?ref=hl
Follow him on Twitter @mysteryimp